© 2012 McSweeney's Quarterly Concern and the contributors, San Francisco, California. INTERNS & VOLUNTEERS: Belle Bueti, Jessica Lee, Emily Myers, Sarah Marie Shepherd, Samantha Abrams, Cayla Mihalovich, Andrew Ridker, Melissa MacEwen, Sabrina Wise, Ida Yalzadeh, Kevin Mosby, Evan Greenwald, Kylie Byrd, Lucie Elven, Craig Dathe, Keziah Weir, Joey Nargizian, Nara Williams, Oona Haas, Hayden Bennett, Francesca McLaughlin, Aimee Burnett, Alessandra Bautista, Naoki O'Bryan. ALSO HELPING: Walter Green, Andi Mudd, Sam Riley, Rachel Khong, Em-J Staples, Ethan Nosowsky, Maren Rusia, Chris Ying. COPY EDITOR: Caitlin Van Dusen. WEBSITE: Chris Monks. SUPPORT: Sunra Thompson. OUTREACH: Alyson Sinclair. ART DIRECTOR: Brian McMullen. ASSOCIATE PUBLISHER: Adam Krefman. PUBLISHER: Laura Howard. ASSOCIATE EDITOR: Chelsea Hogue. MANAGING EDITOR: Jordan Bass. EDITOR: Dave Eggers.

Printed in Minnesota at Shapco Printing. Cover and endpapers by Cassandra C. Jones. Her photo collages are from a series entitled "Lightning Drawings" (2009–2012). Jones collects and digitally arranges stock photographs of lightning bolts to make each collage; by situating the lightning bolts just so, she is able to "draw" pictures ranging in complexity from a circle to a charging pack of greyhound dogs. While some of the individual photographs have been cropped in the assembly process, they have not been otherwise modified. All of the lightning is real. The images appear courtesy of the artist and Eli Ridgway Gallery, San Francisco.

DEAR SENSEI,

I began this letter last year, when you lived here, and then put it away because I was too afraid; then I rewrote it four more times and never finished, because more people died. Then last month your son was born, at the hospital three blocks from my house—the same hospital where I was born, where your uncle was born, where your cousins were born. You stayed awake for two days, and then you came to sleep here—got the key from under the pot on the porch and went up to your old bed. When you called, beforehand, I told you to take off your hooded sweatshirt before you went inside, in case someone who didn't know you was watching.

You look like the reincarnation of Bob Marley, with your angular face and your dreadlocks like black coral and your eyes the color of cloves—even your mouth and teeth seem somehow like his. But you are six-two and that makes you more frightening, even to the kids who listen to Marley while they smoke marijuana; when they see you on the sidewalk, they have been conditioned to think you want something from them, even though you are only on your way to the skatepark. You are a master skateboarder whose favorite song when you lived here was "Midnight Rider" by the Allman Brothers. You were obsessed with the Doors, Jimi Hendrix, and Janis Joplin. Your tattoo is not a gang identification but a devil-grin skateboard clown and the words *One Love*.

When I look into your face I see everyone in our family. You are Ethiopian (according to family legend about one of your first ancestors here) and Samoan and Irish and Cherokee and some other stuff no one knows, because violence drove your grandmother away from her home in Mississippi and no one knew her father or her grandfather. A white man ran your great-great-grandmother down on the road because of a secret, and many of those American secrets are still about race and sex and fear. That has not changed in this country.

Nothing about you "fits the description"—and yet to strangers, maybe everything does. Back in the 1970s, your father and your uncles were hauled in by the police after a shooting and kept overnight in jail because they fit the description. They were on their way to a James Brown concert. They never saw him. They were young black men wearing Converse sneakers, at that time the only sneakers anyone wore.

You made your will at thirteen. Two of your best friends, Anthony Sweat and Markess Lancaster, also thirteen, were shot in separate incidents the summer of 2003—a bad summer. A Latino gang hunted them down, caught one of them running to hide on a porch a few blocks from where you skate now and the other riding in a car with his friends from a store near my house. In trial testimony, documented conversations showed the gang referred to finding black targets as "snail hunting."

You were arrested at eighteen for felony burglary after you walked to the store one morning and two other boys caught up with you. One was carrying a duffel bag, and it turned out he'd taken stereo equipment from an older woman's house. She testified that she'd never seen you, that you were not there, and even so you were in jail for weeks. You explained to us, when you were finally released, that you used the money we sent to buy candy bars.

You turned twenty-one last year, living here, and burst through the door one night with your hood up to keep us from seeing your eyes—you were crying, and you buried your face in the dog's fur for a long half hour before speaking. You'd been skating near that same hospital, on the metal rails you all love, and two older guys came through the parking lot to rob you. (Who expects skaters to have any money?) One demanded your board, and when you held it up as if to hit him, he pulled a gun and pointed it at your chest and called you a name and laughed when you used the board as a shield and ran.

It is fifty years since James Baldwin, my teacher, my mentor, wrote a letter to his nephew James, named for him, the son of his younger brother. I have read that letter countless times over the years. (I named you, accidentally, all those years ago when your father called me and asked how to spell *Sensei*, and I said, "Like the marijuana?" and he said, "Like the teacher in *Karate Kid*," and I called a Japanese American friend to make sure, and then your father said, "Thanks, sis, you just named my fourth son," and I said, "What?" and he said, "I was going to name him Malachai, like *Children of the Corn*, if you didn't know how to spell

Sensei," and I said, "Thank god.")

James Baldwin wrote other words that I have on a pink Post-it taped to this computer, where you and my girls all worked on your essays for English, when you typed here as KrazyAzzSamoan, your Facebook profile pictures making me shake my head. You saw these words every day: *I imagine that one of the reasons people cling to their hates so stubbornly is because they sense, once hate is gone, they will be forced to deal with pain.*

It is thirty years since he was my teacher, and stood in the tiny apartment in married-student housing where I lived with your uncle, and read the words I'd written on a tiny white piece of paper and taped to the wall over my typewriter: *With the rhythm it takes to dance to what we have to live through, you can dance underwater and not get wet.* James Baldwin turned to me with deep lines like staples between his eyes and said, "That's one of the most profound things I've ever read. Who's George Clinton?" We told him, and he laughed.

Fifty years since he wrote the letter to his nephew: "You were born into a society which spelled out with brutal clarity and in as many ways as possible that you were a worthless human being. You were not expected to aspire to excellence. You were expected to make your peace with mediocrity." And now, when I see "aspire to excellence" as an academic or marketing phrase beloved by large institutions and by politicians, when I see "American exceptionalism" shouted as a mantra of defense, I realize that I wish only for you to live. Just to stay alive. That is not an exaggeration. That is how the women who love you—and who love men like you all over the nation—feel fifty years later.

His letter says, "There is no reason for you to try to become like white men and there is no basis whatever for their impertinent assumption that they must accept you. The really terrible thing, old buddy, is that you must accept them, and I mean that very seriously… They are in effect still trapped in a history which they do not understand and until they understand it, they cannot be released from it. They have had to believe for many years, and for innumerable reasons, that black men are inferior to white men."

And now, fifty years later, the children of those men listen to Lil Wayne and wear hoodies, but the Internet lets strangers with cartoon portraits and hilarious names conceal their faces while they say, *The NBA is just f------ jungle bunnies running up and down the court so who cares?* and *Trayvon Martin was a ---- ----- * and *We were right in 1863 and we're right now—send ni----- back to Africa so they can die of AIDS and we won't have to waste bullets.* That is not to say no one believed this before, but when your uncle and I were young, we didn't know what a stranger believed unless he said it straight to our faces, and because your uncle was six-four and had an Afro so big he had to turn sideways to get through a doorway now and then, no one said anything like that straight to his face.

But thirty years ago, the guns still spoke. They spoke in 1983, and they speak now, and that will never change in America, no matter how many letters we write.

You know the stories because you and my girls all had to hear them over and over from every relative, as cautionary tales meant to keep you alive. I remember being dizzy and nauseous when a policeman pointed a shotgun directly at your uncle's ear while we were lined up against a wall, another officer shouting that he "fit the description" of someone who'd been seen on a college campus carrying a shotgun himself. Shouting and shouting. We'd been walking. Not even driving. I remember sweating and nearly fainting when we were pulled over again and again at night, when he got gas before dawn at the station next to the hospital where we were born and the clerk hit the silent alarm—maybe accidentally—when your uncle got out of the car. More guns pointed at his head. (We never tell you this part—that we think we will have heart attacks while we watch—I sat in the passenger seat, that muscle inside my chest hurting so bad that I imagined the small red heart I saw once when I was a child, excised from a bird by a cat on the sidewalk in front of my house, the muscle leaping four more times on the cement, but not bursting.)

It is one hundred and fifty years since the Emancipation Proclamation. You are free. You are free to skate down the street, to ride in a car, to walk down the sidewalk toward the taco place two blocks from here where everyone knows your name. You wear a hood when it is cold. You wear skinny jeans because you are not a gangster, you are a skater. Your dreads are legendary. You wear an old Hawaiian shirt with two buttons missing because your grandfather left it behind when he died, and you miss him. You wear a shark-tooth necklace. You do not fit the description.

Your grandfather came to California because of his own uncle, who was shot in the knee during the Tulsa Riots of 1921, when white Tulsans hunted down and shot black Tulsans in the neighborhood known as Greenwood, the Black Wall Street. After he was shot, Steve Stevenson left for Los Angeles and most of Greenwood burned to the ground. Black Tulsans had to live in tents while ordinances were passed declaring that they couldn't buy bricks. Steve bought a bit of property, ran a junkyard and scrap business, and eventually his sister-in-law Geneva left Tulsa, too, and came to stay with him in California. After a while she brought out her half sister, and her niece and nephews—your grandfather, General, was one. Last week five black Tulsans were hunted down and shot at random.

Some things were easy when you lived here—the taco, taquito, enchilada part, when I made hundreds of them and you lined them up on your plate with unabashed glee; the part where we watched *Dazed and Confused* and *A Knight's Tale* and *Fired Up!*, which contributed mightily to our weird family language. "All right, all right, all right," we would all say in our best Matthew McConaughey. And "You're not an old

lady gardening or a baby on the beach, okay? You shouldn't be wearing Crocs." The part where we had really good shampoo and lotion, that was easy.

Some things were not. The part where you had to go to community-college classes and actually do homework; the part where everyone else in the house was female (my three daughters, their innumerable friends, all the chattering and laughter and gossip like sparrows in the wisteria bush, and when you brought home laconic tattooed skaters of all races and sizes who tried to watch endless skate videos the single television in the house was clearly not enough for you all and I got tired of making taquitos and went on strike); the part where we made you put a timer in the shower because you used all the hot water and then we all screamed at you because we were freezing.

We fought briefly over curfew and the absolutely required phone call every midnight to let me know you were alive. This is part of life when you have children, but it's different when you have black children. I achieved victory with you by shamelessly using the heart— I told you that if you didn't come home one night I might have a heart attack and your uncle would have to raise you, which entailed the end of taquitos, nice shampoo, and everything else you loved, and you never came home late after that.

In February, for the baby shower, I bought an extra gift for you—a Jimi Hendrix CD, so you can teach your son about your favorite music, the same way my brother years ago brought me a Lynyrd Skynyrd CD so I could teach my three girls about his. (He was not a George Clinton fan.) You love considering yourself part of his legacy here in Southern California—he was a famous BMX rider, you a skater, and you share broken bones, an inability to be regularly employed by taxable workplaces, and a love of classic rock about outsiders. My brother who died by his own hand ten years ago last month, being chased by police because his last surviving friend had committed a crime, having written a note saying he wanted to join another friend, his best friend, who'd been killed by police the year before, shot eighteen times in his truck on the freeway divider because he appeared to be a threat even though he had no weapon and his toolbox was in the truck bed, far from his reach.

In March you put on your grandfather's shirt and I drove you and two other nephews and my youngest daughter to the funeral of your cousin, Lareanz, who had been halfway through his freshman year of high school. He was in ROTC and band; he wore skinny jeans and a blond-streaked Mohawk. He was as far from gang life as possible. Yet while he walked back to his grandmother's house with a borrowed DVD, a young Latino man pulled up in a car and another young Latino man shot him. You already know this—it is all we talked about for weeks. He made it to the driveway, where he was found brain-dead. The family kept him alive long enough to donate organs.

You mentioned the smell of the enchiladas I'd put in the back of the car. You joined more than three hundred people lined up outside the church, the military-uniformed ROTC members in formation, white and Latino and Asian and black. His grandfather was your grandmother's first cousin, born in Mississippi to the Ethiopian.

You were two blocks away when he was shot. You had talked my daughters, your cousins, into driving to another cousin's house to visit—my two girls in the red car sitting across the street putting up an umbrella through the open sunroof for a joke while you and your cousin stood in the driveway talking, and fifteen minutes later a car turned down a street two blocks away and someone got out and shot Lareanz six times at close range, shot some of the bullets into his head.

My dungeon shook. My ribs shook. My eyelids shook. You were all on the couch that night, lined up like panelists on a dating show: my girls, you and one of your brothers, his girlfriend who's Mexican American, trying to talk me into letting you all go out, and me shaking and saying No, your uncles calling and saying Hell, no, everyone stays in, for three days, like always.

Like always. For all the years of our lives so far.

I don't want to read the comments about his death. I don't want to read the comments about Trayvon Martin, or think about the comments anyone might make if they even saw your picture here. Your face that somehow causes a smoldering, intense resentment among a loud segment of your countrymen, your very presence and life that make them seethe with rage and hate at welfare and entitlement and crime and rap music and the fraying of the very fabric of what they consider American life, though you are not on welfare (but taquitos) and you do not listen to rap music and you still wear your grandfather's shirt, though it is frayed beyond repair.

James Baldwin's letter says: "Try to imagine how you would feel if you woke up one morning to find the sun shivering and all the stars aflame. You would be frightened because it is out of the order of nature. Any upheaval in the universe is terrifying because it so profoundly attacks one's sense of one's own reality. Well, the black man has functioned in the white man's world as a fixed star, as an immovable pillar, and as he moves out of his place, heaven and earth are shaken to their foundations."

The president your grandfather wanted to vote for, if he hadn't died twenty-one days before the election, the one whose face your uncles wore on T-shirts for weeks afterward—he moved out of his place. As you wish to do. His face in the news makes them seethe, too.

Now you have a son. Dustin Ozzy. Yes, for Mr. Osbourne. Mr. Osbourne has done very well riding the crazy train, but you—can you afford to be a tall brown Dennis the Menace, which is how I always think of you, with your half grin and dreads tied back with one of our shoelaces, your foot iced again with

my last bag of frozen corn because you skated off the rails? You have to get a better job than skating for prize money and working odd construction or clean-up gigs. You have to stay alive.

"You come from sturdy peasant stock, men who picked cotton, dammed rivers, built railroads, and in the teeth of the most terrifying odds, achieved an unassailable and monumental dignity. You come from a long line of great poets, some of the greatest poets since Homer. One of them said, 'The very time I thought I was lost, my dungeon shook and my chains fell off.'"

Your dungeon shakes differently—it trembles, unseen and inexplicable. It is not the bars of the slave jail, the barracoon; it is not the black bars around which civil-rights activists wrapped their fingers while James Baldwin wrote to his nephew. You have a son. This is my letter to say we love you, and we want to see you walking up our cracked cement path, holding your son's hand when he walks next year, and every year after that until there is silver hair in your dreads tied back with a shoelace.

Love, Auntie Susan.

SUSAN STRAIGHT
RIVERSIDE, CA

OPENING SPREAD: *The author's ex-husband, Dwayne Sims, his cousin Eddie Chandler Jr., his brothers Carnell Sims and General RC Sims III (father of Sensei), and Sensei Sims, walking on the corner lot where the house of Sensei's great-grandmother has just burned down and been bulldozed. Photo by Doug McCulloh.*

DEAR KINKO'S!

You have an employee named "Mia" in Oakland, California, at your Lakeside Drive location, in the building with the Starbucks, right to the west of Lake Merritt and on the way to the 19th Street BART stop, which is also kind of close to the Wells Fargo and not too far from Bakesale Betty (whoa, the strawberry shortcake), kind of on the other side of things from the 24 Hour Fitness (do not get me started on that place. Well, okay, real quickly: My dad has been trying to convince me to join a health club for the past nine years or so. I think it's something he enjoys, going to a club, and he thinks I would like it, too. Also, he does not want me to be fat. This past Christmas he was really getting on me about it; maybe I am getting more visibly fat. I told him there was a 24 Hour Fitness near me that I would check out when I got back to New York. I'd heard they had a pool, and I was excited at the idea of being able to go and swim in the middle of the night. But when I went in to ask them how much it cost and to see the pool, the man at the desk said that he needed to call a membership consultant for me. It had already reached a level I wanted to avoid. A guy popped out from the back office and introduced himself, and I went ahead and told him that I wanted to see the pool and find out how much it cost to become a member. He said that he would take me on a tour of the place. I followed him downstairs, past people working out on treadmills and stairsteppers, people sweating a lot and

holding energy drinks, people actually flexing their muscles for other people, and then down a hallway past rooms full of people doing exercises under black lights [I could see their shoelaces; it looked like a futuristic music video was being filmed] to the pool area, which was half a lane and a side nook where two old ladies wearing swim caps were splashing each other. The water was yellow. "Luckily for you, not too many people like the pool!" he said. He also told me that it closed every night at 11 p.m. We continued into the locker rooms, where there were naked men all over and I felt like I shouldn't just be able to walk right in and see that, and he showed me how the lockers worked. He also showed me how they supplied towels [he mentioned this a couple times]. Then he walked me back upstairs. When I said thanks he told me to come into his office. We sat there and he put my phone number and address into the computer. He showed me how much things were going to cost monthly, plus setup. I told him that I was going to think about it. He didn't like that, obviously, and said, "What's stopping you, man?" I said I'd just wanted to see the pool and find out the specifics and now I wanted to think about it. "That's cool," he said. "Sometimes I do that, too. Go into something with my mind already made up that I'm not going to do it, I mean." How was I supposed to respond to that? I ended up just saying, "Ha." "So what are you going to do instead?" he asked. "Probably go home and watch TV on the Internet and eat pizza," I told him. "No, I mean for fitness," he said. "Go home and eat pizza and watch people exercising on the Internet," I said. I don't think he thought I was funny. He handed me his business card and told me that I could either walk out through the front door or the one on the side, which was closer to the office.), the one on Grand, I mean, not the other one. I think there is also a fountain in the building, but it's not always running. Anyway, I just wanted to let you know that Mia was very helpful and nice. So happy you received my last note!

Sincerely,

JASON POLAN
NEW YORK, NY

DEAR MCSWEENEY'S,

He is forty-five years old but in many photos appears to be about twelve: a boy dressed for a family wedding, in a black suit and red tie. With his pale skin, dark and moony eyes, and hair gelled into a pompadour, he looks very much like the hero of a locally produced soap opera. His name is Enrique Peña Nieto, and if the polls are any indication, he will soon be elected president of Mexico.

Peña Nieto is a member of the centrist Institutional Revolutionary Party (a legendary oxymoron) known by its Spanish-language initials (PRI), which ruled Mexico between 1929 and 2000—the longest-running political show in modern history. Between 2005 and 2011, he was the governor of Mexico State, his term marked by infrastructure projects that made work, however

temporarily, for thousands. A multitude of the less fortunate—many in the shantytowns that ring Mexico City—lived in poverty compared by the United Nations to that of sub-Saharan Africa. Nearly all the surveys place Peña Nieto double-digit percentage points ahead of his rivals in the the left-wing Democratic Revolutionary Party (PRD) and the right-wing National Action Party (PAN), which has presided over Mexico (most would say disastrously) during the past twelve years.

He is not infallible. Last December, while presenting a tome he putatively wrote called *México: La gran esperanza* ("Mexico: The Great Hope") at the Guadalajara Book Fair—the most important in the Spanish-speaking world—a journalist asked Peña Nieto to name three books that had changed his life. His stammering response, posted on YouTube, lasted an excruciating four minutes. First he mumbled about novels he'd liked but whose titles he couldn't remember. Then it occurred to him that, although he had not read the entire Bible, some passages of it were inspirational to him during adolescence. Then he mentioned how much he liked historian Enrique Krauze's *La silla del águila*—a novel in fact written by Carlos Fuentes.

He became further confused after that, lost in a labyrinth of books and authors he could not recall, and asked people in the audience to help him out with details. Eventually Peña Nieto came up with the titles of two best sellers by Jeffrey Archer—a British author whose own political career was derailed by a conviction for perjury and a jail term. The candidate's smile and body language were unsettling, as if he thought the exercise was a joke.

Peña Nieto's performance caused a furor in Mexico, if only among the elite. He was widely ridiculed in the newspapers and social media. Those who defended him made matters worse. Peña Nieto's daughter Paulina tweeted the following message: "Regards to the bunch of assholes, who are all proles and only criticize those who they envy."

Peña Nieto is widely known as "Televisa's candidate"—a reference to Mexico's most important television network, which captures the lion's share of viewers. On a talk show called *Third Degree*, presenter Adela Micha said that "being a voracious reader is completely irrelevant when it comes to governing well or badly"; on the same show, newspaper editor Carlos Marin suggested that many people who made fun of the candidate were similarly ignorant themselves.

The reaction to Peña Nieto's gaffe lasted well into the new year. Tweets from an account called "Peña Nieto bookstore" abounded: "Let's read something by Martin Burger King," a representative entry suggested. Other politicians, meanwhile, managed to fall into the same trap. A former secretary of health who is running for governor of the state of Guanajuato mentioned, as a book that had changed his life, *The Little Prince*—written, he said, by Machiavelli.

UNESCO statistics say 93.4 percent of Mexicans know how to read. That doesn't mean many are exercising this ability; when I first came here to live, in 1990, a much-bandied-about statistic said that, on average, Mexicans read half a book a year. More recent studies put the figure at 1.9. If a book sells three thousand copies, it is considered a "best seller."

Other statistics, from the Organisation for Economic Co-operation and Development, tell us that 52 million Mexicans live at or below the national poverty level—about $130 per month, in a country where prices approach those in the U.S. That's nearly half the population, and many millions more hover just above that line. Only 11 percent of the working population earns more than $18.65 per day.

I have visited towns and even small cities in Mexico where there is not even a newsstand, much less a bookstore. If you are one of those people living at or around the poverty level—and it should be noted that more than half the impoverished are children—books are prohibitively expensive. An ordinary paperback costs about $16. Libraries are underfunded, woefully disorganized, and infrequently update their collections.

"Our education system has been replaced by TV," says Sergio González Rodríguez, a columnist for the newspaper *Reforma* and author of various books about politics and culture. "It's a medium that doesn't incite reading. People believe they are informed by TV, and that reading isn't important."

My work as an investigator for legal-defense teams takes me to visit families who live on the outskirts of cities, trying to eke out a living with their backs. Most young men I have interviewed have worked since childhood, shining shoes, delivering groceries, selling candy on the street. The girls help with housework almost as soon as they can walk. They go to primary and secondary school because they are obliged to by law, but after that they go to work full-time to help their parents, who are often spent by the time they are in their forties, with broken teeth and crooked spines.

Adolescents have few, if any, examples of people who have bettered their lot through education. There is virtually no social mobility in Mexico; nearly all those who are born poor are condemned to remain so for the rest of their lives. Those who do manage to claw their way out of poverty traditionally follow one of three channels. The first is hard work, most often in the form of a small business (the likeliest possibility would be to sell food from a stall on the street). The second is criminal activity. And the third—sometimes linked to the second—is politics. Mexican politicians earn higher salaries than their counterparts in the U.S. and Europe, and the sky is the limit for those who use their influence to make corrupt business deals. As former Mexico City mayor Carlos Hank González put it, "Show me a politician who is poor and I will show you a poor politician."

Since his appearance at the book fair, Peña Nieto has made additional slips. At recent public events he demonstrated that he doesn't know what the minimum wage is, nor the price of a kilo of tortillas. (His explanation for the latter lapse was "I am not a housewife.") At the end of January, he told a reporter that during his first marriage, he'd been a serial adulterer and had two children out of wedlock. Novelist J. M. Servín, in response, pointed out that illegitimate children are "normal within the scheme of macho Mexican society," and that his confession might even help Peña Nieto find support among male voters.

The candidate's first wife died under mysterious circumstances in 2007. During an interview, Peña Nieto claimed that he didn't remember the cause, but that it was "something like epilepsy." Plenty have speculated (without evidence) that he killed her, or that she committed suicide. Still, these blunders, revelations, and rumors have barely affected his standing in the polls.

Novelist Guillermo Fadanelli thinks that many Mexicans might approve of Peña Nieto's literary lapses. "An illiterate candidate is an accomplice to an illiterate public," he says. "Among those here, many use the word *intellectual* as a derogatory term."

Peña Nieto is wealthy, and has white skin, good looks, and a beautiful trophy wife, Angélica Rivera, who is in fact a former Televisa soap-opera star. In his TV commercials, he is often filmed sitting in the back of a limousine in shirtsleeves, with his necktie loosened, proclaiming his commitment to the people.

None of these symbols correspond to the reality of the lives of the proles.

Instead, they reflect their aspirations—the kind of person they would like to be if they were not stuck in a life of harvesting beans, shining shoes, selling tacos and tamales, cleaning other people's houses, or washing other people's cars. If Peña Nieto is elected, it will be because he represents that wish, that dream, regardless of whether he has ever read a book in his life.

DAVID LIDA
MEXICO CITY, MEXICO

DEAR MCSWEENEY'S,
Having been whipped—many times in the nipple—onstage for a paying audience, I have never understood how people could claim to derive sexual pleasure from this sort of activity.

It was November 1994, and I was playing Jesus in *Jesus Christ Superstar* at the University of Virginia. I loved the role, and—well, I won't write my own reviews—but once, passing by a giant snowball fight months after the show, a student I didn't know yelled, "Look, it's Jesus! CRUCIFY HIM!!!" And they did. Scores of them, with a barrage of snowballs. I took that experience positively, if painfully: after all, when you can get the crowds to adore and remember you and then turn on you, you've nailed "Jesus" as an actor.

Still, it's not the snowballs that I remember most; it's the whipping scene. It comes in Act II, "Trial Before Pilate (Including the 39 Lashes)," wherein Jesus is whipped thirty-nine times—or so you, the paying audience, would assume. Actually, he's whipped thirty-nine

times for each of the four performances, plus thirty-nine times for each of three full-dress rehearsals, plus as many times as it takes for a few eighteen-year-olds to work out the fake-blood situation. So hundreds upon hundreds of times, really.

The technical team of two women and I worked for hours perfecting the blood mixture, as well as the technique of me not screaming in pain. What we discovered in the process was that in order for our fake-blood combination of water, Karo sauce, and actual human tears to look and act like real blood (so as not to look like Jesus was leaking Kool-Aid), we needed to make it thick. I mean, *thick*-thick. Molasses thick. Charlottesville in August thick.

The problem—well, for Jesus, the problem—was that the thicker the fake blood, the more it stuck to human skin. The whipping was painful enough, but a whip that sticks to your skin takes a piece of Jesus as a souvenir with every lash. Worse, the guy playing the Roman guard who whips Jesus never missed. He didn't know his own strength, either. Every night before curtain, I would say to him, "Please, go light. You're whipping me much harder than you think."

"Got it," he'd say.

Then every night the first blow would come light, and the next thirty-eight at full imperial strength.

He and everyone else agreed: it just didn't look real otherwise. Not that they were telling me to take one for Team Jesus; they just assumed the marks on my body were fake, and out of some noble loyalty to the show's aesthetics, I didn't tell anyone that, actually, every night audiences were paying to see a man flayed onstage.

What can I say? The technical team did its job and did it well. The fake blood looked just like the real stuff.

It was Jesus' nipples that suffered the most, though. You see, the blood needed to flow from a high-enough point on the Messiah's back for the audience to see it. That meant aiming as best you could for the upper torso—and that our Roman friend did with great skill. Unfortunately, every fifth or so blow would snake around front and strike Jesus square on his right nipple. The whip was long enough to occasionally hit the left one, as well.

I don't know if you've ever been bull-whipped in the nipple, say, eight times a night for seven nights in a row, but it's not the fun your secret stash of movies makes it out to be. The pain comes in three stages. There's the initial strike, when it lands, at which point no matter how much you've prepared yourself for it, you still lose your breath. Then—at least in this Jesus' case—there's the pain of the whip making that sticky tearing sound as it's ripped away. One time when that happened—a full shot to the right nipple—I nearly fainted.

But it's that moment in between, when the whip has landed and you have a split second to recover from the pain while letting yourself be mentally terrorized by the tearing to come, that really brings you closer to the role.

Honestly, between the bits of blood and body I gave, I'm one of the few people who can tell you what it's like to *be* Holy Communion, not just take it.

Had my first association with whips and nipple torture not been so ecclesiastical, perhaps I might hold a different opinion on their sexual allure. But I doubt it.

Yours,

JOHN FLOWERS
BROOKLYN, NY

DEAR MCSWEENEY'S,

I hope this letter finds you well. I hope this because you are potentially my biological father.

Recently I found a trove of carefully penned love letters tied together with a single mauve ribbon. In a terse script, these were addressed to my now-deceased mother and dated the year of my conception. Each was signed *T.M.*

I know what you're thinking: Tim McGraw. But that wouldn't make any sense, since I am not a fan of country music. What am I fan of, you ask? Fine cheeses; *Moby-Dick*; edamame. If this isn't enough to prove to you that I am your offspring, then I don't know what is.

Please swab your cheek using the enclosed home-DNA-test kit and write both your name and your identification number on the blue sticky labels. I'll take care of the rest. I look forward to getting to know you!

Yours biologically,

CIROCCO "MCSWEENEY" DUNLAP
BROOKLYN, NY

P.S. Please send cash.

RIVER CAMP

by THOMAS MCGUANE

illustration by MATT ROTA

"ANYTIME YOU'RE on the Aleguketuk, you might as well be in heaven. I may never get to heaven, so the Aleguketuk will have to do—that, and plenty of beer! Beer and the river, fellows: that's just me.

"Practical matters: chow at first light. If you ain't in the chow line by O-dark-thirty, your next shot is a cold sandwich on the riverbank. And don't worry about what we're going to do; you'll be at your best if you leave your ideas at home.

"Now, a word or two about innovation and technique. You can look at these tomorrow in better light, but they started out life as common, ordinary craft-shop dolls' eyes. I've tumbled them in a color solution, along with a few scent promulgators distilled from several sources. You will be issued six of these impregnated dolls' eyes, and any you don't lose in the course of action will be returned to me upon your departure. I don't want these in circulation, plain and simple.

"The pup tent upwind of the toilet pit is for anyone who snores. That you will have to work out for yourselves. I remove my hearing aid at exactly nine o'clock, so snoring means no more to me than special requests. From nine until daybreak, a greenhorn can be seen but not heard.

"Lastly, the beautiful nudes featured on the out-of-date welding-supplies calendar in the cook tent are photographs of my bride at twenty-two. Therefore that is a 1986 calendar and will not serve for trip planning."

Marvin "Eldorado" Hewlitt backed his huge bulk out of the tent flap, making a sight gag of withdrawing his long gray beard from the slit as he closed it. Sitting on top of their sleeping bags, the surgeon Tony Capoletto and his brother-in-law Jack Spear turned to look at each other. Tony said, "My god. How many days do we have this guy? And why the six-shooter?"

Tony, the more dapper of the two, wore a kind of angler's ensemble: a multipocketed shirt with tiny brass rings from which to suspend fishing implements, quick-dry khaki pants that he'd turned into shorts by unzipping them at the knee, and wraparound shades that dangled from a Croakie at his chest. His pale, sharp-featured face and neatly combed hair were somewhat at odds with this costume.

"I have no idea," Jack said. His own flannel shirt hung loose over his baggy jeans. "He seemed so reasonable on the Internet."

Some sharp, if not violent, sounds could be heard from outside. Tony crawled forward in his shorts, carefully parting the entry to the tent to look out. Jack considered his friend's taut physique and tried to remember how long he'd had his own potbelly. Tony was always in shape—part handball, part just being a surgeon.

"What's he doing, Ton'?"

"Looks like he's chopping firewood. I can barely see him in the dark. Not much of the fire left, now."

"What was that stuff he made for dinner?"

"God only knows."

The tent smelled like camphor, mothballs; the scent was pretty strong. When Jack let his hand rest outside his sleeping bag, the grass still felt wet. It made him want to take a leak, but he didn't care to leave the tent as long as Hewlitt was out there.

Tony went back to his sleeping bag. It was quiet. A moment later his face lit up with blue light.

"You get a signal?"

"Are you kidding?" said Tony. "That would only inspire hope."

Tony's wife—Jack's sister—was divorcing him. There were no kids, and Tony said the whole thing was a relief, said that he was not bitter. Jack was quite sure Tony was bitter; it was Jack's sister who was not bitter. Jack had seen Shelley at the IGA and she'd been decidedly unbitter—cheerful if not manic. She'd hoped they would have an "outtasight" trip. This was part of Shelley's routine, hip and lively for a tank town. Tony might have been a bit serious for her, in the end. Maybe he needed to lighten up. Jack certainly thought so.

Jack's wife, Jan, was one of the sad stories: having starred, in her small world, as a staggeringly hot eighteen-year-old when Jack, half cowboy and half high-school wide receiver, had swept her out of circulation, she had since gone into a rapid glide toward what could be identified at a thousand yards as a frump, and at close range as an angry frump. Shelley and Jan had driven "the boys" to the airport for their adventure together, each dreading the ride home, when in the absence of their men they would discover how little they had to talk about. In any case, they could hardly have suspected that they would never see their husbands again.

But the divorce wasn't the reason that Tony was so bent on a trip. He'd made some sort of mistake in surgery, professionally not a big deal—no one had even noticed—but Tony couldn't get it out of his mind. He'd talked about it in vague terms to Jack, the loss of concentration, and had reached this strange conclusion: "Why should I think I'll get it back?"

"You will, Ton'. It's who you are."

"Oh, really? I have *never* before lost concentration with the knife in my hand. Fucking never."

"Tony, if you can't do your work in the face of self-doubt, you may as well just quit now."

"Jack, you think you've ever experienced the kind of pressure that's my daily diet?"

Jack felt this, but let it go.

Marvin Eldorado Hewlitt was now their problem. Jack had tried plenty of other guides, but they were all either booked or at a sportsmen's show in Oakland. He'd talked to some dandies after that, including a safari outfitter booking giraffe hunts. At the bottom of the barrel was Hewlitt, and now it was getting clearer why. So many of the things they would have thought to be either essential or irrelevant were subject to extra charges: fuel for the motor, a few vegetables, bear spray, trip insurance, lures, the gluten-free sandwich bread.

"But Marvin, we brought lures."

"You brought the wrong lures."

"I'll fish with my own lures."

"Not in my boat."

Lures: $52.50. Those would be the dolls' eyes.

"Marvin, I don't think we want trip insurance. I'm just glancing at these papers—well, are you really also an insurance agent?"

"Who else is gonna do it? I require trip insurance. I'm not God, but acts of God produce client whining I can't deal with."

Trip insurance: $384.75.

"Tony, give it up. There's no signal."

Tony looked up. "Was that a wolf?"

"I don't think it was a wolf. I think it was that crazy bastard."

The howl came again, followed by Marvin's chuckle.

"You see? That was him."

Tony got out of his sleeping bag and peered through the tent flap.

"He's still up. Sitting by the fire. He's boiling something in some kind of a big cauldron. And he's talking to himself, it looks like. Or it's more like he's talking to someone else, but there's no one there that I can see. We're in the hands of a lunatic, Jack."

"Nowhere to go but up."

"You could say that. You could pitch that as reasonable commentary."

Jack felt heat come to his face. "Tony?"

"What?"

"Kiss my ass."

"Ah, consistency. How many times have I prayed for you to smarten up?"

Jack thought, I've got him by forty pounds. That's got to count.

The two fell silent. They were reviewing their relationship. So far, Tony had come up only with "loser," based on Jack's modest income; Jack had settled for "prick," which he based on the entitlement he thought all doctors felt in their interactions with others. This standoff was a long time coming, a childhood friendship that had hardened. Probably neither of them wanted it like this; the trip was supposed to be an attempt to recapture an earlier stage, when they were just friends, just boys. But the harm had been done. Maybe they had absorbed the town's view of success and let it spoil something. Or maybe it was the other thing again.

Outside, by the fire, Marvin was singing in a pleasant tenor.

Way down yonder on the Indian Nation
I'll ride my pony on the Reservation
in the Oklahoma hills that I call home

There was some accompaniment. Jack said, "See if he's got an instrument." Tony sighed, and climbed out from his sleeping bag again. At the tent flap, he said, "It's a mandolin." And in fact at that moment a lyrical solo filled the air. Tony returned to his bag and the two lay quietly, absorbing first some embellishment of the song Marvin had been singing, and then a long venture into musical space.

Shortly after the music stopped, Marvin's voice came through the tent flap.

"Boys, that's all I can do for you. Now let's be nice to one another. We've got our whole lives ahead of us."

In a matter of minutes, the camp was silent. Stars rose high over the tents and their sleepers.

Morning arrived as a stab of light through the tent flap and the abrupt smell of trampled grass and mothballs. A round, pink face poked through at them, eyes twinkling unpleasantly, and shouted, "Rise and shine!"

"Is that you, Marvin?" Tony asked, groggily.

"Last time I looked."

"What happened to the beard?"

"Shaved it off and threw it in the fire. When you go through the pearly gates, you want to be clean-shaven. Everybody else up there has a beard."

The flap closed and Jack said, "I smelled it. Burning." Then he pulled himself up.

Jack fished his clothes out of the pile he'd made in the middle of the tent. Tony glanced at this activity and shook his head; his own clothes were hung carefully on a tent peg. He wore his unlaced hiking shoes as he dressed. Jack was briefly missing a shoe, but it turned up under his sleeping bag, explaining some of the previous night's discomfort.

Tony said, "It's time for us to face this lunatic if we want breakfast."

The sunrise made a circle of light in the camp, piled high with pine needles next to the whispering river. Hewlitt had hoisted the perishable supplies up a tree, to keep them away from bears; a folding table covered by a red-and-white-checkered tablecloth was set up by the small, sparkling fire. Stones on either side of the fire supported a blackened grill, from which Hewlitt brought forth a steady stream of ham, eggs, and flapjacks.

Jack rubbed his hands together eagerly and said, "My god, it's like Chef Boyardee!" Tony rolled his eyes at this and smiled at Hewlitt, whose surprisingly mild and beardless face had begun to fascinate him. The beard, it was explained, was something Hewlitt cultivated for sportsmen's shows: he hated beards.

"I'm not ashamed of my face," he said. "Why would I hide it?"

Hewlitt had already eaten, and so Jack and Tony sat down at the table while he headed off toward the trees. Halfway through the meal, Jack noticed the man making slow, strange movements. Tony, thoroughly enjoying this breakfast, which was miles off his diet, hadn't looked up yet.

Finally Jack said, "I think the guide is having some kind of a fit."

Tony glanced up, mouth full of unsaturated fats.

"No, Jack, that's not a fit. That's *tai chi*."

"Like in the kung fu movies, I suppose."

"No."

They continued to eat in a less-pleasant silence until Hewlitt bounced over and joined them. Tony smiled as though they were old friends and asked, "Chen?"

"Uh-uh," said Hewlitt.

"Yang?"

"Nyewp."

"I'm out of ideas," Tony admitted modestly.

"Wu," said Hewlitt, in subdued triumph.

"Of course," said Tony. "What was that last pose?"

"Grasp-the-Bird's-Tail."

Jack listened, and chewed slowly. He let his eyes drift to the other side of the river: an undifferentiated wall of trees. The water seemed so smooth you'd hardly know it was moving at all if it wasn't for the long stripe of foam behind every boulder. Invisible behind the branches, a raven seemed to address the camp.

Fried eggs on a metal plate. Jack ate more cautiously than usual: Tony was always on him about his weight. But then Tony was a doctor, and Jack felt he had his well-being in mind despite the often-annoying delivery. It was pleasing to notice these signs of old friendship, such as they were. Jack knew he should take better care of himself, and he had complied when Tony had wanted him to give up the cigarettes. It had been hard, and they were never completely out of his mind. In an odd way, that had been his own gesture of friendship, despite Tony's main argument having been that financially Jack really couldn't afford to smoke.

Tony was telling a story to Marvin that Jack already knew. He'd heard it a hundred times.

"We went on vacation to Mexico one year, and I brought back these little tiny super-hot peppers to cook with. We had Jack and his wife Jan over for dinner one night, and I told Jack what I just told you, that these were the hottest little peppers in the world. Well, Jack, he's had about five longnecks in a row, and he says, 'Nothing's too hot for me!' right before he puts a spoonful of them in his mouth. Buddy, that was all she wrote. Tears shoot out of his eyes. His face turns... *maroon*. His head drops to the table, and what do you think he says?"

"I don't know," said Hewlitt.

"He says, 'Why is it always me?'"

Hewlitt stared at him for a moment. Then he said, "What's the punch line?"

Tony's face fell with a thud. Hewlitt got up to feed the fire.

"Our host doesn't seem to have much of a sense of humor," Tony said, when the man was gone. Jack just smiled at him.

There were a lot of Italians around the meatpacking plant, and that's where Tony's people had settled. He had come a long way. Jack's family was cattle, land, and railroad: they'd virtually founded the town, but hadn't had a pot to piss in for generations. Shelley liked to point out that half of her and Jack's relatives were absolute bums, which generally made Jack's wife respond that Tony's family was right off the boat. Nobody crossed Jan: she wasn't witty, she was angry. *He may be a doctor to you, but he's a wop to me.* Jack was fundamentally too fragile for this kind of badinage, unfortunately, because he had to admit that Tony and Shelley were far less snippy when Jan was around. She'd say to Jack, "You want respect, you better be prepared to snap their heads back." Or she'd put it the way Mike Tyson did: "Everybody's got an attitude until you hit them in the face."

Jack's roots in town were so deep that he thought that Jan's bellicosity was just a result of having grown up somewhere else. She was from Idaho, for crying out loud. This was before he found out Jan had had a slip-up with Tony back in the day, while Jack was off doing his time with the National Guard.

When Tony and Shelley took them to New York to see *Cats*, that's when it really hit the fan. Tony had made a big thing about *Cats* winning a Tony Award, which Jan thought was such a hoot because Jack had no idea what a Tony Award was. He'd thought Tony was flirting with Jan again, with his so-called humor. Jack and Jan moved to their own hotel, leaving the room Tony had paid for empty. In their new room, Jan went on the defensive and blamed alcohol for the flirtation. She seemed to think that with this citation, the issue was settled. Jack didn't buy it, but he'd never been willing to pay the price for taking it further. Instead, he absorbed the blow. Having Tony know he just took it was the hardest part.

But somehow the problem between the two of them evaporated when they were back in town. "New York just wasn't for us," Tony said, amiably, and Jack accepted this gratefully. Jan, however, twisted it around; she took it to mean that she and Jack just weren't *good enough* for New York.

"Who wants to go there anyway?" she'd say. "All those muggers, and that smelly air!"

Meanwhile her slip-up was consigned, once again, to history. Full stop. Jack couldn't stand any of it.

They all pitched in to tidy up the camp, and then they headed for the boat. It was tied to a tree, swinging in the current; a cool breeze, fresh and balsamic, was sweeping up the river. Hewlitt carried a Styrofoam chest— their lunch—to the shore and put it aboard. Fishing tackle had been loaded in already.

A moment later the three men climbed in, and Hewlitt started the engine. Once he was sure it was running properly, he stepped ashore and freed the painter from the tree, sprang aboard again, and turned into the current. Tony said, "This is what it's all about."

Jack nodded eagerly and then felt a wave of hopelessness unattached to anything in particular. Maybe catching a fish, maybe just the day itself. Hewlitt gazed over the top of their heads, straight up the river. He seemed to know what he was doing.

He had looked more competent when he'd still had the beard. Now he looked like a lot of other people. God was always portrayed with a beard— for Jack it was impossible to picture Him without one, even if he strained to imagine what he assumed would be a handsome and mature face. The only time you ever saw Jesus without a beard, He was still a baby. Tony had grown his own beard right after med school. Sometime later Jan had told Tony that he needed to get rid of it; that was one of the worst arguments Jack and Jan had ever had. Jack had said it was for Shelley to say whether or not she liked the beard, since it was her husband. Jan said that a person was entitled to her own opinions.

"Who taught you to cast?" Tony said. They had started fishing.

"You did," Jack replied.

"Obviously you needed to practice."

Jack just shrugged it off. He was still getting it out there, wasn't he? Maybe not as elegantly as Tony, but it shouldn't have made any difference to the fish. The casting was just showing off. It seemed to have impressed Hewlitt, though, because he took Tony upriver to another spot, leaving Jack to fish where he was, even though nobody had gotten a bite. Jack thought it was probably a better spot, this new one, and of course it was perfectly natural that Hewlitt would take Tony there, since it was Tony who was paying for the trip. Nevertheless, after another hour had passed, he felt a bit crushed, and no longer expected to catch a fish at all. He thought, None of this would be happening if I had more money.

The sun rose high overhead and warmed the gravel bar. Jack's arm was getting tired, and eventually he stretched out on the ground with his hands behind his head. The heat felt so good, and the river sounded so sweet this close to his ear. Let Tony catch all the fish, he thought; I am at peace.

"How are you going to catch a fish that way, Jack?"

Tony was standing over him. He hadn't even heard the motor.

"I'm not. Did you catch anything?"

"No."

"See? You could have had a nice nap."

Tony sat down next to Jack on the gravel and glanced over at Hewlitt, who was carrying their lunch box from the boat to the shore. "You know what old Eldorado did before he was a wilderness outfitter? Guess."

"Lumberjack?"

"Way off. He was a pharmacist."

"I'm surprised they even had them up here."

"This was in Phoenix."

Jack thought for a moment, and then asked, "Do you think he knows what he's doing?"

"No."

"Are we going to catch fish?"

"It seems unlikely."

They were interrupted by a cry from Hewlitt, whose rod had bent into a deep bow.

"Jesus. I didn't even see him cast," Jack said.

The two men hurried over. Hewlitt glanced at them and said, "First cast! He just mauled it."

The fish exploded into the air and tail-danced across the river.

"Looks like a real beauty," said Tony grimly, his hands plunged deep in his pockets.

After several more jumps and runs, Hewlitt had the fish at the beach and, laying down his rod, knelt beside it, holding it under its tail and belly. It was big, thick, and flashed silver with every movement as Hewlitt removed the hook. Tony and Jack craned over him to better see the creature, and Hewlitt bent to kiss it. "Oh, baby," he murmured. Then he let it go.

"What'd you do that for?" Tony wailed. The fish was swimming off, deeper and deeper, until its glimmer was lost in the dark. "We could have had fresh fish for lunch!"

Their guide, in response, got right in Tony's face. "Don't go there, mister," he said with an odd intensity. "You don't want that on your karma." Then he walked back to the boat and dragged the anchor farther up the shore.

"My god," Tony said. "What have we got ourselves into?" But Jack was simply pleased with everything.

A few minutes later, he even made a possibly insincere fuss over the bologna sandwiches. "Is there any lettuce or anything?"

"Doesn't keep without refrigeration. Where do you think you are?"

"The Aleguketuk. You already told me."

"Nice river, isn't it?"

"I wish it had more fish," said Tony. "Although it's obviously not a problem for you."

"Nyewp, not a problem."

As Hewlitt went to the boat to look for something, Tony said, "Ex–pill salesman."

"But fun to be with."

Jack had gone through times like this with Tony in the past: just be patient, he knew, and his friend would soon be chasing his own tail. It had already started. Tony had come unglued once when both couples had gone to a beginners' tennis camp in Boca Raton—thrown his racket, the whole nine yards. Jack had just let it sink in with Jan, what she had done with this nut. He knew he shouldn't feel this way: Jan had made it clear she regretted the whole thing, but he felt doomed to rub it in for the rest of their lives, or at least until she quit marveling over how fit Tony and Shelley were. He always suspected she included Shelley only as camouflage, when she mentioned it. He'd seen this fitness language before: buns of steel, washboard abs, power pecs—all just code for Tony hovering over Jan like a vulture. And now, because Tony and Shelley were divorcing, Jack feared that further indiscretions might be on tap.

Tony threw his bologna sandwich into the river. "I can't eat it."

Hewlitt had his mouth full. "Plan on foraging?"

Tony sat down on the ground, elbows on his knees, and held his head in despair.

No other fish were caught that day, and neither man slept well that night. The next day a hard rain confined them to their tent; Tony read Harvey Penick's *Little Red Golf Book*, and Jack did sudoku until he was sick of it. The weather finally lifted in time for the third night's evening fire, and Hewlitt emerged wearing only his long underwear to prepare the meal, which was a huge shish kebab with only meat the entire length of the stick. When it was cooked, Hewlitt flicked the flesh onto their tin plates, which were so thin you could feel the heat through their bottoms. Afterward Hewlitt recited a Robert Service poem—"There are strange things done 'neath the midnight sun"—so slowly that Tony and Jack were frantic at its conclusion.

"Where exactly was that drugstore you worked in?" Tony asked.

Hewlitt stared at him for a long time before speaking. "A pox on you, sir."

Back in the tent, Jack asked, "Aren't you concerned that he'll confiscate the impregnated craft-shop dolls' eyes?"

"What difference does it make? They haven't worked so far."

"Tony, it was a joke. Jesus, for a fancy doctor with a five-thousand-square-foot home on the golf course, you sure haven't lost your sense of humor."

"Fifty-two hundred. Get some sleep, Jack. You're getting crabby."

Jack had worked for the county all those years since the National Guard. In '96 he had denied Tony a well permit for his lawn-sprinkling system, and

Tony had never gotten over it. It was payback for the little nothing with Jan, he was convinced, even though in reality it was no more than a conventional ruling on the law, which Tony, as was often the case, thought should be bent ever so slightly. Jack had explained the legal basis for his decision without denying that it was pleasant seeing Tony choke on this one. Tony had put his hand in Jack's face and said, "This is for surgery, not for holding a garden hose."

"You might want to tone down the square footage, if your time is limited," Jack had replied. "That's an awful lot of lawn."

"What the fuck are you talking about!" Tony had shouted back. "You don't even have a lawn, you have fucking pea rock!"

Hewlitt must have been throwing more wood on the fire. You could see the flare of the flames through the walls of the tent. From time to time, he laughed aloud.

"Do you suppose he's laughing at us?" Tony asked.

"Things can still turn out. We have time."

"At least we got away together," Tony said. "We used to do more of this. It's important. It makes everything come back. We're kids again. We're who we used to be."

"Not really," said Jack. "You used to be nicer to me."

"You're joking, aren't you?"

Jack didn't answer. He wished he hadn't said such a thing, and his throat ached.

"What about Cancun in 2003? It didn't cost you a nickel."

Jack didn't know how to reply. He was in such pain. The tent fell silent once more. When Tony finally spoke, his voice had changed.

"Jack. I don't have another friend."

Jack wanted to make Tony feel better then, but it wasn't coming to him yet. Tony was right about one thing: they *were* who they used to be. Jack was still doing okay in his little house, and Tony was still just as lonely by the golf course as he'd been by the meatpacking plant. He had to take it out on somebody.

In the morning, there was frost on everything. Jack and Tony, arms stiff at their sides, watched as Hewlitt made breakfast and merrily reminisced about previous trips.

"Had an English astronaut here for a week, just a regular bloke. Loved his pub, loved his shepherd's pie, loved his wee cottage in Blighty."

Tony and Jack glanced at each other.

"Took a large framed picture of the Queen Mother into space. Ate nothing but fish and chips his whole month in orbit, quoting Churchill the entire time."

Tony whispered to Jack, "There were no English astronauts."

"I heard that," Hewlitt said, standing up and waving his spatula slowly in Tony's face.

"Did you? Good."

Hewlitt resumed cooking in silence. The silence was worse. He served their meal without a word, then went to his boat with his new bare face and in his hand he grasped a handful of willow switches he had cut from the bank. With these, he scourged himself. It was hard not to see this as a tableau, with the boat and the river behind him and Hewlitt, in effect, centered in the frame. His audience, Jack and Tony, turned away to gear up for a day of fishing and standing with their rods at their sides like a sarcastic knockoff of *American Gothic*.

Right out of the blue Hewlitt stopped his thrashing and turned to fix them with a reproving gaze. "I've spent my entire life as a liar and an incompetent," he said.

"Don't be so hard on yourself, Eldorado," Tony said, with poorly concealed alarm.

"Bogus vitamins on the Internet? How about swingin' doors and painted women?"

"That's all behind you, now."

"If only I could believe you!" Hewlitt cried.

Tony was paralyzed by the strangeness of this, but Jack stepped forward and snatched the willow switches away. He got right in Hewlitt's face.

"How much of this do you think we can stand?"

"Well, I—"

"We're not on this trip to hear about your problems. We don't even know you. I came here to be with my friend because we need to talk. This is a freak show, and we shouldn't have to pay for it. We thought we'd catch some fish!"

This seemed to sober Hewlitt, who replaced his look of extravagant self-pity with one of caution and shrewdness.

"I'm the only one who can get you out of here, son. No brag, just fact.

You make me feel respected or you're S.O.L. I'd like to be a fly on the wall when you try backing this tank down a class-five rapid. That's the only way home, punk, and I'm unstable."

"Jesus," said Tony. "This is insane! This trip was my reward as a vassal of Medicare!"

Hewlitt responded by pretending to play a violin and whistling "Moon River." Jack raised a menacing finger in his face, and he stopped. Then he was talking again.

"How about you try going broke on eating-disorder clinics to wake up to find your wife still gobbling her food? Forty K in the hole and she's facedown in a ham!"

Jack turned back to Tony. "I don't know what to do."

Hewlitt's lament rushed onward. He had dug deep in his pharmacist days to throw a big wedding for his daughter, apparently; she had married way above their station thanks to her big blue eyes and thrilling figure. It was, in Hewlitt's words, a hoity-toity affair with the top Arizona landowners, the copper royalty and the developers, and Hewlitt's caterer food-poisoned them all. Several sued, his wife and daughter blamed him, and in this way Hewlitt found himself at the end of his old life and the beginning of the new. He took a crash course in wilderness adventures at an old CCC camp in Oregon, graduating at the top of his class and getting a book on the ethics of forestry in recognition. Hewlitt seemed to think that this was all an illusion, that no one really cared about him at all.

Tony and Jack maintained compassionate, respectful smiles throughout this tirade. By the end Hewlitt was so upset his cheeks trembled. When he finished, Jack raised an imploring hand in his direction, but to no avail: Eldorado Hewlitt walked past them and into his tent.

"Doesn't look like a fishing day," Jack said.

Once they were back in the tent, Jack stretched out on his sleeping bag and Tony turned to grab a thick paperback from his pack, a book about zombies with the face of someone with white eyeholes on the cover. He slumped back on his bedroll, drew his reading glasses from his shirt, and was on the verge of total absorption when Hewlitt flung open the tent flap. Tony slowly lowered the zombie book.

"Sorry to disturb you," the man said, though there was no evidence of that. "I have to ask: what is *your* problem? 'Old friends'? Is that what you are, 'old friends'? Grew up together in the same little town? I know I have problems; I'm famous for my problems. I'm told by qualified professionals that I have ruined my life with my problems, but these few days with two 'old friends' have completely unnerved me. What did you two *do* to each other? Where is this bad feeling coming from? I'm terrifically upset and I don't know what it is. But it's coming from you two, I've figured out that much. Can't you work this out? You're killing me!"

Hewlitt hurled down the flap and left. Jack and Tony looked at each other, then quickly glanced away.

"What was that all about?" Tony asked, unpersuasively.

Jack said nothing. He had found his box of lures, and was lifting one up as though to examine it. A blue frog with hooks.

After a minute he got to his feet. He went out of the tent, looked around, and came back in with their rods. He made a show of breaking them down and putting them back in their travel tubes. Tony, staring determinedly now at a single page of his zombie book, barely lifted his eyes to this activity, which caused Jack to raise the intensity of it. He held up a roll of toilet paper in his hand. Tony couldn't look at him.

"Might as well take a shit. Nothing else to do around here."

Tony kept his eyes on the book and gave him a little wave.

A short time later, the toilet paper flew back into the tent, followed by Jack. He slumped on his bedroll with a sigh.

"I've got another book," said Tony.

"I hate books."

"No, you don't. You loved *The Black Stallion*."

"I was twelve."

"So don't read. Who cares?"

"What's the other book?"

"*Silent Spring*."

Jack snorted. "Thanks a bunch."

Tony dropped the book to his chest. "Jack, what do you want?"

"In the whole world?"

"Sure."

"I'd like you to tell me in plain English what my wife saw in you."

Tony exhaled through pursed lips and looked at the ground. "We did this a long time ago. Either you shoot me or throw her out, but otherwise there's nothing more to say. The whole thing is both painful and negligible to me, and kind of an accident and kind of ancient history. We have managed to stay friends despite my very serious personal crime against you. It is a permanent stain on my soul."

"What do you mean by that?" Jack said. "You don't even believe you have one."

"Well, you do, and you're innocent. *I* have a soul that is blemished by shame. All right? I'm not proud of myself."

Jack lay facedown on his bedroll, chin on laced fingers, and looked miserably toward the tent flap. He fell asleep thus, after a while, and so did Tony, glasses hanging from one ear. Hours later, they were awakened by the cooling tent and diminished light.

Jack got to his feet abruptly, seeming frightened, and rifled through a pile of clothing until he found his coat.

"You going to find us something to eat?" Tony asked.

"I am like hell. I'm going to have a word with our guide."

Tony raised a cautioning hand. "Jack, we're dealing with a very unstable—"

"Well put, Tony. That's exactly what I am, but I plan to do something about it. I'm upset. And it's his fault."

"Jack, please—"

But Jack had already gone. Tony slumped back with his hands over his face. It went through his mind that patiently putting up with Jack was an old habit. That's what had started their mess. Jack had done something dumb—gotten drunk and driven his car on the railroad tracks, in fact, nearly ruining it—that had caused Jan and Tony, in an accidental encounter at the post office, to commiserate with each other, and the next thing they knew they were in bed, bright sunlight coming through the thin curtains of the Super 8. It wasn't anything, really, but Jan threw it into an argument with Jack the next year during the Super Bowl and the half-life was promptly extended to forever.

Jack came back in through the tent flap, slapping it open abruptly. He crouched down, staring at Tony. Then he said, "He's dead."

Tony sat up. The zombie paperback splattered on the dirt floor. He stood and walked straight past Jack, out through the flap, then came back in, kicking the book out of his way, and lay down again.

"He sure is," he said.

"So what happened?"

"He took something."

"Jesus. Did you see this coming?"

"No. I thought it was an act."

"Is the food in there with him?"

"He hauled it back up the tree. Where the bears couldn't get it."

"Bears. Jesus, I forgot about bears." Jack dashed out of the tent once more. When he returned, dangling Hewlitt's gun by its barrel, he had a wild look in his eyes. Tony knew what it was and said nothing.

"I'll get a fire going," Jack said. "We've got to eat something. Why don't you get the food down and see what we've got."

Outside they felt the strangeness of being alone in the camp, the cold fire, Hewlitt's silent tent. The boat meant everything, and separately they checked to see that it was still there. Tony ended up crouched by the fire pit, shaving off kindling with his hatchet, while Jack puzzled over the knots on the ground stake: the rope led upward over a branch, suspending the food supplies out of reach. Once the rope was free, he was able to lower the supplies to the ground and open the canvas enclosing them: steaks, potatoes, onions, canned tomatoes, girlie magazines, schnapps, eggs, a ham. He dragged the whole load to the fire and stood over it with Tony, not quite knowing what to do next.

"If I'm right about what's ahead, we go for the protein," Tony said.

It was getting darker and colder; the flames danced over the splinters of firewood. Jack was quite still.

"What's ahead, Tony?"

"The boat trip."

"Oh, is that what you think?"

"That's what I think."

Jack looked up at the sky for a moment but didn't reply. Instead, he lifted two of the steaks out of the cache and dropped them onto the grill.

The bedrolls became cocoons without refuge. They were in a dead camp with a dead fire and a corpse in a tent. They thought about their wives—even Jan's misery and Shelley's demand for freedom seemed so consoling now, so day-to-day. Tony's small slip with the scalpel was now nothing more than a reminder of the need for vigilance—a renewal, in a sense. Jack had a home and all his forebears buried on the edge of town. He could wait for the same. No big deal, just wink out. Nothing about this bothered him anymore. He had sometimes pictured himself in his coffin, big belly and all, friends filing by with sad faces. He belonged.

They couldn't sleep, or they barely slept; if one detected the other awake, they talked.

"I don't know what the environmentalists see in all these trees," Jack said. "Nature hates us. We'll be damn lucky to get out of this hole and back to civilization."

"Well, you want a little of both. A few trees, anyway. Some wildflowers."

"You try walking out of here. You'll see how much nature loves you."

There was no point worrying about it, Tony said; they would have the whole day tomorrow to work on their problems.

"So what do we do with the body?" Jack asked.

"The body is not our problem."

It couldn't have been many hours before sunrise by the time the bears came into the camp. There were at least three; they could be heard making pig noises as they dragged and swatted at the food that had been left out. Tony tried to get a firm count through a narrow opening in the tent flap while Jack cowered at the rear with Hewlitt's gun in his hands.

"It's nature, Tony! It's *nature* out there!"

Tony was too terrified to say anything. The bears had grown interested in their tent.

After a moment of quiet they could hear them smelling around its base with sonorous gusts of breath. At every sound, Jack redirected the gun. Tony tried to calm him, despite his own terror.

"They've got all they can eat out there, Jack."

"They never have enough to eat! Bears never have enough!"

Tony went to the flap and tied all its laces carefully, as though that made any difference. But then, as before, the sound of the bears stopped. After a time he opened a lace and looked out.

"I think they're gone," he said. He hated pretending to be calm. He'd done that in the operating room when it was nothing but a fucking mess.

"Let's give them plenty of time, until we're a hundred percent sure," Jack said. "We've got this"—Jack held the gun aloft—"but half the time shooting a bear just pisses him off."

Tony felt he could open the flap enough to get a better look. First light had begun to reveal the camp, everything scattered like a rural dump, even the pages of the girlie magazines, pink fragments among the canned goods, cold air from the river coming into the tent like an anesthetic. Tony said, "Oh, god, Jack. Oh, god."

"What?"

"The bears are in Hewlitt's tent."

Jack squealed and hunkered down onto the dirt floor. "Too good, Tony! Too good!"

Tony waited until he stopped and then said, "Jack, you need to take hold. We've got a long day ahead of us."

Jack sat up abruptly, eyes blazing. "Is that how you see it? You're going to tell me to behave? You're a successful guy. My wife thought you were a big successful guy before she was fat. So tell me what to do, Tony."

"Listen, start by shutting up, okay? We're gonna need all the energy in those big muscles of yours to get us out of this."

"That's straight from the shoulder, Tony. You sound like the old guinea from down by the meat processor again."

"I'm all right with that," said Tony. "Up with the founding families, piss poor though you all are, it must have been hard for you and Shelley to know how happy we were."

"Somebody's got to make sausage."

"Yes, they do."

"Linguini, pepperoni, abruzzo. Pasta fazool."

"I can't believe you know what pasta fazool is, Jack."

Jack imitated Dean Martin. "'When the stars make you drool, just like pasta fazool.' Asshole. Your mother made it for me."

He was gesturing with the rifle now. When the barrel swung past Tony's nose, the reality of their situation came crashing down on them as though they had awakened from a dream. Jack, abashed, went to the front of the tent and peered out. After a moment, he said, "All quiet on the western front."

Tony came to look over his shoulder, saw nothing.

"They're gone."

The two men emerged into the cold, low light, the gray river racing at the edge of the camp. There was nothing left of the food except a few canned goods scattered among the pictures of female body parts. The vestibule of Hewlitt's tent was torn asunder, to the point that the interior could almost be inspected from a distance. Jack clearly had no interest in doing so, but Tony went over gingerly, entered, then came out abruptly with one hand over his eyes. "Oh," he said, "Jesus Christ."

They picked through the havoc the bears had left until they'd found enough undamaged food for a day or so in the boat. They put their bedrolls in there, too, but the tents they left where they were. Any thought of staying in camp was dropped on the likelihood of the bears returning at dark.

"We'll start the motor when we need it," Tony said. "All we're doing is going downstream until we get out."

Jack nodded, lifted the anchor, and walked down to the boat, coiling the line as he went.

The river seemed to speed past. As they floated away, Tony thought that this was nature at its most benign, shepherding them away from the dreaded camp; but Jack, looking at the dark walls of trees enclosing the current, the ravens in the high branches, felt a malevolence in his bones. He glanced back at their abandoned tents: already, they looked like they'd been there for hundreds of years, like the empty smallpox tepees his grandpa had told him about. This might be good country if someone removed the trees and made it prairie like at home, he thought. With the steady motion of the boat, he daydreamed about the kinds of buildings he'd most like to see: a store, a church, a firehouse.

Tony said, "My dad was a butcher, and I'm a surgeon. I'm sure you've heard a lot of jokes about that around town."

"Uh-huh."

"The funny thing is, I didn't want to be a surgeon—I wanted to be a butcher. The old second-generation climb into some stratosphere where you'll never be comfortable again. Where you never know where you live."

"I don't think you'd like it back there at the packing plant."

"Not now—I've been spoiled. But if I'd stayed... I don't know. Dad was always happy."

"And you're not?" Jack asked.

"Not particularly. Maybe after Shelley goes. Now that I'm used to the idea, the divorce, I can't wait. I think I'm over spreading my discomfort around."

"Jan and I don't have the option," Jack said. "There's not enough for either one of us to start over on. We're stuck together whether we like it or not." He was thinking of how life and nature were just alike, but he couldn't figure out how to put it into words.

Boulders, submerged beneath the water, could be felt as the boat rose and fell, and the river began to narrow toward a low canyon. In a tightening voice, Tony said, "Most of humanity lives beside rivers. By letting this one take us where it will, we'll be delivered to some form of civilization. A settlement, at least." He reached inside his coat and pulled out a wallet. "I thought we better bring this."

"Is that Hewlitt's wallet?"

"That's not his name. There are several forms of identification, but none of them are for a Hewlitt." He riffled it open to show Jack the drivers' licenses and ID cards, all with the same picture and all with different names.

"He had a lot of musical talent," Jack said, and let out a crazy, mirthless laugh.

"See up there? I bet those are the rapids he was talking about."

"Oh, goody. Nature."

Indeed, where the canyon began, and even from this distance, the sheen of the river was surmounted by something sparkling, some effervescence, a vitality that had nothing to do with them. Shapes appeared under the boat, then vanished as the river's depth changed, the banks and walls of trees narrowing toward them and the approaching canyon walls. You couldn't look up without wanting to get out through the sky.

At the mouth of the canyon was a standing wave. Somehow the river ran under it, but the wave itself remained erect. A kind of light could be seen around it. Tony thought it had the quality of authority, like the checkpoint of a restricted area; Jack took it for yet another part of the blizzard of things that could never be explained, and that pointlessly exhausted all human inquiry. Carrying these distinct views, their boat was swept into the wave, and under; and Jack and Tony were never seen again.

WORDKEEPERS

by AIMEE BENDER

illustration by GRACIA LAM

I CAN'T REMEMBER the words of things. The words for words. I have lost my words. What's this from? Is it the Internet? Texting? Email? I see it in kids, too; it's not an aging thing. An aging issue. I do know that at the supermarket yesterday, I asked the guy where the weighing thing was, the thing that weighs other things, flailing around with my hands, indicating, and he crumpled up his forehead and said, "You mean the scale?"

"Yes!" I said, beaming, pumping his hand—"The scale!" As if he were the winner of an SAT giveaway.

At the doctor's office, I told my doc that it was sore.

"What's sore?"

I pointed to my neck. "This."

"Your throat," he said.

"Of course," I said.

We went over my symptoms. He gave me a subscription.

With hand gestures, you can fill in a lot of gaps. The words *thing* and *stuff* and *-ness* also help. *Patientness* instead of *patience*, *fastness* instead of *speed*, *honestness* instead of *honesty*. At the shoe store, I watched a lady walk up to the mini socks and point right at them. The salesguy knew just what she wanted.

*   *   *

"Cavemen point," said Susan, my neighbor, one Saturday morning. "You can always point at what you want, but you'd be returning to Neanderthal standards."

"Well, maybe we're going back to caveman times," I said, pouring a circle of wet pancake into the pan. "Tech forward, language back."

"Reverting," she said.

"What?"

"*Reverting* to caveman times."

"That's not my word choice," I said, picking up the flipper thing. "I said 'going back' on purpose. I don't like that word, *reverting*."

"If it was on purpose, then fine," she said, standing a fork on its end.

I flipped the pancake. "Oh, fuck off," I said.

Once the edges were all gold, I put one on her plate. A perfect goldy circle. She smiled at me. But not a thank-you smile, no; a self-satisfied one. She always looks so smug. Smug, smug, smug. I like that word very much, and I won't forget it easily.

Susan calls social websites silly distractions. She refuses to even look at an electronic book, because she says she must have pages, must. Fine; I read pages, too. I too enjoy the book smell everybody goes on and on about. Time for the perfumists to wake up, right? A perfume called *Book*? With its cologne follow-up, *Newspaper*? The question is, does she have to be so goddamn righteous about it? Does she have to raise her eyebrows like that, when I mention an app? She looked over my shoulder once while I was texting, and when I wrote *lol* she made a very clear point to me about how I was silent and not laughing out loud, not at all. I said it was just an expression, and that I was laughing out loud inside my own mind. She rolled her eyes, then, way back into her head. She's not even my girlfriend. We did sleep together once, right when I moved in, yes, but then it sort of drizzled away. We both got busy and I woke up to the neighbor problem. The neighbor-lover problem. And sure, fine, I do check my phone about every two minutes, but so do a lot of people, and it's better than smoking, that's what I say. It's the new, lung-safe cigarette.

"Those breathing things," a student of mine said last week, gesturing at her chest. She was trying to explain to me why she had to miss the history test. I nodded. I got it.

"Pneumonia," she said.

"You okay?"

"I think so," she said. "The doctor gave me drugs."

"Drugs?"

She thought for a second. She made that little wheeze sound. "Anti-robotics?"

I couldn't help smiling. "So you will not become a robot," I said.

"Hope not," she laughed.

In the daytime, I work at a school where I teach junior-high-school history. I have been working there for eight years, since I had a crisis of identity in law school and realized I hated reading red and beige books. Teaching's way better. I teach American history, and true, we do spend a lot of time on the Revolutionary War, more than on any other war, but junior-high-school kids like the idea of people throwing tea in the water.

You'd think in school it might be better with the words, but it's worse. When we have a good class discussion, my students will sometimes raise their hands with enthusiasticness, jumping up and down in their seats, but by the time I get around to calling on them, most of them can only say "I forgot what I was going to say." A good 50 percent of the time, this is true. I have taught now for eight years and this did not happen even five years ago. It is new.

"Where did it go?" I ask.

"Where did what go?"

"Your point?"

They shrug. "Don't know," they say. "Sorry," they say. "We are holding a lot of small things in our heads."

"What things?" I say.

"Things," they say. "In our..."

They point to their heads.

"We are holding a lot of them."

Half the time, as soon as they leave, I have a thing I am planning to do and I walk into the center of the room to do it and whatever it was flies away. Half my days I find myself standing in the centers of rooms.

*   *   *

In some study, they say phones and computers are replacing our cerebral cortexes, externalizing our thoughts so that we do not need to think them— the same way certain couples will have one quiet meeky person who trails off all the sentences and one overeager type who leaps in to finish. We're the trailer-offer, and Google's our jumpy mate. Susan is worried about this, but is it so bad? Sure, Shakespeare knew ten thousand words, or a million words, just a lot of words, and he was real good at what he did, but also no women were allowed in his shows and if you got sick with pneumonia you'd just die, probably in two days, and only half the children made it to age ten. So it's a trade-off, is what I say.

Susan shook her head when I told her this. "It's no trade," she said. She was over again, with wine. "Meaning," she said, "you can improve your vocabulary and still get your amoxicillin and vote. It's not like there's a checklist and for each era we only get ten helpful options, and everything else goes to shit."

"I like that word, *option*," I said.

"Are you kidding me?"

"*Optional*," I said. "*Opt. Opting*. Nice."

She poured herself a second glass of wine.

"I'm so sick of dating," she said, leaning back in her chair and lifting up her legs to sit cross-legged.

"Online?"

"Yeah," she said, sighing. "I hate picking a name for myself, you know? What am I supposed to name myself? Yesterday I saw a man and his Internet name was Fido. What am I supposed to do with that?"

"What'd you name yourself?"

"Nothing."

"You have to name yourself something," I said. "Or they don't let you on the site."

She finished her wine. Eyed the bottle. I refilled both of us, so it looked like it wasn't just her.

"Wordkeeper," she said.

"Your dating name is Wordkeeper?"

"Shut up," she said.

"Sex-y," I said.

"Well, maybe to someone it will be." She took off her glasses, and touched the middle top of her nose, a jester she does that I do like.

"It has a little bit of a dom tone," I said, sipping. "Like you're hoarding all the words and you'll give them out when you feel like it. Some guys will like that."

She had her eyes closed. She was thinking something private.

"Some guys," she said.

I went to open a bag of peanuts and poured them into a bowl. Susan and I have talked about dating since that one thing, but I have always said no. I'm not completely sure why. We are like the couple on the sitcom that have good sparks but never get together, for the sake of ratings.

"You know I can't," I said, putting the bowl on the table. "I'm your neighbor."

"So?" she said. She opened her eyes. "We get along. I see you almost every day."

"Too risky," I said.

"That is such bullshit!" she said. She glared at the table. She began to shell peanuts. "Are you just not... attracted?"

Susan is a good-looking woman, I'll give her that. She wears blouses with one button unbuttoned right where you'd want that to happen. Her glasses make her look like you want to take off her glasses. She gets plenty of dates, or she could, if she wanted.

"You're smug," I said. I laughed at myself, surprised.

"What do you mean?"

"'Wordkeeper'?"

"Is smug?"

I winced. "Yeah," I said. "Kind of."

"I'm old-fashioned," she said. She swept her shells into a little pile.

I smiled, but not an agreement smile.

She shook her head. "I don't mean to be," she said. "I just like the feeling of finding the right word in my mind and employing it. I get pleasure from that feeling. I prefer language to gesture. I figured other people might, too."

"Sure," I said.

"I don't think I'm better than you."

"It's okay. You probably are."

We sat there for a while. She liked to run her long nail down the length of each peanut and then open it up like a present.

"I suppose sex is all gesture," she said.

"Not even really gesture."

"I guess not. Not indicative at all."

"No."

She ate the peanuts. She was flushed from the wine. She wanted to take off her clothes, I could feel it, the same way she was undressing the peanuts, and I felt it as cruel then, how I didn't want to do anything with her. Maybe cruel to both of us. But the truth is, there was probably already email to check. I could masturbate faster. It was safer, in terms of fallout. Who wants to be in an argument with your neighbor?

She held the bottom of her wine glass down hard with her fingers, like otherwise she might just toss it across the room. I checked my phone. Sent a couple of quick texts. After a few minutes, she left.

The phone is about the same size as a cigarette pack. It's no surprise to me that the traditional cigarette lighter in the car has turned into the space we use to recharge our phones. They are kin. The phone, like the cigarette, lets the texter/former smoker drop out for a second to get a break. It lets you make a little love to the beautiful object. We need something. We can't live propless.

It wouldn't bother me except it bothers me. In the shower I gave myself a test. That stuff I put in my hair for suds? Is called shampoo. The silver tray hanging over the shower top? Is a caddy. The string I use to get crap out of my teeth? Is known as dental floss. She's in my head all day, Susan, so why have sex with her too? All day I hear her chiding me.

She doesn't come over for a few days, which is unusual. On Saturday I walk up to her place. I had a dream about her and it was nice. In the interest of living in the moment, I made a tray of chocolate-dipped strawberries. I made them Friday night. Good chocolate. Good with wine. Organic strawberries, because they are very high on the pesticide list otherwise. She opens the door.

"Yeah?" she says.

She looks tired. Her hair is less planned than usual. I step in. I give her the tray.

"You brought me these?" she says, suspicious.

"I did."

"What for?"

I was in the middle of her living room. I had a plan, I knew that. But the rest of it had vanished.

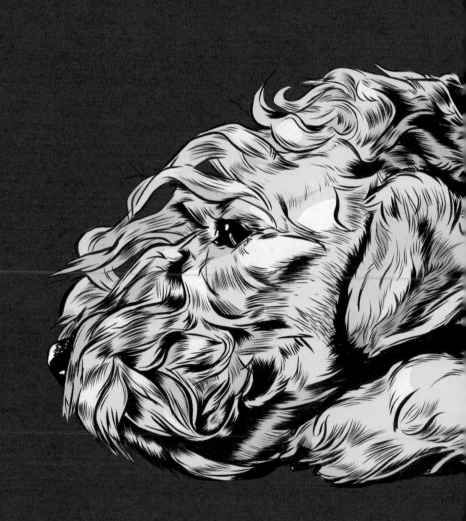

AMERICAN TALL TALE

by STEVEN MILLHAUSER

illustration by KELSEY DAKE

OF GREEN RAIN AND PORCUPINE COMBS;
OF HOT BISCUIT SLIM AND THE AMAZING GRIDDLE

LET ME TELL YOU a story about Paul Bunyan. You've all heard a tale or two about Paul Bunyan. You know the kind of man Paul Bunyan was. He could out-run out-jump out-drink and out-shoot you. He could out-cuss out-brag out-punch and out-piss you. He could swing that ax of his so hard, the wind it made would blow the needles clean off all the pine trees in ten acres of good timberland. Those pine needles, they'd come raining down for days. There never was a logging man could swing an ax like Paul Bunyan. Work! Why, he'd leap out of his bunk before the sun was up, jump into his greased boots, and finish buttoning up his mackinaw before his eyes were done opening. He'd step outside and pluck up a pine tree to brush his beard. Comb his hair with a porcupine. Then over to the cookhouse while his men were snoring away like a plague of mosquitoes and Hot Biscuit Slim standing there waiting at the griddle. You've heard about Paul Bunyan's griddle. That griddle was so big that to grease it you had to have three men skating on it with chunks of bacon fat strapped to their boot-soles. Paul Bunyan would swallow those hotcakes whole. He'd wash them down with a keg of molasses. He'd swallow so many hotcakes that if you laid them end to end they'd stretch clear across Minnesota, and that was before he got serious. After that he'd drink down two kettles of black coffee and a barrel of cider and head out to the woods. You never saw a man like Paul Bunyan for laying down timber. He'd swing that ax so hard the blade would cut through a white pine high as a hill and wide as a barn and just keep going. Time his swing was done he'd have two hundred trees laid out at his feet. He could log off twenty acres of good pine forest before lunch. Meantime the swampers would be cutting trails to the riverbanks, the limbers'd be chopping off branches, the sawyers cutting the pines into hundred-foot logs, and the hitchers hitching the logs to Babe the Blue Ox, who'd snake them over the trails to the riverbank landings. A forest never did stand a chance against Paul Bunyan. You know what they say about North Dakota. Used to be all timber till Paul and his shanty boys came by. They cut their way from Maine to Michigan and from Michigan to Wisconsin and from Wisconsin clear on over to Minnesota. They sawed their way from Minnesota through both Dakotas and on into Montana, swamping and chopping and limbing like men on fire. There never was anything like it. You know all that. You've heard the stories. But there's one story you might not have heard. You might not have heard the one about Paul Bunyan's brother.

IN WHICH I TELL YOU ABOUT PAUL BUNYAN'S BROTHER

Paul Bunyan never talked about his brother, and no wonder. That do-nothing dreamer drove Paul wild. Just the look of him was enough to set a logging man's teeth on edge. He had Paul's height all right, but that was all he had. He was the skinniest man alive enough to move. He was so skinny the sun couldn't figure out how to lay down his shadow and gave up trying. He was so skinny and scrawny that when he turned sideways all you could see was the end of his nose. He was a slump-shouldered knob-kneed stick-shanked droop-reared string-necked pole-armed shuffling husk of a man, with shambly shovel-feet that went in two different directions. His shoulders were so narrow he had to loop his red suspenders around his scraggy neck to keep his saggy pants from falling off. His knees were so knobby, when he walked it sounded like cookhouse spoons banging in tin bowls. But worse than the broomsticky look of him, this poor excuse for a mother's son was so lie-around lazy he made a dead dog look lively. He'd get up so late in the day it was time to go back to bed again. And what did this drowsy loafer like to do when he dragged himself out of bed slower than a log rolling uphill? Not one thing. He was so lazy it took him two days just to scratch the side of his head. He was so dawdly it took him six days just to finish a yawn. He was so loafy that when he blinked his eyes during a lightning storm, by the time he unblinked them the sun was shining. This spindly splintery slivery slip of a half-dead half man didn't eat enough in two days to feed a starving spider. If he found an old green pea at the back of a cupboard he'd cut it up into seven pieces and have enough dinner to last a week. If he found a crumb on the table he'd break it in half and wonder which half to have for lunch. And when he wasn't spending his time eating nothing and doing less, you'd find this skin-and-bonesman bent over some book like a hungry man leaning over a haunch of venison. Books! Why, you've never seen such a heap of books as that string-bean snooze-man had. There were books in the cupboards and books spilling out of the sink. There were slippery stacks of books on chair-seats and books on the bedcovers and piles of books sticking up so wobbly high you couldn't see out the windows. You couldn't walk in that house without books falling down around you like shot ducks. And when he was done blinking over his books, do you think that slumpy dozer would rouse himself to do a decent day's work? Not likely. Next thing you knew, he'd be taking a walk in the woods with his hands in his pockets just as cool as you please or sitting under a tree staring off at a sunbeam on a tree root or a moonbeam on a pond. If you asked him what in thunderation was he doing sitting under that tree, he'd look at you like maybe he'd seen a human being before but couldn't be sure of it just yet. Then he'd say: Just dreaming. Dreaming! That James Bunyan never drank whiskey, never put a plug of Starr tobacco in his cheek, never spat a sweet stream of tobacco juice over the rail of a porch, never shot a possum or cut open a rabbit or skinned a deer. He didn't know a pike pole from an ax-helve. He couldn't tell you how to shoe a draft horse or fix a split spoke in a wagon wheel. And yet this slope-backed dreamer, this walking cornstalk, this drift-about bone-bag and slouchy idler was brother to Paul Bunyan, who could tie a rope around a twisty river and straighten it out with one mighty pull.

HOW THE GREAT CONTEST GOT ITS START

Now, whatever you may say about Paul Bunyan, with his strut and his swagger and his great blue ox that measured forty-two ax handles and a plug of tobacco between the eyes, there was no denying he had his share of family feeling. Paul Bunyan felt duty-bound to visit that no-work all-play brother of his twice a year. That was once after the spring drive when the men rode the logs downriver to the mill and once near the start of the fall season. James Bunyan lived in a rundown house in the middle of whatever was left of the Northeast Woods, up in Maine. Paul would leave things in the hands of Johnny Inkslinger or Little Meery and go on over to the stable and give Babe the Blue Ox a good tickle behind his ears. Then he'd shoulder his ax and head out east. He'd start out fast with those mighty strides of his, one foot splashing down in the middle of Lake Michigan and the other making waves on the shore of Lake Huron, but the closer he got to Maine the slower he moved, cause the last man on earth he wanted to see was that leave-me-be brother of his. Well now, on this visit that I'm going to tell you about, he arrived on a fine September afternoon with the sun shining and the birds chirp-chirping and not a cloud in the sky. He found that joke of a brother of his flat on his back in bed just opening his eyes to take a look around. So there was James Bunyan lying there looking up at his brother Paul standing over him like the biggest pine tree you ever saw, and there was Paul Bunyan looking down at his brother James lying there like a long piece of rope nobody had any use for, and each one thinking he'd rather be standing up to his neck in a swamp with the rain coming down and the water rising than be there looking each other over like two roosters in a henhouse. Not a one of them could think of anything to say. How's Ma. How's Pa. That's good. Paul was just standing there fidgeting and squidgeting and eyeing the books and the apple cores lying all over the bedcovers and a boot on the chair and a shirtsleeve sticking out from under the bed, and he's burning for his neat bunkhouse with the rows of bunks against the walls and the washbowls with their pitchers all in a row and the boots at the bottom of the beds. You get up now, Paul says, and I'll find somethin to eat. But in the kitchen all he could find was the other boot in the sink, a raccoon on the table, and nothing to eat but a bunch of dried-out berries and a jug of sour cider. In the front room his brother and him sat down to talk, but there was no more to talk about than there ever was. Paul told him about the spring drive down the river when Febold Feboldson fell off a log and was picked out of the rapids by the hook of a peavey, and he told him about the good timber to be had out in Oregon, and James listened with a look on his face like a man who can't make up his mind whether to close his eyes and take a quick nap or open his mouth and take a slow yawn. The more Paul talked, the more James said nothing, till Paul couldn't stand it no more and said I don't see how a man can live like this and James said It suits me fine and before you know it Paul was shouting Why don't you make somethin of yourself instead of lyin around all day like a dog doin nothin and James was saying I'd rather lie around all day like a dog doing nothing than spend my time killing off good trees that weren't doing anybody a bit of harm and that got Paul so mad he said I can out-run out-jump out-drink and out-shoot you and I can out-chop out-cut out-saw and out-swamp you and James said Maybe you can out-run out-jump out-drink and out-shoot me and maybe you can out-roar out-scream out-howl and out-shout me but there's one thing you can never do not if you live five hundred years and that's out-sleep me. Well now, Paul had never heard words the like of that coming out of his brother's mouth before. And when Paul heard those words coming out of his brother's mouth like a swarm of angry bees he didn't know whether to laugh till he cried at the sight of his bony brother challenging him like a man with muscle on him or cry till he laughed at the thought of himself Paul Bunyan taking up a challenge thrown out by that bloodless no-man brother of his. Then he said I can out-bash out-gash out-mash and out-smash you and there's one other thing I can do more than anyone ever can and that's out-sleep you. So that was how the Great Sleeping Contest got its start.

THE BIGGEST BED THAT EVER WAS

Well now, first thing Paul Bunyan did when he got back to camp was step into his bunkhouse and give a good look at his bed. That bed of his was so long that when it was morning at one end it was midnight at the other. That bed of his was so wide, Johnny Inkslinger once reached the middle of it riding a fast horse all day. Paul Bunyan took a look at that bed and knew it wasn't a bad bed as beds go, a little cramped maybe, good enough to lie down in for thirty-nine winks before you jumped back to work, but there were bunks all up and down the other wall with men snoring and grunting and talking in their sleep, and sometimes old Babe would stick his head in through a bunkhouse window and lick Paul awake. What he needed was a bed set off by itself somewhere, a bed where a man could settle in for a good long sleep and turn over any which way he pleased and not wake himself up. The more he thought about it, the more he knew what he had to do. So he hitched up Babe to a supply wagon and headed out to Iowa. You know what they say about Iowa. In Iowa the corn grows so tall it takes one man to see halfway up the stalk and another man to see the rest of the way. In Iowa the corn grows so tall you find hawks and eagles building nests up near the top. They say those Iowa cornstalks grow so wide, the farmers have to hire loggers from the Michigan woods to chop everything down and haul it all off to the silos. They say there's so much corn growing in Iowa, if you want to lift up your arm to scratch your nose you have to cross over into Nebraska. Now, what Paul did was this. He hired himself out to harvest half the corn in Iowa. He and big Babe tramped right into the middle of that Iowa corn. Paul swung his ax and stalks began falling so fast and hard the ears popped right out of the husks and landed smack in the wagon. Paul hauled the ears over to the silos and loaded up the stalks in the wagon till the sides creaked with the weight of it. He spit out some tobacco juice and headed out of Iowa by way of Nebraska and then Colorado and made it down to Arizona before the tobacco juice hit the ground. He went on over to the Grand Canyon and looked down into it. You know the story of the Grand Canyon. That was back when Paul Bunyan was traveling west and dragged his peavey behind him. The hook of the peavey is what dug up that canyon. Now, what Paul did there on the rim was this. He tipped his wagon over and watched those cornstalks go crashing down. The cornstalks spread out over the canyon bottom and rose halfway up the cliffsides. Paul liked what he saw but he wasn't done yet, not by a long shot. That layer of cornstalks made a pretty good mattress for a man of his size, but it was scratchy as a pack of alley cats. He stood on the rim of the canyon looking down and thinking hard. Just then a big flock of geese came flying over and Paul got himself an idea. He sucked in his breath till his chest looked like a mainsail in a storm. He raised his face to the sky and blew so hard you could see the sun flicker and almost go out. That big breath of his blew all the feathers off those geese. The feathers came floating down nice and soft and settled over the cornstalks. When another flock flew by, Paul puffed himself up and gave another blow. He kept blowing feathers off so many geese, by the time he was done he had himself a thick cover of feathers lying all over the cornstalks like a big quilt you could slip inside of and keep warm. Only thing missing was a pillow. So Paul, he traveled back to camp and ordered some of his boys to buy up five thousand head of good merino sheep. You know those ranches out in Montana and Utah where they have so many sheep you can take off your shoes and walk river to river on sheepback. Well, while his men were off buying up sheep, Paul set about clearing the stumps from fifty acres of logged-off woods. How he did it was this. He walked along and stomped those stumps into the ground one after the other with one stamp of his boot till they were all set even with the dirt. Soon as the boys came back with the sheep, Paul drove every last one of those merinos onto his cleared-off land. He sharpens two axes and sets the handles in the ground with the ax-blades facing each other. Then he sets up two more axes with the blades facing each other only lower down. Then what he does, he runs the sheep between those double axes so you have strips of fleece dropping off on both sides clean as a whistle. That was the first sheep-shearing machine. He loaded up the sheared-off wool in his wagon and headed back down to the Grand Canyon. He lifted out those strips of wool and laid them down along one end of his goosefeather quilt and had himself a pillow so fine and soft that before he was done, three ringtail cats, two mountain lions, and a mule deer lay curled up asleep.

UP IN MAINE

While Paul was blowing a storm of feathers down from the sky and running merino sheep through his four-ax shearer, that droopy drag-foot brother of his was spending his time sitting slumped on his backbone in a broke-legged armchair next to a spiderwebby window or leaf-shuffling his sloggy way along a soggy path in the woods with three floppy mufflers wrapped around his stretchy neck and a beat-up book sticking out of his peacoat pocket.

IN WHICH PAUL SHOULDERS HIS AX AND SETS OFF

The Great Sleeping Contest was set to begin a good month into the fall season, first night of October at nine sharp. To keep things fair, Paul went and hired up a crew of sleep-checkers to work three-hour shifts keeping an eye on each dead-to-the-world stone-faced snorer. You could twitch in your sleep and you could turn over in your sleep, you could groan in your sleep and moan in your sleep, but if you opened an eye so much as half a crack you were done sleeping. These sleep-checkers were shrewd-eyed rough-living no-nonsense men known for rock-hard character and knife-sharp sight—a couple of keelboatmen who worked the Ohio River, a buffalo hunter from

Oklahoma, three Swede farmers from Minnesota, a Kentucky sharpshooter, two trail guides from the high Rockies, a frontiersman from Missouri, a cattle rancher from Texas, two Utah sheep ranchers, a Cheyenne Indian from Colorado, and two fur trappers from Tennessee. After a cookhouse dinner of thick pea soup and spiced ham baked in cider, Paul Bunyan stood up and addressed his shanty boys. He told them he could out-jump out-run out-fight and out-work any man who ever logged the North Woods or walked the face of the earth in spiked boots and he was off to prove he could out-sleep out-nap out-snooze and out-doze any man big enough to brag and fool enough to try. Johnny Inkslinger would take over camp operations while he was away. Any trouble and Little Meery and Shot Gunderson would take care of it with four hard fists and a six-foot pike pole. Then Paul Bunyan said goodbye to his men and specially to Johnny Inkslinger and Little Meery and Hot Biscuit Slim and Big Ole the Blacksmith and Febold Feboldson and Shot Gunderson and Sourdough Sam and Shanty Boy and then he went over to the stable and gave old Babe a big hug around the neck and a big tickle behind his blue ears and set off walking with a swing in his stride and his ax over his shoulder. He stamped through forests and along river valleys, took one step over the Missouri River onto the plains of Nebraska, and dusted off his boots in Colorado. First thing he does in Arizona is pluck up a fifty-foot saguaro cactus to comb his beard. Gets to the Grand Canyon two minutes before nine. One minute before nine he's down on his crackly cornstalk bed. Went and laid himself out on his back and sank into those goosefeathers with his feet up against a cliff and his head on his pillowy wallowy wool. He set his ax steel-down in the cornstalks with the hickory handle sticking up beside him, and right at nine sharp he shut his eyes and fell into a mighty sleep.

IN WHICH JAMES GETS HIMSELF READY

The day the Great Sleeping Contest is set to begin, the sun's going down in Maine and James Bunyan is dragging himself out of bed slower than a one-horned snail in an icehouse. He goes yawning his way into the creaky kitchen and looks around for anything to eat but all he can find is a dead mouse in a cupboard and one stale raisin in a box. He sits down on a three-leg chair at a tilty table with a hungry cat on it and looks at that dried-up raisin like it's a plate of bear stew served with brown beans baked in molasses. He sets to work slow on that wreck of a raisin and when he's done he's so stuffed he just sits there like a dead branch leaning against the side of a barn. He stares at his left hand so long it starts looking like a foot. He stares at his right foot so long it turns into a nose. He figures it's time to rest up after his exertions, so what he does, he goes back to his room and crawls into bed and stretches out on his bone-bumpy back with his hands behind his bootlace of a neck and his stringy legs crossed at his stalky ankles and looks at the ceiling beams jumpy with shadows thrown up by the candle on the bedside table. He sees blue horses riding over hills. The clock hand on the cracked old clock on the wall crawls over to nine slow as a cat on crutches. James closes his eyes and starts snoring.

HOW THE SHANTY BOYS SPENT THE NIGHT

Back at the camp the men swamped and felled and limbed from sunup to noon. They sat on stumps to gulp down sourdough biscuits and black coffee brought over by wagon and went on logging till the sun dropped down. None of it was the same without Paul Bunyan. After the cookhouse dinner they swapped stories round the bunkhouse stoves but they all of them knew they were just sitting there waiting. Paul Bunyan was the no-sleepingest man they'd ever seen. He'd throw himself down on his back and before his head hit the pillow the rest of him would be standing up raring to go. Some said he was bound to come back before midnight, others said he was already back out there chopping in the dark. Little Meery said they ought to get themselves some rest cause he knew in his bones a man like Paul Bunyan wouldn't be back till next morning. Past midnight there was a crashing noise in Paul Bunyan's bunkhouse and the men sat up ready to yell out a cheer and dance him a welcome-home but it wasn't anybody there but big Babe, busted out of the stable to knock his head through a bunkhouse window. All next day the men swamped and chopped and sawed but their hearts weren't in it. That night not a story got told round the bunkhouse stoves. The men stayed flat in their bunks with ears open wide as barn doors and eyes shut tight as friz oysters waiting for Paul Bunyan to come on back from his cornstalk mattress and sheep pillow down there in that faraway canyon under the stars.

THE LONG SLEEP

Johnny Inkslinger could push the men hard when he had to. He told them

Paul Bunyan was bound to sleep for a week and they ought to stop dreaming about it and get to work. Why, a man like that could sleep two weeks, maybe three. Weeks passed, the first snow came. It snowed so hard you couldn't see the end of your ax. One day the sun came out, birds sang in the trees. The men drove the logs downriver to the mill and broke camp for the summer. In the fall they hitched the bunkhouses and the cookhouse and the stable to Babe the Blue Ox, who hauled the whole lot of it over hills and across rivers to a fir forest that grew so high the tops of the trees were hinged to let the moon go by. Nights they still talked about Paul Bunyan round the bunkhouse stoves, but it was like telling stories about someone who was long gone and maybe never had been there at all. Remember the winter of the blue snow? Member the time old Paul Bunyan walked across Minnesota and his boot-prints were what formed the ten thousand lakes? Member the time Paul Bunyan dug that watering hole for Babe the Blue Ox? That watering hole is Lake Michigan. Then there was the time Paul Bunyan chopped a dog in half by mistake. Put it back together wrong, with two legs up and two legs down. Remember the hodag? The whirling wampus? In the cold weather the men rose late and stopped work early. Johnny Inkslinger cussed and howled but it was no use at all. Babe was so sad he stayed put in his stable and wouldn't come out for anything. The men forgot all about him, all except Hot Biscuit Slim, who brought barrels of hotcakes out to the stable every morning. That winter the snow fell for forty-seven days. Snow was so high you had to cut tunnels to get to the trees. The trunks were hard as whetstones. When the ax-heads dragged against them, the blades got so sharp they could cut a snowflake in half. Some of the new men said they'd heard about Paul Bunyan, but it was so cold their words froze in the air and didn't thaw out till spring. In the warm weather the men drove the logs downriver to the mill, and when it was over some of the crew went to work in the mill town and didn't return to camp in the fall. Johnny Inkslinger moved the camp to higher ground that looked out over miles of fresh spruce forest. The men cut trails and felled trees and hauled them to the river landings. Snow howled down from black skies. In the warm nights the men sat outside the bunkhouses, spitting tobacco juice into the fire. Some said Paul Bunyan had gone to sleep down there in the Grand Canyon and drowned when the river rose. Some said Paul Bunyan was a story men used to tell at night around the bunkhouse stove.

AMERICAN TALL TALE

IN WHICH JAMES DOES SOME DREAMING

While Paul Bunyan was sleeping the stony sleep of an ax-swinging man dead to the world on his mighty bed, that no-account brother of his was doing what he was always doing up in the woods in Maine: dreaming his life away. There was nobody ever dreamed so much as that dodge-life brother did. Dreamed all day on his bone-hard backside and dreamed all night on his brawnless back. Now he was nose-up in his bed dreaming so many dreams you'd think his head would be crackling like a pinewood fire in a bunkhouse stove. He dreamed he was a fish swimming in a river. He dreamed he was flying through the sky like a buzzard or a red-tailed hawk. He dreamed about things you weren't supposed to see, like what it was like walking around up in heaven with angels going by and what it was like far down under the earth where things looked at you in the dark. He dreamed he was red fire. He dreamed he was dead. He dreamed he was so big his brother Paul could stand on the flat of his hand with his little ax on his shoulder. He dreamed he was throwing fistfuls of pine cones into every state and great pine forests sprang up all over the land. Those trees grew so high they brushed up against the Big Dipper. There wasn't anything but trees every which way you looked. Towns and cities got swallowed up. Birds spoke words you could understand. People lived on riverbanks and grew what they needed. Bears and coyotes lay down with wild turkeys and deer. Loggers turned their axes into harmonicas. It was summer all the time. They say James Bunyan dreamed so hard it plumb wore him out and he had to go on sleeping just to keep himself alive enough to dream some more.

IN WHICH THE GREAT CONTEST IS DECIDED

You know the kind of man Paul Bunyan was. Once he set his mind on something, there was no stopping him. He slept down there in that canyon when it was so cold you could see ten-foot icicles hanging from his chin. He slept in that canyon when it was so hot, red rocks melted away in the sun. He slept with coyotes and bobcats curled up in his beard and two bald eagles nesting in his hair. He slept when howling winds sent boulders crashing down cliffsides right onto his bed and he slept when raindrops the size of McIntosh apples whipped against his face and soaked through his mackinaw. One day a strange thing happened. Paul Bunyan opened his eyes. Just like that. Up above him, a crowd of people standing on a rim trail pointed down and started shouting. Somebody called out, Ten years and twelve hours! Paul stood up so fast, goosefeathers flew all around him like a storm of snow. First thing he did, he plucked a spruce tree off the top of the North Rim and combed his beard. That beard was so long it grew down to his feet and wrapped around his wool socks and kept going. It kept going till it reached a cliff and grew halfway up like ivy. Next thing he did, he stepped up out of the canyon all covered in feathers like a giant goose. He brushed off his mackinaw with a ponderosa pine and put his ax on his shoulder. A powerful hunger was in him, but he needed to do one thing before he ate and that was see that brag-mouth brother of his. He headed east and got to Maine so fast he was knee-deep in ocean before he realized he had to turn back. The house in the woods wasn't the same. Bushes rose up over all the windows, wildflowers grew on the roof. The porch was mashed in by a dead pine covered in moss. Inside, long branches stuck in through the smashed-up windows. Squirrels and possums scampered over the mossy furniture. The door to the bedroom stood open and in the dark of the room he saw a stranger sitting in a chair at the side of the bed. In the bed his brother was stretched out on his back with his broomstraw arms crossed over his twig of a chest. His stringy beard was so long it came slithering down over his legs and curled around his chicken-hawk feet. From there it dropped to the floor and twisted itself around a bedfoot. A bony dog lay up on the bed next to him whimpering for all he was worth. Moss and wild mushrooms grew in that beard. His brother's long nose was thin and sharp as an ax-blade. The whimpering dog, the dark room, the stranger in the chair, the graveyard silence, it was all making Paul mighty uneasy. He looked at his brother's caved-in cheeks and forgot the Great Sleeping Contest. He forgot everything in that dead-quiet room. All he wanted to do was get out of there quick as a fox on fire and go back to his loggers, but he couldn't hardly make himself move. He bent down to look close at his brother. Those nothing shoulders stuck up through his shirt like chicken bones. Paul wondered what it would feel like to touch him. He wanted to give him something. He took his ax off his shoulder and put it down on the bed next to his brother. He laid it out real slow. Just then James opened one eye and looked at him. The stranger in the chair said, Ten years twelve hours and sixteen minutes. Paul jumped back and gave out a roar. He roared so loud the bony dog who was licking James's face went flying off the bed and rolled into a corner. Paul Bunyan roared so loud the branches blew away from the windows and let in the sun. James scrunched up his eye in the sunlight and laid a spidery arm across his face. He said, Can't a man get a little shut-eye around here? Then he rolled over and went back to sleep.

AFTER

Paul knew he was beat, and beat by his own rickety bone-pile of a no-good brother. But before he had time to feel powerful bad, a mighty hunger rose up in him. He hadn't had a bite to eat in ten years twelve hours sixteen minutes and then some. He was so hungry he could've eaten his own boots fried in butter. He was so hungry he could've bitten off half of Maine and washed it down with the St. Lawrence River. In his mind he saw Hot Biscuit Slim standing over his griddle with the batter spattering and the hotcakes flipping over in the air. Paul picked up his ax and left that cabin in a hurry. He was in such a hurry he jumped onto a hurricane going his way but got off fast when he saw it was blowing too slow. He got one foot wet in Lake Huron and the other foot wet in Lake Michigan. Time he reached camp the men were looking up from the middle of the woods wondering what all the ruckus was about. When they saw Paul Bunyan standing there like the tallest tree in the forest some let out a cheer, some looked surprised, and some scratched their heads in wonder. Paul went straight to the stable and hugged his blue ox so hard they say Babe turned green and then red before he went back to his rightful color. Then over to the cookhouse so fast his hug had to catch up with him later. They say Hot Biscuit Slim out-cooked himself that day. He set up a big chute at the side of the griddle and sent those hotcakes down one after the other so's they'd fall smack on Paul's platter and stack up all by themselves. Ten men kept filling the batter kettle and twenty men kept throwing split logs and brush under the griddle to keep the fire roaring. Paul ate so many hotcakes that morning that rivermen and sawmill men came from far away as Idaho just to watch that ax-man eat. He ate so many hotcakes there wasn't any flour left from Maine to Oregon and they had to haul it down in barrels on flatboats from Canada. Paul kept throwing hotcakes into his mouth and washing'm down with a kettle of molasses till he figured it was time to pick up his ax and do a little work. He went out into the woods and swung his ax so hard, when the trees hit the ground they split into piles of trim pine boards. He worked so quick he felled an acre of white pine before you even heard the sound of his ax. As he swung he roared out: I can out-run out-jump out-drink and out-shoot you and I can out-bash out-gash out-mash and out-smash you and my own little brother up in Maine can out-sleep out-nap out-snooze and out-doze you even if you're a grizzly bear holed up in a cave in winter. All that night the men in the bunkhouses could hear trees falling and no sign of Paul Bunyan. They say he swung that ax fourteen days and fourteen nights before he stopped to wipe a drop of sweat from his cheek. Some say he chopped his way over the Rockies clear past the coast of Oregon and stood knee-deep in the Pacific chopping waves in half. He chopped so hard he never did have time to see that no-muscle brother of his again. They say James Bunyan was so almighty tired after battling it out with his brother he spent all his time trying to catch up on his sleep. Some say he's sleeping still. I wouldn't know about that. These are stories you hear.

A LAND RUSH IN IRAN

ONCE HOME TO SWEDISH ARCHITECTS
AND THE PARTYGOING SET, CHANGE IS COMING
TO IRAN'S RICHEST NEIGHBORHOOD

nonfiction by VIVECA MELLEGARD

I

A T 6 A.M. THE sun casts a swath of hot light over Elahiyeh. From my grandmother's balcony, there is a view of the whole neighborhood, Tehran's garden suburb, nestled in the purple shadows of the Alborz mountain range. Cranes like mechanical trees swing across the skyline. Even now, a woodpeckering of machines—drilling, boring, smashing, scraping—disrupts the early-morning calm. In Elahiyeh, and all across the city, construction is king.

I can see Amin Street, and my family's old plot of land, between the various emerging monoliths. The brick wall that surrounds the property is still there, buckling like an old man's creaky knees, but within its perimeter, in place of the villa built by my grandfather, stand two white-stone apartment blocks, three stories high, with dark and dusty balconies. Of the gardens, only the plane trees along one side of the narrow street remain, flanking a meltwater stream that flows down from the mountains—a typical sight in Tehran, one that hasn't yet changed.

The city's population is expected to swell to 15 million in the next four years; multistory apartment buildings have replaced the big single-family houses along my old street. Despite increasing pollution, overcrowding, and the threat of earthquakes like the one that injured

---

ABOVE LEFT: *The view of Elahiyeh from the author's grandmother's balcony.*
BELOW LEFT: *A new building on the author's family's former plot of land. Photos by Viveca Mellegard.*

a hundred people in northern Iran in January—despite, even, the threat of economic collapse, and war—skyscraper construction continues unabated. The capital is in the throes of a housing boom.

II

Change came abruptly to Elahiyeh. In 1979, when the embassies closed their gates and the wealthy families abandoned their houses, the new government appropriated many of the properties that they left behind. Islamic charities, invited in by the nascent regime, laid claim to land belonging to the Shah's ministers and the international crowd. A different set of neighbors moved in—well-connected supporters of the new government, and, guided by the charities, the homeless and the poor.

A year later, when Iraq invaded Iran from the west, floods of people fled the towns and villages on the border and sought refuge in and around the capital. By 1986, Tehran's population had mushroomed; more than a million new residents had arrived in the years since 1976. The revolution and the war's demands for cannon fodder, meanwhile, pushed the birth rate upward; the new government dismantled the Shah's family-planning clinics, and pressed its citizens to help keep their country's numbers strong. Girls as young as nine were allowed to marry. By 1988, Iran's population had grown to 52 million people—nearly double what it was twenty years before. In response, the government found good use for the empty plots in Elahiyeh. The era of skyscrapers had begun.

In 1990, Gholamhossein Karbaschi, Tehran's newly appointed mayor, came up with a series of controversial policies to make the municipality financially independent; the most lucrative involved development. By 1998, Karbaschi's administration had collected $6 billion in taxes and fees relating to construction. Karbaschi became known as "the man who sold Tehran's air"—for the right price, his administration allowed developers to bypass Tehran's height limits, and turn one-story buildings into structures with as many stories as their builders could afford.

Karbaschi's administration also pushed through plans for public parks, libraries, cultural centers, and sports facilities; the mayor himself helped found Iran's first full-color newspaper while in office. But in 1998, as the national political climate swung in a more conservative direction, he was imprisoned on corruption charges. His swift departure appeared to inaugurate a pattern. Outnumbered by conservatives in parliament, reformists like Karbaschi and the succession of mayors who followed him were inevitably found guilty of either embezzlement or mismanagement.

Elahiyeh's skyline had already been thoroughly reshaped by the time the next mayor, Morteza Alviri, came to office; the problem was that no one could decide how high the buildings should be allowed to go. Alviri attempted to reestablish a five-story limit. When he resigned, in 2002, under his own cloud of accusations, the next mayor, Mohammad-Hassan Malekmadani, lowered the limit to two.

Meanwhile, land prices skyrocketed. More and more of Elahiyeh's garden estates were giving way to construction sites, and again attempts at regulation, and preservation, did little to slow the pace of change. Since the 1980s, there had been calls to safeguard the quality of the city's air; at one point the Revolutionary Council asked the municipality to levy taxes on the felling of the city's trees in order to protect them. Walnuts and mulberries were valued at up to 5 million *tomans* each (roughly $4,000, today).

Reaction to the new law was swift. The tax applied only to healthy trees, not to those that were diseased or dead, so people stopped watering their trees, or poisoned them, and fires consumed many of Elahiyeh's remaining gardens. Not even Tehran's latest mayor hewed to the city's guidelines. In January 2003, Malekmadani was given a five-month jail sentence for approving construction permits that threatened the preservation of green spaces, and ignored the minimum standards for distance between buildings.

III

The garden is a Persian invention. In the old Iranian language of Avestan, according to Mehrdad Fakour in the *Encyclopaedia Iranica*, "The word *pairidaêza*, Old Persian *paridaida*, Median *paridaiza* ('walled-around,' i.e., a walled garden), was transliterated into Greek *paradeisoi*, then rendered into the Latin *paradisus*, and from there entered into European languages, the French *paradis*, and the English *paradise*."

Elahiyeh means "paradise" in Farsi. From my grandmother's balcony, some greenery is still visible through the skyscrapers—the remnants of walled gardens that date back to 1921, when the whole of Elahiyeh, once composed of three estates, was broken up after the fall of the last Qajar king. While it's nearly impossible for me to imagine the wheat fields and cherry orchards that once dotted the neighborhood, my grandmother cherishes such memories. She and her family would make the daylong journey from southern Tehran by donkey, riding toward the coolness of the Alborz foothills. All summer long the children raced up and down the hills and soaked themselves under waterfalls, and at night they slept on the roof, under a dizzying canopy of stars. They woke at dawn, sheltered from the mountain chill by thick blankets. Elahiyeh was their Eden.

In the 1930s, my Swedish grandfather came to Tehran and established the construction company Svenska Entreprenad AB. He won large contracts from the government of Reza Shah, father of the last Shah; SENTAB constructed bridges, hospitals, and roads in every corner of the country. It built the University of Tehran and Mehrabad Airport. Whenever I'm there, I think of the stories my parents told me about the city in the 1960s, of partygoers from all over the world heading to Mehrabad for breakfast after dancing all night. The imprint of that era is very faint now.

My grandfather fell in love with Iran, and relinquished his share of the family farm in Sweden, though he remained very close to his siblings and made an annual visit home. Toward the end of one of those trips, he was invited by one of his brothers to a party, and there he met my grandmother. At the end of the night, knowing he would soon have to return to Iran, he proposed to her. She accepted, enchanted by the idea of an adventure.

Back in Tehran, he eventually built the house where I spent the first years of my life—a redbrick one-story villa with a porch and a sloping roof. There was a patio paved with large stones, and a swimming pool, and beyond that a garden fringed by rosebushes and tall trees. It was the style of architecture favored by Tehran's Europeans at the time.

There is a photograph of me on the day I was brought home from the hospital, with my mother and three brothers standing by a garden wall covered with spring climbing roses. During my formative years I played in that garden, making flower-and-leaf stew for the dogs or searching for Oscar, our pet tortoise. Sometimes I called over the wall to Reza, the boy who lived next door. If he was home, he climbed over, and we chatted together before deciding where to play. I remember thinking the family next door was odd because Reza's mother wore a *chador* inside the home. My own mother taught aerobics to her friends in our grandparents' house, on another of our garden's adjoining properties.

That house was at the top of the garden, separated by a wrought-iron gate. Steps led up to a yard in which my grandmother planted daisies, corn-flowers, and tall grasses, attempting to make the garden resemble a Swedish meadow. There was a small paddling pool for me; inside the house, my grandfather kept a low-standing bookshelf for a game I liked to play, which involved pulling out his architecture books and piling them into a heap on the floor. The odd trips to the baker at the end of Amin Street were filled with wonder for me: the sight of the bric-a-brac man, the smell of corn on the cob grilled on a brazier and dipped in saltwater and butter.

Occasionally, city life intruded. In spring a man brought carts piled high with mounds of camel dung, which he tipped onto the lawn, creating an unbearable stink. Later it was evidence of revolutionary change that spiked the serenity of the garden. First the muezzin's call to prayer, unheard of until then in that part of the city, and then bullet shells hurled over the walls by marauding young men.

IV

Whenever I come home to Elahiyeh now, I like to wander through our old neighborhood and take in the changes. I do this despite the fact that, as a woman walking alone, I tend to attract unwanted attention. Men stare, and mutter under their breath.

At first I was rattled by this; if there are any benefits to the compulsory Islamic garb that has been enforced inconsistently since the revolution, it is the occasional equality between men and women that it seemed to establish. By observing the dress code, women from conservative families could participate in activities that, before the revolution, would have been deemed unsuitable. A woman who might have expected a future as a wife, mother, and homemaker had the option to study at a university and pursue a career, all thanks to the headscarf.

In more recent years, however, an ambiguous space has opened up between modesty and the subversion of it. Prostitution lies at one end of the spectrum; there are parts of the city well-known for being pickup points. For everyone else, the gaze has usurped any possibility of sexual temperance. As the only public contact between men and women, the eyes have become weapons of mass desire. Nowadays most people prefer to drive.

Two women walking together is still somewhat socially acceptable. Twenty-eight-year-old Samaneh Ghadarkhan, a city reporter, agreed to accompany me on my last visit. Samaneh, who was born after the revolution, is fascinated by Tehran's past—one that she, too, believes is on the verge of disappearing completely. (She has herself, in fact, emigrated to Canada since the trip described here, having found it too difficult to continue her work uncensored.)

On that walk, I take us on a shortcut that avoids the ever-present traffic, leading us from my grandmother's apartment block down the hills to my old street. Huge green stone steps have been cut into one hill; few people use the path anymore, but I can remember my grandmother and myself walking it, and the challenge it posed for a three-year-old. Going down the massive steps now, I see they are beginning to fall away on one side, where the foundation for a new building has been laid.

Directly ahead of us is Amin Street. Ten meters wide, it seems narrower with the cars racing along it, hugging the stream on one side and our old brick wall on the other. At the end of the street, alongside the apartment blocks, the smell of fresh bread has attracted a breakfast queue outside the still-functioning bakery—mostly Afghans and construction workers waiting for sheets of stone-baked *lavash* to be folded into steaming piles once they've been pulled from the *tanoor*. A young man named Nasari sits outside the last remaining brick villa on the street, tearing into the hot, thin bread and rolling strips of it around a bit of cheese.

Some Swedish neighbors of ours lived in that house before the revolution. When they left, an Islamic charity took it over, and as far as I know no one has lived there since. A glimpse through the garden door reveals that the roof has fallen through; branches are growing into the windows. Nasari, who speaks quietly and doesn't ever glance up at us as we talk, looks after the property. He came to Tehran from Kabul, and quickly found that his nationality gave him an advantage. Afghan migrant laborers are preferred for caretaker jobs, as Afghans are thought to be generally more skeptical than other ethnicities, and less likely to allow snoopers onto the property. When I explain that I used to live on the street, though, he agrees to show us the house and garden.

Samaneh, in response, whispers to me that it would be unwise. She could ask her husband to come back with us another time, she says. Later she explains that many of the rapes that happen in Tehran are thought to be committed by Afghan men.

"Who would know where we were, if anything happened?" she says.

Since the demonstrations of the Green Movement in 2009, a new sense of vulnerability is palpable. Foreigners are hardly the only source of potential danger; the more-pressing threat comes from the *basij*, the regime's religious enforcers, and even from the ordinary traffic police. There is a sense that anyone can be hauled in for questioning, on whatever charges, and with little to no recourse to justice. I heard a story from a family member of a woman in her forties who was shopping with her mother one day: the mother suddenly heard screaming, and ran out of the shop she'd gone into just in time to see her daughter being pushed into a patrol car. She pummelled the policeman and yelled blue murder until a crowd formed, and eventually the man backed down. The daughter was released; her crime seems to have been nothing more than being an attractive woman, one who might have been easy pickings for a bored officer who fancied exercising his power.

Samaneh and I walk back up the street to the lot where my old house once stood. The address on the wall is the same, but now there is a buzzer for the flats occupying what used to be our garden. Mr. Sadekhi, a distinguished gray-haired man in his sixties, comes to the door when we ring. When I introduce myself, he immediately recognizes my surname. He tells me that the electricity meter is still registered to the Mellegards, and I joke that I hope we won't have to pay twenty-six years' worth of bills.

Mr. Sadekhi bought the plot from the woman to whom my mother sold the property, and for six or seven years he lived in our former house. The only thing he neglected was the swimming pool; he had been afraid he might be reported for having decadent Western habits, so it lay empty, and withered. While his children were earning their degrees in Germany, he built apartments on the property for each of them. By 1999, the villa, garden, and pool had given way to the flats. My grandparents' house next door had already been built over.

That transition coincided with a black period before the 1997 presidential elections, when journalists, writers, and political activists were murdered in a brutal purge. The thread of suspicion that weaves through most societies in a state of flux knotted itself into the fabric of everyday Iranian life. People who lived on their own, in houses, became fearful that they were exposed to prying eyes, and the attention of the secret police. Many moved into what they considered to be the relative safety of the new apartment blocks. There were economic incentives, too: interest rates abroad were at a high, and profits from Tehran property sales could be tucked away in foreign bank accounts.

Mr. Sadekhi asks how it feels, to stand where my old house used to be. In many ways, I tell him, I'm glad that it no longer exists. The fact that there's no physical trace of the world I knew means that there's nothing that could challenge my memories of it.

A faint breath of wind lifts up the dust; traffic crawls along. There is never enough parking, now. A few of the old single-family dwellings have been replaced by twenty-story buildings, with their concomitant demands on the public space around them.

Samaneh and I make our way down the street, dusk encircling the neighborhood, and I wonder again: How did the largest and most obviously illegal tower blocks come to be built in the first place? If the law prevented anyone from building more than two stories, or five, how was it ignored? A twenty-story building isn't exactly easy to hide. We're walking past an estate agent's office; I figure someone in the property business should be able to tell us.

"Construction is more powerful than the law of the land," explains the agent, who asks to remain anonymous. He takes us a few streets away, to the site of the old Swedish embassy, a seventy-thousand-square-foot property where a giant skyscraper is under construction. A notice has been placed on the gate: in October 2003, a waiver was granted allowing the developer to build to a height of twenty stories. When I ask the agent what happened, he shrugs.

"Property, power, and politics—they're intertwined," he says.

Elahiyeh has the most expensive real estate in Tehran, if not the country—some plots sold for 1.5 billion *tomans* ($1.2 million) last year. It is no surprise that high-ranking government insiders and their families long ago snapped up a significant portion of the area. As the streets start to darken, though, the neighborhood draws a different crowd; Kurds selling binoculars appear, and begin to do a roaring trade. Because the buildings are packed so close together, a new pastime has emerged: peering into other people's flats.

V

One summer I accompanied a cousin to the eye hospital in downtown Tehran and realized that it was one of my grandfather's buildings. The manager, recognizing my grandfather's name, told us that a new wing had been added a few years ago. "During the last earthquake," he continued, "that's the wing that suffered damage. You can see the cracks in the walls. But your grandfather's building is as solid as rock."

Japanese seismologists who made an assessment of Elahiyeh concluded that a small tremor, like the ones commonplace in the country, would not put the neighborhood at risk. A larger quake, though, above 6.5 on the Richter scale, could reduce 90 percent of the neighborhood to rubble. Because of the narrow streets, it would be difficult to reach any survivors.

You would have thought that the possibility of such a catastrophe would lead the government to make the nature of the risk more transparent to the public. But whenever Samaneh calls various borough offices for statistics, she is always told—very courteously—that someone will have to call her back. They never do. Both of us wonder if comprehensive information exists at all.

Eventually we reach a Mr. Zahedi, a member of Elahiyeh's city council. He is in his eighties, and seems focused on other problems. In the past, he tells us, water management was a primary concern; years ago, some of the big houses used to release their sewage into the streams running alongside the streets in the dead of night. That doesn't happen anymore, but the sewage system that was built to solve the issue is now being overwhelmed itself. In some places, sewage burning through the old pipes has seeped into the drinking water.

Next to the bakery on Amin Street is a corner shop that has been in business for more than fifty years. It's crowded with packets of biscuits, cartons of sour cherry juice, squares of white cheese floating in water, and boxes of tissues with smiling, brashly colored cartoon faces on them. From behind his counter, the owner, Mr. Heyderi, has spent decades observing the changes in the neighborhood. When Elahiyeh was dominated by the embassies, he says, Americans were his best customers and Europeans his worst. Now his store has become a place where the nouveau riche buy milk alongside the Afghan workmen, a few old-timers, and gangs of chic youngsters from the nearby cafés.

Business is much better for Mr. Heydari now; he prefers the social melting pot. In the past, he says, the only contact he had with the wealthy residents was through their servants, drivers, and gardeners. The people in the big houses were from a higher social class, and thought a lot of themselves, he says. He sums it up using an expression I've never heard before: *Haser naboodan ba shah faloodeh boghoran.* "They wouldn't have deigned to eat ice cream with the Shah."

Mr. Heydari has a vivid memory. He reminisces about the day my parents got married, and about my grandmother ordering boxes of fruit juice from the shop; he can recall my grandfather whizzing about with snow chains on his Volvo, diligently wearing a seat belt. Mr. Heydari's face wrinkles into a chuckle. Only a Swede could handle the icy winter roads of Elahiyeh at that speed, and only a Swede would have bothered to buckle up. Even now most people wear their seat belts only begrudgingly, pulling them down when they pass a policeman and then releasing them again.

In the fizzy orange streetlight glare, Elahiyeh's streets thicken with exhaust fumes. Cars pass by carrying rosy-lipped beauties and sultry-eyed young men. Jammed side by side and inching along, there's enough time and plenty of inclination for them to flirt through their windows. Even though the cafés here still display signs reminding women to remember their proper *hejab*, there's more freedom in this part of town.

On our way home, Samaneh and I pause in front of a tiny, pistachio green van parked outside the last house on Amin Street. It's filled with keys and key-cutting tools; Hassan, who minds it, says it has been here for eight years. His uncle, the owner, makes a very good living. A string of colored bulbs like fairy lights hangs across the open side. Hassan taps into the bakery for his electricity supply.

Back again on my grandmother's balcony, I see the pallor of skyscrapers in the making. Construction is like a death rattle in this city. Yet whispers of something else still float over the stream running down my old street, where my house and garden once lay. Even for someone like Samaneh, who has only known life after the revolution, that garden remains an ideal. She confided to me that she, too, would one day like to have one, "if any are left."

In 1926, when the British writer Vita Sackville-West visited Tehran, she wrote, "I call it a city, but it's more like an enormous village." Perhaps Tehran has come full circle—more a cluster of villages, once again, than a cohesive capital. Those who can afford it live, shop, and entertain themselves locally, while others wake up in the early hours to beat the traffic and get themselves to work. Places like Karaj, to the west, which used to be on the outskirts of the city, are now connected to it by a continuous stream of buildings. It's possible that Tehran will reach its limits only when it overtakes those towns entirely. Another future is suggested by recent government incentives offered to those willing to resettle elsewhere in the country, in order to ease the strain on Tehran's infrastructure—or, perhaps, to scatter the activist base that congregates in the capital.

To my eye, the city's skyline paints a picture of some of the stresses playing out in the country as a whole. The towering buildings, far exceeding legal limits, suggest a separate reality for those with the money and political clout to live above the law. The restive bustle below suggests that such an arrangement may be unsustainable.

At night I look to the north, and the mountains, away from the glittering sprawl. Even there I can see threads of light delineating the seams of the Alborz. Construction creeps upward, toward cleaner, cooler air, and toward some degree of privacy. It's easier to escape the latest round of worries over an uncertain future and extended economic sanctions when surrounded by nature, peace, and freedom. These are not romantic, sentimental meanderings. A young Tehrani woman, when I asked her what dreams she had for the years to come, told me that "the day I can feel the breeze on my naked neck, that's when I'll feel really free."

THE WOLF AND THE WILD

by JESS WALTER

illustration by MATT ROTA

1

THEY FANNED OUT in the brown grass along Highway 2 like geese in a loose V, eight men in white coveralls and orange vests picking up trash. In the center, in the hump between lanes, Wade McAdam found himself explaining futures trading to a drug dealer named Ricky.

"Wait," Ricky said. "So you're just betting on whether the price goes up? You need a fuckin' finance degree for *that*?" He grabbed something with his trash-picker and showed it to Wade: a shit-filled diaper. Then he flicked it back into the weeds. "Sick."

Wade snagged the diaper and put it into his bag. "Yeah, but the wheat, the stock, the energy, whatever—it never changes hands. The *thing* is beside the point. You're selling a contract. You're selling the instrument itself—"

"Wait, what?"

Wade shielded the sun from his eyes. "See, the underlying asset can be anything: a hedge fund, an interest rate. Hell, you can sell futures on futures. The thing doesn't matter. All you're doing is spreading risk. You make money no matter what." Wade smiled at the irony of saying this while wearing a prison jumpsuit. "You know, within a certain algorithmic range."

"Goddamn it, Beans, you totally lost me."

Wade didn't know why the men called him Beans.

Ricky grabbed a Taco Bell bag with his picker, flicked it into his garbage sack. "You're like them scientists on TV explaining black holes. More you talk, less I get."

2

At group, Wade just listened.

Ricky always got emotional in the big circle. He twitched and wept and said he could see "the patterns I been chained to my whole life." The social worker in the wheelchair asked if that meant he was "ready to go straight now."

"Oh fuck, definitely," Ricky said.

After group Wade asked Ricky if he was really going to quit dealing drugs.

"Oh, that ain't what I'm here for, Beans," Ricky said. "I diddled my neighbor's kid."

3

Wade didn't even know they still made Fanta, but there were two empty cans in the weeds along the highway.

"How'd you get caught, Beans?" Ricky asked.

Wade paused over a cigarette pack. Pall Malls. Did they still make Pall Malls? This stretch of highway was a time machine. "One of the partners had a girlfriend," Wade said. "Anna. After his wife found out, I started seeing Anna. Next audit, my partner pointed out some internal controls that I'd let slip. Trust-account funds that had mingled into my..." Wade stopped and stared up at the sky. "Black holes," he said.

"How much you take?" Ricky asked.

Wade looked back down at the sandy tufts of grass along the highway, at the line of orange-vested men with their garbage-picking spears and trash-bag shields. "Not enough," he said.

4

Another time, Ricky said, "Don't be so hard on yourself, Beans. Everybody up in this shit for some kind of greed or fucking."

5

Wade's lawyers said they could get him transferred back to Seattle for community service, but he didn't want some old client seeing him cleaning pigeon shit in Pioneer Square. His kids wanted nothing to do with him. And until the divorce was finalized, he didn't even know which house to go to.

No, he said, he'd just do his community service in Spokane.

At the hearing, Densmore got the judge to agree to shorter probation in exchange for a steeper fine and Wade's involvement in a community-service pilot program. Wade had never worked with the criminal side of the firm before; Densmore was crudely efficient, brusque even, as if this business was beneath him. The hearing took all of four minutes. It was between the lawyers. While they talked at the bench, Wade looked down at the white socks he had on beneath the suit Densmore's secretary had brought for him.

"We'll see you back in Seattle in six weeks," Densmore said when it was over. He closed his briefcase. "Now if you don't mind, I'm going to try to catch the four p.m. flight."

Back at Geiger, Wade looked for twitchy Ricky to say goodbye, but apparently he'd been caught flashing one of the female prisoners on the federal side of the fence and been shipped back to the sex farm at Shelton.

6

Real estate was practically free in Spokane. Wade had known that, of course, but it seemed somehow profane to be standing in a fully furnished, two-bedroom downtown loft that went for half the monthly price of his sailboat moorage. He walked from room to room, the property manager a step behind. She explained that Wade would need to provide "bank statements, pay stubs, references, that sort of thing." In the kitchen, Wade used her laptop to call up his personal checking account. The property manager said not to worry about the references and the pay stubs.

She suggested a nice restaurant a few blocks away and Wade went alone, took a seat at the bar. He had a scotch and water, his first drink in sixteen months. He closed his eyes as he drank it. His counselor at Geiger had once asked him if booze wasn't perhaps "the first knot in your life." How to answer something like that? It was knots all the way down.

"Want me to pour the next one straight down your gullet?" the bartender asked.

Wade looked down at his empty glass, then up at the bartender. She was in her thirties, attractive, with short black hair. She smiled at him, a little warily. Then she filled him up again.

"No sense dirtying a glass if you're going to inhale it," she said.

He tipped it, barely let the whiskey touch his lips, then put it down.

"Attaboy," she said.

7

The volunteer coordinator was a thin woman with a flesh-colored eyepatch and an atrophied left arm that curled into her breast like a hawk's claw. Wade wondered if she'd had a stroke.

"This is a very controversial pilot program," she explained. "We don't typically let ex-cons work with children. But our test results call for drastic measures, and since you white-collar assholes are the least likely to volunteer, we're targeting a few hand-picked, nonviolent offenders to supply supervised, one-on-one tutoring." She closed his file. "Now, this program is my baby and I'd really hate to lose my job, so I'd consider it a personal favor if you could refrain from having kids bring you their mom's checkbooks."

"I'll try," Wade said.

She slid a contract across the table. "You check in at the school office every time. If you go walking alone down a hallway or contact a student outside school, anything like that? Start some Ponzi lunch-money scheme? It's back to Geiger for you, my friend, and my little program dies. Understand?"

Wade nodded.

"Four hours a day, four days a week," she went on. "Two days at a high school, two days at an elementary school. Sophomores and second-graders. We're assigning you to two very good, veteran teachers. Any questions?"

"I didn't get your name."

She seemed uncomfortable with this and looked away from him with her good eye. "Sheila," she said.

"Well, Sheila," he said, "thanks for this opportunity. I'll do my best."

8

Megan's mouth hung as if on a loose hinge, her eyes half-lidded. She blinked, sighed, stared at the page, at the equation, at oblivion. Wade had to fight to keep from reaching over and gently closing her jaw.

"Come on, Megan. We just went over this. The coefficients are…"

"Ni-i-ine," she said, "and… fi-i-ive?"

"That's right. And the variables?"

"Are the letters?"

"Right, although technically a letter could be a coefficient, too, if there're no assumed variables."

"What?"

"Nothing. Sorry. So how would you go about solving this?"

Megan looked over her shoulder, back into the classroom, where Mr. Watkins was going over more-complex equations on the board. Then she leaned in closer to Wade. "Were you really in jail?"

"Let's just concentrate on these problems, okay?"

"Did you do a murder or something?"

"No," Wade said. "I didn't pay attention in algebra."

9

This boy Drew kept trying to crawl up into Wade's lap to read.

They were on a couch just outside the office. When the boy didn't move, Wade looked up at the secretary and shrugged, as if to assure her that he hadn't put the kid on his lap, that he wasn't a pervert. But the secretary was giving some other kid his Ritalin from a drawer in her desk and didn't seem to notice.

"Why don't you sit over here," Wade said, and gently moved the boy.

Drew was tiny for a second-grader. At first Wade had wondered if he'd just forgotten how small seven-year-olds were, since his own kids were seventeen and nineteen now, but then he saw Drew with his class and the boy was a head smaller than everyone else. He moved his tiny index finger along each word as he read, as if each one were a story unto itself.

The boy brought the same book for their one-hour reading session every time. *The Wolf and the Wild.*

"Don't you want to bring another book?" Wade finally asked him.

Drew considered this for a moment. "But I don't know what's in those other books."

"Isn't that the fun, finding out?"

Drew looked dubious.

10

"Is it the... associative law?"

Wade pointed to the problem again. "No, it's the other one."

"Associative?"

"No, you just said 'associative,' J'mar. It's the other one."

J'mar stared at him.

"Dist..." Wade said, his eyebrows arching.

J'mar stared.

"Distrib..."

J'mar stared.

"Dis... trib... u... tive."

"Distributive?" J'mar said, as if he'd just come up with it.

"Nice," Wade said.

11

The bartender's name was Sonya. She was married. Wade was a little disappointed, but also a little relieved.

"I like working with the little kids," Wade said, "but the high-schoolers are stupid. Distracted."

"You had to go to prison to learn that?" Sonya refilled his whiskey.

"On on the bright side, I *have* figured out how to fix the American educational system. End it at sixth grade."

"Brilliant. Then what?"

"Lock them up in empty factories, give them all the Red Bull, condoms, and Taco Bell they want, pipe in club music, and check back when they're twenty-five. Anyone still alive, we send to grad school." Wade pushed his glass forward. "How's that for a campaign issue?"

"Hate to break it to you," said Sonya, "but I'm pretty sure you can't run for office."

12

In *The Wolf and the Wild*, a little boy lives on a farm without any brothers and sisters. Every night he hears a wolf howling. One day he sees the animal at the edge of their farm.

That night his mother makes round steak. The boy hates round steak. He sneaks it into his lap and then into his pocket, and later that night he leaves it at the edge of the farm for the wolf. Every night after that, he takes some food out to the edge of the farm. Then one day he gets lost in the woods.

After a few hours, he sees the wolf in the distance, and eventually it leads him home. The boy tells his parents how the wolf saved him, but they only laugh, in a kindly way. "You probably just imagined it," they tell him.

On the last five pages of the book there are no words at all. The boy is older, and he's going for a walk with a sack lunch. In one panel he walks through the wheat field. In the next, he walks through the woods. In the next, he comes across the wolf. In the final panel, he is lying back with his head on the curled-up animal, staring up at the sky while he and the wolf share his lunch. This was Drew's favorite part of the book.

"And that's the end," Drew said every time they got to that last page. Then he'd sigh, look up, put his hand on Wade's arm, and smile.

13

Wade rolled over and watched Sonya put on her bra. She wouldn't look back at him.

"The funny thing is, it wasn't that bad, being in prison," he said. "They put you with other nonviolent offenders, the white-collars and the frauds. Stone liars. It wasn't until work-release that I even met any *real* criminals. And even they were okay. You think it's all going to be beatings in the yard and gang rapes in the shower, but it's just a bunch of fucked-up guys at summer camp."

She stood and zipped her skirt. She looked miserable. "I can't do this," she said.

He leaned back and stared up at the ceiling of his apartment. "The only thing I could never figure out was why they called me 'Beans.' I thought they meant that I spilled the beans. But I didn't. Who was I going to testify against? It was all me."

"I won't be able to live with myself," she said.

14

"And that's the end," Drew said. He closed *The Wolf and the Wild*, put his hand on Wade's arm, and smiled.

15

Wade kept detailed reports on all the kids, the sophomores and the second-graders: Megan's progress in algebra, Tania's struggles with geometry, J'mar and his quick mind for figures but inability to grasp concepts. The way DeAndre was working on sounding out longer words and Marco was anticipating story elements and creating voices for characters. And, of course, Drew.

"Most of these kids have no parental involvement in school," Sheila told him one day at the office, as she looked over his notes. "These classes are ninety to ninety-five percent free and reduced lunch. Every kid is essentially living in poverty. Single-parent homes are the best case; a lot of them live with aunts, grandmothers, foster parents, random people."

He always wanted to ask Sheila what had happened to her arm and her eye.

"But I have to say, you're doing great with them," she said.

"Thank you," Wade said.

16

Wade finally talked Drew into bringing another book, *Dog Day.* The boy tried to crawl up into Wade's lap again, but this time the secretary was watching. She opened her mouth to say something, and Wade nodded at her and gently pushed Drew back onto the couch. His own son, Michael, had been a lap-reader, and Wade felt a tug of regret just thinking about that little boy, now a big greasy kid who lived in a dorm room and wanted nothing to do with him.

Dog Day was about two brothers who volunteer at an animal shelter, and who organize an adoption parade with the dogs through downtown Scottsdale, Arizona. Drew struggled, his finger vainly pointing at each word.

"Reh... Reh... Ret..."

Wade was supposed to just let him sound the words out himself, but the wrinkles in the boy's forehead got to him. "Retriever," he finally said. "It's a kind of dog."

Drew closed the book and rested his hand on Wade's arm. "Can't I just bring the wolf book again next time?"

17

Sonya leaned against the bar. All the chairs were up except Wade's. "So how much are we talking?"

Wade shrugged and acted as if he had to think about it. "Total worth?"

"Yeah. I'm just curious."

"Well, okay. Figure I'm going to lose almost half of it to the divorce, and I've still got restitution to deal with, and there's a civil suit we're about to settle…"

"How much?"

"I don't know. Exactly."

"Yes, you do."

Yes, he did. He took a drink of his whiskey. "Thirty," he said.

Sonya's eyes got huge. "*Million?*"

Of course, it was closer to forty. That's how much he figured to have left when the dust settled. He wondered why he did that. Shaved off just a little bit. "Give or take," he said.

She covered her mouth.

"What's the matter?" Wade asked.

"I don't know," she said. "It's kind of… sick."

18

Wade requested a meeting with the second-grade teacher, Mrs. Amundson. She was an attractive young woman, maybe thirty, with curly black hair and a patient smile. They sat after school on tiny plastic chairs in her classroom, surrounded by leaves pasted to construction paper. Wade brought out the notebook he kept on the students' progress.

"Marco is doing especially well. He seems to have a real grasp of context and he's anticipating stories, which is pretty high-level stuff. I'm not sure he even needs one-on-one attention. DeAndre—I don't know if he's been tested for dyslexia, but he really struggles with blocks of text and complex sentences."

Mrs. Amundson nodded patiently.

Wade flipped to his report on Drew. "Finally, I'm not sure what to make of Drew. He just keeps bringing the same book, this wolf book; he's basically just memorized it. I want him to be comfortable, but he's just repeating the story now. I went online, and it looks like there are three more books in that series. I thought if you could have the librarian request the other books, I could work on some word-attack strategies with him—"

The teacher looked up.

Wade shrugged. "I've been doing some research." He held out the note-book.

Mrs. Amundson took it. "This is very thorough, Mr.–"

"McAdam."

"Mr. McAdam." She looked down at his report. "Unfortunately, our district cut its library funding last year. We have no librarian. We're not allowed to request any new books."

He stared at her. "You can't request *books*. But this is a school."

"Yes." She smiled.

"So a kid gets hooked on a series and he's just... on his own? That's crazy."

She closed his notebook and looked up at him. "Look. This is very nice, what you've done. But I need to tell you, all of these boys already work with a reading specialist. I just sent them with you because they're boys who have no male relationships in their lives, and there are no male teachers at this school. I thought they should have some casual, normal time around a man. That's all."

She handed Wade back his little notebook.

19

"I can't, Wade," Sonya said. "Just... please."

Wade's head felt like it was on a swivel. "I know," he said. "I'm sorry."

She turned away and began washing glasses.

Wade looked around the bar, at the chairs up on the tables. Then he looked down at the bill she'd left for him an hour ago. "I know," he said again. His eyes were bleary. He couldn't focus. The bill looked like it was for forty bucks. As always, Sonya had charged him only for every other whiskey. He opened his wallet. He stared at the blossom of dull, greenish-white bills. He took out three fifties, then a fourth, and a fifth, and finally all of them. He set the money on the bar and left.

20

Wade stood in the children's section of Auntie's Bookstore, staring at all the books. All the fucking books.

21

"I brought something for us," Wade said. He pulled Drew up on his lap and took out the book he'd bought that morning, the second in the series, *The Wolf and the River.* The secretary cleared her throat, but Wade held the boy tight on his lap and this time he read the whole thing to Drew himself, working to keep his voice steady.

In the book, houses are going up in the fields around the boy's family farm. Trees are being cut down and the boy is worried, because the wolf has had a litter of six pups. At one point, a bulldozer nearly takes out the wolf's den. Eventually the boy buys a pool raft to help the wolf move her pups to the safe side of the river, where there are no houses. On the last five pages, as they cross the river, there are no words.

When Wade looked up, the secretary was walking across the office toward them. She was bringing along the vice principal, who was speaking angrily ("...the boy's on his *lap!*") into her cell phone.

Wade hung on.

"And that's the end," Drew said.

STAY WHERE YOU ARE

by DEB OLIN UNFERTH

illustration by GRACIA LAM

A MAN IN FATIGUES stepped out of the brush and onto the gravel. He must have come off a small path of some sort because no branches snapped when he came out. He turned and pointed a machine gun at them—maybe more like *toward* them. He called out something neither of them understood.

"Now what," said Jane. "What's this soldier want?"

Max lifted a hand in greeting. "Hullo, we're waiting for the bus," he called.

The man in fatigues walked over and said some sentences in Spanish. He kept the gun casually pointed their way. He was young. One of his boots flapped on the ground.

"Maybe it's about the chairs," Jane suggested. Max had borrowed the chairs from the coffee farm off the road. She had told him not to, because there might not be time to run them back when the bus came, but Max had done it anyway.

"You can take the chairs back," Jane said to the gunman now. She stood and pointed at her chair.

The gunman didn't seem interested in the chairs. He moved the gun from side to side, explaining. He wore an army cap pulled low over his eyes.

"We're waiting for the bus," Max said. "The Tuesday bus?" He sighed. "They give these kids these weapons to go out and wave around like hands." He slapped his thighs and got to his feet. He was at least a full head taller than the gunman.

The gunman waited, listening. He spoke again, louder this time, and gestured with the gun toward the place in the trees he'd exited from.

"You want us to go with you? Take us to the station, is that it?" Max turned to Jane. "Could be there's a hurricane coming through. An evacuation?"

"Hummm," said Jane. She studied the sky for a storm. "Too bad he doesn't speak English."

Max frowned.

They'd argued the night before because she wanted to stop in the next country and take a language. Six weeks. Spanish school. Learn something. Hordes of people were doing it and it looked like fun. But Max detested school—being rooted to the ground, potted. He'd been to fifty-eight countries and never learned a language other than his own. He was no good at language. He never had a problem making himself understood. He could pantomime. "Besides, everybody speaks English these days," he'd said.

So they would accompany the gunman. But now what were they supposed to do with their packs? Max and Jane stood over the packs, deciding. The gunman waited. If they weren't going to be long, they could just leave the packs here. No one came down this road. Max and Jane had been walking up and down it for days and had seen hardly a soul. Even if someone did come along, Max didn't think they'd make off with the packs. On the other hand, Jane said, the two of them might be kept awhile at the station.

What damn luck.

The gunman interrupted them irritably.

Max and Jane looked up. "We'll probably miss the bus, you understand," Max said. "The Tuesday bus?"

They got their packs on.

The three of them entered the rainforest in the same spot the gunman had come out. Indeed it was a very small footpath, so small it could overgrow itself in days. It must have been well used despite its thinness. Max, then Jane, stepped through the trees, the gunman behind. Max and Jane walked easily, without the usual timidity of the tourist. Wet leaves hit their faces and arms. The rainforest hung in loops around them.

In fact they'd been stopped by the authorities before, many times—mostly in order to be herded back onto the tourist tracks or pumped clean of any cash they were carrying, and once in Morocco to make Jane put on more clothes (she'd been wearing a [really rather modest] bathing suit). Never been delayed more than a few hours but it would be unfortunate to miss the bus, Max thought. On the other hand these military men might arrange a ride back to town for them, might even bring them themselves in a jeep. You never knew. Might as well make the best of it. Was Jane listening to all these species of bird?

"How close are we to the river?" Max called back to the gunman, who didn't respond. "We saw a waterfall yesterday that couldn't be beat. I say, my dear, was that a waterfall?"

"All right," she said. "Okay."

"Would you believe," Max called back to the gunman, "I have a wife who complains about being on a tropical vacation? Other women say, 'You never take me anywhere.'"

"Vacation?" said Jane. "Who takes a vacation for eighteen years?"

She'd been sixteen when they met, an English schoolgirl. He liked to say he stole her from her father and it wasn't a big stretch. He'd been working on an oil rig twenty miles out on the ocean. Three-month shifts. All men. The boss, her father, had brought her on board. What sort of a dull-headed move was that, to bring your sixteen-year-old daughter out to a place like that?

Oil rig: square island, salt and steel, concrete, fish, everything the color of water.

Max had been thirty-four at the time, married with a daughter in Sussex. He was thirty-six and divorced when he took Jane away. The first place they'd gone was Africa, where they'd stayed for years, far from anything she'd ever known, Max the only familiar object for thousands of miles, anyone else days away. It was like being the last two people on Earth. It was like you yourself had sent everyone off, except for the man with you—the only man left on Earth. It was like being in one of those movies about that, about you being the only ones who had ever done this, your great idea, and his. At first.

But then the movie keeps going, five years, eight years, twelve. Eventually you want a movie like that to be over, you want to see a different movie, change the channel, but it keeps going. Then one day fifteen, sixteen years in, you're suddenly sick of it—not horrified, not scared—just annoyed and sick to death of it, sick of yourself, sick of him. It was like waking up in someone else's bed and knowing just how you'd gotten there.

They'd been going like this for eighteen years, half her life, never stopping.

The gunman prodded Jane with the gun when she stopped behind Max. "Ow," she said. "Max, he just stabbed me with that monstrous weapon!"

The gunman said something angrily in Spanish.

"Hey, watch where you direct that thing, kiddo," Max said, and moved Jane, rubbing her elbow, around him. "You go ahead of me."

They all continued walking.

Of course they stop, Max would counter. They ran out of money every few years. Remember she'd been a postal lady in New Zealand? Carried sacks of mail. And she'd swabbed decks on a ship like a man, all the way across the Indian Ocean. Spirited girl, always had been. One of the first things he'd liked about her.

And how about the time they became citizens of New Zealand? he'd say. You have to hold still for an honor like that. Nobody just throws citizenship papers into the airplane after you. Remember they got to meet the president on New Year's Day? They got to shake hands with the president.

His favorite defense. How about the time in New Zealand?

Yes, but they left the next day! The *very day* after they received their citizenship, they left, Jane would say. And now they didn't even own anything other than the belongings in their packs and it might be nice to.

Didn't own! Max said. They still had some carpets in New Zealand, remember? They'd gotten them in India and brought them along, left them with the neighbors in Wellington. They could go back and get those carpets anytime they liked. Is that what she wanted? Carpets?

She didn't want carpets.

Citizens of New Zealand, he'd say. Hands in pants. Looking around. As a matter of fact, this is a nice spot. Maybe they could be citizens here too.

They were deep in the rainforest now, dense damp foliage, vines like arms crossing in front of them, sun blocked by a canopy of leaf-knotted trees meters overhead. Bugs whipped past them, loud as motors, biting their hands and getting caught in their sweaty hair, sticking to an eye. Jane brushed them aside.

God she hated this now. She could almost imagine another story for herself but she had no faith in it. No faith in herself. She couldn't really imagine what that other story might be. It had been seven years since she'd seen her father. Nine since she'd seen her sister. Imagine going nine years without seeing your sister.

Max thought she didn't even like her family. He certainly didn't. But why not invite them out if she missed them so much? Meet up in Peru for some hiking. Like his daughter had done that one time. That had been good fun.

Was he referring to the time his daughter met them in Africa and got so sick she nearly died, and so afraid she flew home halfway through the trip? The time his own daughter had to fly six thousand miles and risk death to see her dad?

She used to not like her family.

Yes, well, she used to be a teenager.

The three of them rounded a corner, stepped into a clearing, a gathering of huts. "Ah, here we are," said Max. He stopped and surveyed the patch of border trees, the tents strung between the clotheslines, the overturned crates. "Not much of a station. What is this, an outpost camp?"

The three walkers rounded the corner, stepped into the clearing. The gunman looked around and stopped.

He was thinking (in Spanish): Where the fuck did they go? Fuck.

He kept his gun trained on the Americans.

*   *   *

The bus comes on Tuesday, Max thought. All the people at the coffee farm had told them that. Mimed it. Mimed Tuesday.

Jane was thinking: Shit.

The gunman was thinking: Shit. They'd gone off without him, the bastards. What, they'd woken up, seen he was gone, and left? Or, worse, had they not even noticed he was gone and just marched off without him? And here he'd been so crafty, bringing back two Americans, surprise, surprise! Now who's the champion? But no one was here.

He took out his cell phone.

He told the Americans to shut up.

And another thing was America. The argument always went like this: Max despised first-world countries, but Jane wanted to go. Might be fun to ride a tandem bike across America. Picnic basket on the back.

Oh no, Max always said. They'd been to America once already and they weren't going back. America had been exactly as they'd expected, exactly as they'd always heard. First thing that happens, they buy a cup of tea and the lady says, "Have a nice day!" Just like an American on the television. He and Jane got on a bus and a fight broke out between a young man and the driver. The two of them screaming at each other until the man got off the bus, cursing. Violent country. He's surprised they didn't get killed.

Jane: They spent one day in America on their way to Mexico. Nineteen hours.

Max: And it was just as they thought it'd be. No reason to go back.

Jane thought, Shit. That is, she was thinking about shit. She couldn't see a camp like this one—strung canvas, fire pit, encroaching foliage—without the image coming into her mind of a camp they'd stayed in at the edge of the Sahara. The latrine had filled to the top and then run over. People had to stand on the seat to shit into the pile. Soon the latrine was so full of shit, you just shat nearby it. It became a sort of "latrine area," and you tried to get your shit in the vicinity of it on the ground there without getting too close yourself and stepping in it and tracking it back into the camp. Then, of course, the rains came and drained all that shit right into the camp. It all came floating in, getting into everything. The tents, the mosquito nets, the clotheslines. It got onto hands and smeared onto hair.

The gunman now very decidedly had the gun pointed at them, which was unfriendly, for one, and dangerous, but Max and Jane were both determined not to make a thing of it. It wasn't as though they'd never had a gun pointed at them before, and to complain like an American usually made things worse.

"He's asking to see our passports," Max said. "Here you go, then."

The gunman took the passports. He noted they were not blue and didn't want to think about that. He put them in his pocket and paced. His boot flapped. Too big. He almost tripped. He'd been given a fucking mismatched set of shoes. He told the Americans to stop looking at him and go sit by the pit. He had to make some calls.

The gunman said something in Spanish. Max and Jane didn't understand, but they understood the waving gun and went where the gunman said.

Yes, they'd been captured before. In the late nineties, by a tribe. In order to pass through certain territories you had to ask permission of the head of the tribe. Usually it was no trouble. But one time a tribe took the opportunity to lock them up. Jane had been certain it was the end. But Max had charmed them all, chattered away in English—which none of them understood. The tribe leader had offered Max a dark mixture, the kind of thing that could kill a man not used to it, but Max had drunk it down and asked for more, and by the end of the night they were all singing songs.

They squatted in the dirt with their packs on. A line of ants was re-forming itself around them. The gunman poked at the tents with the gun, making agitated sounds into his cell phone.

Jane slapped the bugs. The ground was burnt moss and forest and soot. The sun coming on full by now, breaking into the clearing. Sweat was coming down their faces and arms. They took off their packs.

The gunman came back over to them with something else in his hand.

The gunman was thinking they had to be at the main camp by now. Were they not answering on purpose? He didn't have a second piece of rope, but in his experience, Americans were an obedient bunch, as long as you had a gun. They'd just stare, or weep—though they always talked, you couldn't shut them up. He couldn't herd these two fourteen kilometers, he knew. When were those assholes coming back?

Yes, Max could talk all day to people who didn't understand him, but with tourists who spoke English, he did just shut up. He let her take over, had never been much for small talk. He'd nod out on the stair or watch the light play on the plaza tile though the trees—who knew what he was thinking— while she talked to the tourists about wristwatches that stopped in the tropical air, places to use the bathroom. All travelers love to talk about shit and bugs. He didn't need anyone but her.

Last month in Nicaragua, they'd met two sisters who had been too scared of getting robbed to do anything but hide in their room, mosquito nets lowered around them. Max and Jane had brought the sisters along with them for a few days, showed them the ropes. They'd been in awe of Max—in the old way. (People used to be so impressed with Max.) Last fun he and Jane had had.

What she herself had been in awe of at one time, she couldn't quite reach anymore when she looked at him. She'd been thinking for two years now about leaving him.

But what was left for him without her? Middle age giving way to old age and the difficulties of that, disenfranchised family, cemented-in views that were now outdated, no friends, no money, no hobbies that one could do while sitting still, no abilities of any kind other than not speaking fifty-eight languages, a keen knack for spotting animals no one else could see in the trees, a knack for drinking the locals' water anywhere in the world (this last was no cheap trick, you had to be determined, unafraid of illness or death, although in most places consuming water wasn't considered a special skill, you don't get a paycheck for being thirsty).

All either of them had was this thing they'd created, this two-ness between them. If she left (or made *him* leave, rather—there could be no question of her walking off and leaving him somewhere, unimaginable, he, the walking man), what was left for him?

Did he think about that? What did he think about? All these years with him and she still didn't know.

For her, sure, there was enough. She was still young enough to create more for herself, to make it someplace, find someone. An adequate life, a job in retail, maybe, or being a company rep or an exec or something. Maybe she'd find that life exotic after the one she'd led. Or nicely quaint. So far she hadn't done it, because of what it could become in the long run—what they'd always feared, what they'd always been running from, the drab, the dull, the stupid, and then death. She'd always said she could never go in for a regular job, house, kids, vacation a few weeks a year. Avoidance of this had been their mainstay, their mythology. But now this option seemed inviting compared to what Max would become by himself, alone, aging. Might as well be dead.

So that's how Jane thought of him, and Max, in a place deep inside himself, knew it. And knew, too, that she might be right. But he also knew it didn't matter, for he had already done the one great thing he would do (not travel all over the world, anyone could do that—didn't even need the resources, just the desire): he'd loved this one woman for eighteen years.

The gunman held the piece of rope in his hands. He put down his gun and began to forcibly tie Max's hands together behind him.

"Now is this really necessary, mate?"

Jane looked on, uncertain. All right, no, they'd never had their hands tied before, but that didn't mean they should get excited, right? She couldn't stop him somehow, could she? How? Grab the gun? "I wonder if this is a stitch-up," Jane said.

Max was nodding. "They've mistaken us for foreign intruders. These fellows are trained to think that anyone near the mountains is trying to take over their government."

They were sitting facing each other by the fire pit. The gunman was sulking by the clotheslines with his phone. Jane was parched.

"You know," Max said, "I don't think this is a military man. I believe what we have here is an insurgent. A rebel of some kind."

They both looked at the gunman.

"I'm sure I'm right about this," he said. "Look at the uniform. It's not a proper military uniform. The top and bottom don't match."

"That doesn't mean anything. Who can tell who wears what?" Jane said.

Max considered. "What war do they have going on here? Do they have one?"

"I thought it was over ages ago."

"Insurrections, maybe? Mountain revolts?"

"Well, if we read the paper," said Jane, smartly. "If we spoke Spanish." She couldn't resist.

"Hey," Max called to the gunman, "are you a revolutionary or a soldier? We can't tell."

The gunman didn't know he was being spoken to.

"Some new revolution," Max said, looking back from the gunman.

"No doubt," Jane said. One they hadn't heard of, since they didn't read the papers, since they didn't speak the language, since they didn't care what was going on around them other than what they could see before them. Only way to know a country is just to be in it, he'd always said. Walk the land. Be among the people. The political stuff was so boring. It changed every month.

"This is the stupidest thing that's ever happened to us," she said.

"Get off," Max said. They'd been through worse, Max thought. This wasn't going to be something they always talked about. Besides, what was this—a situation? Were they being kidnapped? If so, Max wondered whom this guy thought they were going to call for money. No one in *Max's* family was going to donate to the cause. And these revolutionaries or whoever they were better have someone who spoke a little English, because if you thought *Max* was bad at languages, he doubted his family believed other languages *existed*.

Things had been better in Africa, Max was thinking. Things had been better in New Zealand. Only the Americas. The Americas got them all right. Every time.

"Cállate," the gunman called to the American, who blinked at him and stopped talking for a moment but then went on talking. The gunman went over and punched the American in the face and came back.

As for the gunman, we may wonder who he was and where he came from. He was much like a regular gunman for the insurgents: he'd been born not ten kilometers from this spot and loved it here, despite the rain, the poverty, the fighting. He'd grown up doing gunman activities and wanting to do them. He'd learned how to shoot at age nine (he was now nineteen), he knew people who'd died by bullet, he'd shot people he hadn't known, he loved the cool nights of the dry season, he'd had his share of fistfights and knife fights and preferred fists because knives were too psychological and fistfights ended fast. He believed in no land tariffs. He believed in school for kids (he himself had gone three years). He'd buried his mother and two brothers.

He was different from a regular gunman in that he'd been to the States once, had hated it, and had not wanted to stay. He preferred to stay here, where he had the hope of one day being a leader, though he knew those who knew him would say there was little chance of that: he lacked charisma, they would say. And maybe he was different in that he didn't hate all Americans, though he wished those two over there weren't there.

One other fact about the gunman: he'd never loved. He wasn't a psychopath or anything so ugly as that. He'd had women (and once a man) but he couldn't say he'd ever felt love, and he understood this was strange, since the men he knew were always loving their heads off all over the place. He just felt dry. He had desire and lust but never longing, and this bothered him.

But it was only a fact about him, not a defining characteristic, one short fact among others—another being that he could fall from anywhere and not hurt himself, had been like that since he was a kid, could fall out of trees, off roofs. He was known for it, had earned nicknames.

What was that sound? That faint roar in the distance? Was that the bus?

Jane looked over at Max. He'd heard it too. But what were they going to do about it?

The gunman listened for his men but heard only the Wednesday bus, a day early this week apparently.

As for Max, he'd already done the great thing he would do.

They were quiet, all of them, contemplating the glassy future. "Look," said Max at last. "There's going to be a moment when you can get away. I want you to take that moment and do something with it."

"What am I supposed to do with it?"

"Get away."

"How? Where? What about you?"

"Don't sit there asking questions like that when the moment comes, okay?"

Jane was thinking: See? He had a plan. If this fellow with his gun thought a piece of string would hold Max back, well, he had another think coming. There wasn't a knot Max couldn't untie. It was as if he'd been a sailor. And Max had vision. He knew how to see monkeys in the trees. When no one else could see anything but green, Max would spot dozens.

Max was brave, had always been brave. She knew that. He had talents. A punch in the face was nothing to him. She'd seen him stand still when the gorillas came after you. *That* was brave. They had gone to the gorilla preserve in Tanzania some years back, the one people make films about. The gorilla experts, they say to you, "Okay, listen up, folks. This is what's going to happen. The gorillas are going to come after you. They'll make a big noise and run right at you. It's something they do, the gorillas. It's a test. You have to just wait it out. When they charge, don't move—stay where you are." They tell you that and you repeat it in your mind, *Don't move, don't move,* but then when this five-hundred-pound gorilla charges at you, you just throw up your hands and run screaming. Supposedly it took months to learn how not to. Only way to make friends with the fellows, the guides said.

Max was the one who hadn't run. Even the experts—the newer ones, anyway—ran. The scientists ran, but Max didn't. Jane had been amazed. Everyone had been.

Maybe she'd go back to England, see her sister. Maybe she'd go back to New Zealand, where she had friends. She wouldn't go back to Africa, though things had been better there.

Jane looked up and realized Max had scooted to his feet, hands still behind him, so fast she hadn't heard him. The gunman strode over shouting and Max shouted back. The gunman raised the gun to his face. Jane was screaming. But she got up and ran screaming into the forest (didn't sit there asking questions) because what else was she supposed to do? He'd told her to do that and if he had told her to, it meant that this was his plan for her and so he had a plan for himself, too—which was what? That he get punched in the face again? That he get shot? That he get himself killed? That he not care about himself as long as she got away? What kind of a plan was that? She realized she was still screaming so she stopped. Then she heard a shot and started screaming again.

He would one day love. By the time he got around to it, this day with the two Americans would have been long ago (two years) and so much would have taken place in the meantime (he'd leave the insurgents, move to the city with his uncle) that he wouldn't even think of them anymore, except when he had to use his right arm (constantly), because that's where the American (Brit, actually, and New Zealander, but the gunman would never know that) had shot him, and the place still ached after all this time. The American had brought out his hands, untied, and grabbed the gun with a grip the gunman never would have expected—not so hard that he couldn't have wrenched it away, he was trained for this sort of thing, after all, had killed a man in four minutes with his hands. But the problem was the shoe. It was too big, his foot slid in it and at the very moment he needed to have it he couldn't get a good grip on the ground and the American toppled him over and shot him in the arm and then stood over him, staring like a fucking American, gun hanging at his side. The last thing the gunman saw, before the blood made him lower his head, was the two of them running, turning away, the woman pulling the man's arm.

Later that image, the two of them in that instant, would come into his mind again and again, but it would no longer be there when he finally did love, because his own image, his own love, came back at him instead. But the Americans (New Zealanders, rather) stayed in his mind for longer than most things.

You would have thought that going through something like that would keep them together and it did for a while, but humans go through all sorts of things, and it doesn't always settle their hearts.

At the end of it all, after she'd left—well, after he left (because she made him) and, not knowing what she was doing, she left too—and after they both found themselves in countries far away from each other, in places that didn't have the energy or beauty the two of them had once found in such places together (although there is nothing unique in that, the world dims over time—though maybe it wouldn't have had the evil tint that it eventually seemed to Max to have, or the lifeless, meaningless tint that it seemed to Jane to have, if they hadn't parted ways)—after all that, each of them installed on separate continents, she wrote a letter to no one of significance: one of the sisters they'd met in Nicaragua with whom they'd traveled for a few days. Jane wrote to explain, felt she had to explain to this stranger why she'd left him (or made him leave, the walking man) and what it had felt like.

It was like leaving him in the clearing with the gunman. That's how it felt. Like she'd been given a chance to get away, and he hadn't. He'd given her a chance and she'd taken it, knowing where she was leaving him and in what condition, knowing the fear and loneliness he must have felt, but she'd done it, run on a bed of leaves and needles, under a canopy of trees (didn't ask questions)—or that had been the plan, though it hadn't turned out that way.

At first she was running. She realized she was still screaming and she closed her mouth. She heard the shot and started screaming again. She was moving away, running over beds of leaves, the sun coming through the branches.

Then she slowed, and stopped. She didn't move, thinking.

She turned and went back.

She could see a break in the trees and was moving toward it. Should she go in there? She didn't know who had been shot—Max or the gunman. She was pushing away the branches, she was pushing herself through, and then she stepped out to greet him (*I came back for you*) or to be shot.

THE VIRAGO

by HENRY BEAN

illustration by KELSEY DAKE

1

ALLENBY WAS LATE, as usual, so Richter ordered a sparkling water and passed the time making phone calls, answering email, reading the trades, Nikki Finke, a few blogs, and finally, in quiet desperation, playing *Double Dare* online with someone in Florida named KRalph. At 1:19, Allenby's assistant called to say that "the man," as she put it, was running late but was barely a block away. Which could mean a mile, or ten miles, or that he was already parked outside in the valet spot, stuck on a phone call. Richter acted preoccupied, as if this were actually a welcome delay rather than an insult.

At a nearby table, four young women were having a voluble networking lunch. Richter recognized none of them, but she knew the type: development interns, agency assistants, freelance readers, Ivy League drips just bright enough to get hired, wearing the usual designer knockoffs. Fifteen years ago, she would have known exactly where they shopped, though no doubt there were new places now. There was a pretty one who ran the show, more or less; a giant with the face of an ax murderer; a short, fat, bright-eyed girl with a raucous laugh; and a dark little thing who five years from now, Richter sensed, would either be out of the business or dead, assuming there was a difference.

They had reached the point in their conversation where the exchange of data and rumor, progress reports on various scripts and projects, casting, financing, personnel changes, job opportunities, everything that went under the rubric of "intelligence"—the ostensible purpose of the lunch—had given way to the pleasures of gossip: accounts of the wounds and slights they had suffered, their tiny triumphs, and, above all, attacks on the many people they had come to hate.

This was fun. Their voices, low and confidential a few minutes ago, grew louder as if they had been drinking, which they most certainly had not. They trashed anyone they could lay hands on, the enemies list quickly expanding beyond their colleagues and immediate superiors to include other names, better known, persons whom, Richter was certain, they had encountered only secondhand, if at all; at most they'd placed calls to them for their bosses, who, in turn, worked with these eminences, or against them, dealt with them, hated them, feared them, despised them, needed them. The girls had taken on the hatreds of their superiors, whom they also hated, and by attacking people so far above themselves—people who didn't even know their names—they inflated their own importance. Richter did this, too, albeit at a different level. Everyone did it.

It was a minute shy of 1:40. She peered toward the street, looking for Allenby's blond head or his yellow car. At what point did you become a schmuck for waiting? That was always the question. You could get up and walk out, it was easy, but then you couldn't come back. And what if you were paranoid, taking things personally when they weren't meant that way? That, too, was schmucky. Schmuckier.

"...She is a complete, howling bitch," the pretty one was saying, loud enough for half the restaurant to hear, and the others roared their agreement. The girls had turned their attention to someone new, and here at last they seemed to find a target commensurate with their anger. They each had a story about her; the bitch was also "a liar," "a pig," "a moron," "a slut," "a skank," "a cunt," "a ho," and "a virago." It was not until the pretty one described having to make an availability call about one of the virago's clients, Dickie Meister, and recounted in chilling and hilarious detail how rude the woman had been, how arrogant, cold, terrifying, and, really, inhuman—the others were in stitches—that Richter realized they were talking about her.

The girl was imitating Richter's voice, her flat, abrasive accent, her dismissive scorn, her enraged snarl—"like a feral dog," one of them drawled, and they gagged with laughter. Other diners were looking over. The giant signaled them to keep it down, and they quieted briefly in sheepish glee, leaning toward each other, whispering and giggling, until the fat one—wearing a disastrous orange angora sweater that only made her look fatter—said something Richter couldn't hear, and they erupted again, rising up like horses, snorting and pawing the air.

She barely made it to the bathroom before everything came out of her. Vast inner waterways emptied themselves in an instant, a lifetime of sludge. Like vermin fleeing. In the middle of it, the door opened, and a man stood there, an enormous, ungainly, backlit asshole, gaping at her as if she were a corpse until Richter hissed at him, "Shut the fucking door, you twit." He shut it fast, and then she managed somehow to get over there, lock it, and return without further mishap.

She was trembling so hard she had to hold on to the sink. She drank at length from the spigot and made her way unsteadily back to the table, where Allenby was now seated with an ice tea, speaking quietly into an earpiece. He smiled and kissed her without interrupting his conversation. Richter lowered herself delicately into the chair.

At the next table, the girls were signing credit-card slips and gathering their things. On her feet, the pretty one was not so pretty, a clunky body, but the fat one, though still fat, had a vitality Richter liked. Her eyes scanned the room to see who was there, passing over Richter without pause or comment.

"Who are you looking at?" Allenby asked. He had gotten off the phone as invisibly as he did everything.

She pointed with her chin. "Who are they?"

He gave the girls a glance and shrugged. As in, Why do you care? Why are you asking about such nothings? Not simply nothings now, but nothings forever. Richter laughed; she felt a little better.

"What's a virago?" she asked. It was the fat one who'd said it, she was sure of it.

"A what?"

"A virago. It's some kind of monster, isn't it?"

"I think so. A woman monster. A Woman Is a Monster. Where did you see it? In a script?"

She nodded.

"Dialogue or exposition?"

"Exposition," she said. "I mean dialogue. Dialogue."

"Which is which?"

She smiled and looked around. She saw the girls outside by the valet, hugging each other goodbye, their hair lit up in the sunlight.

"Any good? It sounds pretentious."

"Abysmal. Some dorky comp-lit grad student."

"Let me see it." It was funny how they latched onto things. Hold it out of reach, and they had to see it.

"It already sold."

"Abysmal and pretentious, and it already sold? Amazing. Who bought it?"

"Paper Rock Scissors."

"Never heard of them."

"Canadians. They're tiny."

"Virago," he said to himself. "Let me see it anyway. For the writing. It sounds interesting."

"It's not."

He smiled. "Do I have to call Andrew?" He was reminding her how important he was; that he could have her boss beat her up.

She sighed. "I'll have Clark email it."

"Can you send a hard copy?"

"Just get somebody to print it out for you."

"*Please*, Marsh? Pretty please." He was suddenly goofy, pleading. "I like the red covers." He grinned at his own silliness.

Twenty-one years earlier, exactly half her life ago, Richter had been a set P.A. on a creepy little horror flick for New Line, basically her first job in the business, when Allenby appeared one day as an unpaid assistant to the director. He was small, handsome, charming, and had, in Richter's youthful estimation, not a brain in his head, yet by the end of the show they were giving him four hundred a week. He was twenty-two. Three years later she opened the trades one morning to learn that Allenby had been named head of The Hard Way, Teddy Wells's new production company. This was Teddy Wells before *The Wretched*, even before *Dieterle's Army*, when he was still just a sitcom actor—Richter figured it for one of those specious housekeeping deals studios give a TV star to keep him happy on a series.

But Allenby took the job seriously. He went around town meeting all the sharper young agents, of which Richter was by then one, and over the next eighteen months the company produced three movies. Two of them made money, and the third, starring Teddy in a script Richter had sold them, was actually pretty good. Wells had gotten *Dieterle* off that performance.

Before long, Richter had found herself claiming Allenby as an old friend, though she often reflected on how far beyond her he had landed—and he had not landed yet. She was perhaps smarter than he was, by some ancient standard. Back on that first film she had certainly worked harder, given better notes, made more "useful" suggestions. Allenby himself had been the first to say so. She should have seen in that generosity a glimpse of what he had that she didn't, but she was too busy fighting for some bit of ground to stand on. Allenby would always yield today's ground because he planned to be somewhere else tomorrow. He never fought stupid battles.

She wondered why he still called her. Out of kindness? Superstition? Because she always had good material? (Not too good, of course. She didn't try to impress you with the irrelevance of her taste.) Or maybe he simply liked her. That wasn't impossible. Richter was an eccentric flavor, but she had her fans. She was smart, funny, loyal in her way. You knew where you stood with Richter. Some people appreciated that. They sat there until after four, the only ones left in the restaurant, laughing and gossiping and finally sharing a glass of daiginjo.

She drove back to the office with a slight buzz and didn't bother to roll calls on the way. If someone had told her that four little girls she'd never heard of had been trashing her at Hiro's, she would have taken it for the compliment it was. The more she troubled their dreams, the better. But stumbling onto it like that—their faces, the laughter—was different.

Not so long ago, she'd finished a business call, pleasant enough as far as she could tell, clicked off, and clicked back on to call someone else only to hear the guy she'd just been speaking to say, "Every time I talk to that bitch, I feel like I'm being spit on," followed by his assistant's little voice going, "I know."

Spit on, Richter had thought, really? She tried to think of what she might have said or done, but nothing came to mind. Since then, whenever she stumbled onto the tail of the previous call like that, she hung up fast.

She wished the four girls could have hung around Hiro's for another hour or two, somehow, four flies on the wall—there was an image—as she and Allenby whiled away the afternoon. She pictured it slowly dawning on them, as they heard the big names tossed about in the most natural, unpretentious fashion, that the droll duo at the next table were not just bright, witty, and sophisticated, but remarkably well connected—even intimate—with titanic figures whose *assistants* these little chickadees could barely get on the phone. And only at the end, as the two of them were getting up to go and kissing

HENRY BEAN

goodbye, as the check girl brought Richter her fabulous new Claudia Hill coat,
would it be revealed that the man who'd been sitting right in front of them all
that time, and whom not one of them had recognized—you dorks! you flies!—
was, in fact, Bryan Allenby, and that the tall woman with short, dark hair was
none other than the virago herself, Marsha Richter. You stupid, fucking twats.

Clark was on the phone when she got back, deep in one of his furious snits. He
didn't even look up as he handed her the call sheet. Fifty-three names. Not so
many. Richter got anxious when the number dropped below sixty, then played
a tormenting game with herself, trying to clear them as fast as possible, get it
down under thirty, under twenty, get it low enough that Clark would wonder
what was wrong, mention it to the other assistants, and everyone would begin
to smell blood. She wasn't sure what would happen after that.

She cleared thirty in less than two hours, chiefly because half were
just leave-words, and most of the rest irrelevancies she could have handled
by email. Afterward, as a kind of penance—but for what?—she called
up a couple of the unemployables she usually ignored, reporting on her
efforts to find them work. She described the projects she'd put them up for
(though of course she hadn't put them up for anything) and endured their
complaints, diatribes, and outbursts of self-pity without comment, without
really listening. What could she say to these people—writers and directors,
mostly—about the fact that they could no longer find work? Well, she could
have said, when they "threatened" to get out of the business altogether, "But,
don't you see? You're already out."

She remembered how her mentor, the great Eileen Schwabb, had put it
when a producer had called to ask about the availability of one of her clients,
a legendary cult director. Festivals had retrospectives of his films, two books
had been written about him. "Honey," Eileen had said in that smoky voice
she didn't yet know was lung cancer, "I couldn't give him away with a set of
dishes."

All of the unemployables had been hot once, respected, in demand; now
they were jokes. The way you told the joke was simple: you said they were
available. The moment in which the business liked and wanted these people
had ended. This was not a lull; it was the silence that followed an interval of
sound. But Richter said none of that. She simply sat there, responding only
when necessary, and answering emails as they talked.

*　　*　　*

There was a Will Wierasol premiere that night at the Grove, and in the crowded lobby Richter saw what she thought for a second were the dark eyes of that meaningless fourth girl from lunch, the one she'd imagined dead. They were fixed on her with such hatred that she felt a sudden panic, wondering which of her forgotten sins were about to be thrown in her face. Only then did she realize it was actually Michael Gruber's wife, whose name she could never remember—Sheila? Sarah?—and so, trying to be friendly, trying not to be such a virago, she walked over to say hello. As soon as the woman saw her coming, or so it seemed, she looked around for someone else to latch onto. But Richter was undeterred. "Sharon?" she said, sweetly, hopefully, as if unsure she had the right person.

The woman turned to her with a look of such fury on her little face that Richter felt almost a thrill. She pretended not to notice, trotted out the charm, asked after the kids (Evan, Myra), their trip to the Galapagos. Mrs. G was having none of it. She grew even colder, in fact, and harder, as Richter tried to think what in god's name she might have done to this person. She had never slept with Gruber. Had she lied to him, broken promises, stolen his clients, bad-mouthed him around town, and fucked him over for no other purpose than to shove his face in the dirt and teach him who was stronger? Yes, of course she had. That was why she was Marsha Richter and he was merely Michael Gruber. Gruber, of course, would have told wifey only about the sins committed against him, not the ones he'd committed—or would have, if he weren't such a pussy—but Suki or Shiva or whatever the fuck her name was should have been able to figure it out. How did she think they got that house in Rustic Canyon to which Richter had been invited more than once?

They came to a pause, the Gruber woman glowering darkly while Richter smiled on as if oblivious. The two of them stood there a moment in the rumbling silence, and then Richter turned and walked away without a goodbye or a see you inside or anything at all. She felt invigorated for about two steps before she saw that she'd blown it. She'd burned another bridge and, worse, she'd let the bitch get to her. She flushed, furious with her own stupidity, and it put her in such a daze—she would realize later, with fresh horror—that she didn't even notice two or three people trying to say hello, but walked past as if snubbing them.

It was not a glamorous premiere, more a glorified cast and crew filled out with agents, managers, mid-level executives—people like Richter who had some fractional interest in the picture. She stopped here and there to say hello, and let the banter switch click on; she could do a minute or two with anybody. A few had empty seats beside them, but when she asked, it turned out that these were being saved for Ruthie, for Keith, for Jimmy, for the Gabels, for Narissa and Pam, for our friends, our pals, for the people who come for Sunday dinner, the ones we go to Vail with every year, who come for our book group, our wine tastings, our bondage-and-torture evenings. Here and there, a seat was graciously offered, like alms to the poor, but nowhere Richter could quite bring herself to sit.

So she smiled and thanked them—her nice, slow smile—and indicated that there were people farther up the aisle she needed to say hello to. As, in fact, there were. She was a person. She had her friends; they just didn't cluster in protective little circles. She was probably still young enough to marry Roger and have a kid. Would the circle girls like her then, and be her best friend, and call her up just to chat? What in god's name would they chat about?

She found a seat at the very back, among the pimply assistants who'd been given invitations their bosses didn't want. And then, as she waited impatiently for the lights to go down so the movie could start, so the movie could end, so she could go home and read the three scripts she had to get through that night, so she could go to sleep and get up and go to work and do the work and go through the years and finally die and be dead, she remembered what she'd done to Michael Gruber.

Once upon a time, Gruber had discovered a young director at some obscure film festival. After Richter had watched the kid's movie—fifteen minutes of it, anyway—she had dropped him a note saying how much she had liked it, really liked it, and could she possibly take him to lunch? At lunch they'd talked about what he wanted and how to get there and how Richter might help, at which point he'd felt compelled to mention that he already had an agent. And who might that be, she had asked, as if she didn't know. Michael Gruber, really? She'd made a face, one of her favorites, at once neutral and amused, as if the kid had fallen for an old joke often played on rubes.

By then she knew he was gay and pretending otherwise, apparently even to himself, so it was easy—too easy, almost unavoidable—to steer him to the thought that, despite his marriage and children, Gruber, too, had certain inclinations. The look that settled over the boy's face when he realized what she was saying—that he was giving his secret away, *that everyone would know*—chilled her heart and made her wish she'd never written him the note or watched his pointless movie. A week later, after he had jumped to Steve Jacobs (not to Richter), the rumor had already begun to spread.

Gruber had had to fight if off without offending any of the numerous gay titans to whom he kowtowed daily, and Susan, the wife, had been enlisted in the effort. This had required public displays of affection that had no doubt offended her natural reserve. Now, it seemed, they had traced the rumor back to its source.

The funny thing was, there had been no malice in what Richter had done, no wish, really, to harm Gruber. It was mandatory behavior. If you didn't steal clients, you got fired; if you didn't lie and bad-mouth, you usually couldn't steal them. She was simply trying to survive, like everybody else. But she had done it, yes. She would do it again. Mercifully, at that point, the lights went down, and there was that wonderful pause in the darkness between two worlds.

The film was a comedy that a client of Richter's, Larry Balint, had done a rewrite on a year earlier. That draft—brilliant, hilarious, heartbreaking—had gotten the project a director, a star, and a green light, and Richter had found herself thinking that this might actually work, Larry would become hot, the film would be huge, and, most remarkable, it would be something they could all be proud of. Then the studio switched directors, the script was rewritten two or three times by other people, and, in the end, Larry was getting neither a credit nor a bonus. Still, there were those who saw him as the guy who'd "gotten the picture made." Now, as Larry put it, they were going to find out if that was a good thing or a bad thing.

Before the opening credits were over, the verdict was in. The credits were not funny, and neither were the music, the color, the performances, the sets, the costumes, the sound design, nor, least of all, the dialogue; nothing was funny except the desperation with which the thing tried to get a laugh. After ten minutes, Richter slipped out the back door. Larry was in the lobby with his actress girlfriend, two people from the studio, and some others Richter didn't know. They were massively depressed and laughing hysterically. When Larry saw her, he made a face.

She said, "They ruined your script."

"It was never mine." He wasn't laughing now. "When you do fucking middle relief, you don't get the W or the save. You just mop up."

"And clean up," the girlfriend said, putting her arm around him. He looked ready to hit her.

"I wrote stereotypes," he went on, chiefly to Richter, "and they turned them into real people. Don't they know real people aren't funny?"

She smiled, touched his shoulder. She was desperate to go. Other people were starting to leave, and she didn't want to run into the Grubers. Larry took her arm and walked her away from the others. He knew how she got around people sometimes; he was the same way. He said quietly, "We've got to talk."

The words hit her in the heart. His big, weak, handsome head hung heavy and miserable, and though he wouldn't say it here, in front of these people, it was obvious: he was going to fire her and switch agents. She felt something buckle inside, but she smiled and said, "I'll call you tomorrow." As she walked away, she knew he'd think for a minute that he was making a mistake. Marsha was hip; he could talk to her. But then he'd think, no, his career sucked, he was fixing movies so other people could ruin them, he had to change something. If it didn't work out, he'd come back.

Then she was out the door and into the blessed night alone.

She drove without thinking. It was too early to go home and too late to go back to the office. She called Roger at the studio and on his cell, but both went straight to voicemail. She wasn't hungry. She'd seen everything in the theaters. The stores would be closing in a few minutes. There was always the gym, but she wasn't in the mood. She needed something.

On Beverly, she pulled up in front of Hiro's. She drank a quick pinot grigio at the bar, then ordered another. Hiro's was a good place for meeting the sort of people Richter liked to meet. She always did well here. But tonight even that most reliable of distractions did not seem to be happening. There was no one of interest. Or maybe she was on the wrong frequency.

She carried her drink over to the greeter's desk, where Bette, who had been on at lunch, was still working. "Twice in one day," the girl said, as if pleased or impressed or perhaps faintly critical. She checked her seating chart. "Are you alone?"

Richter smiled. "I'm not eating."

Bette cocked her head as if to say, Then what? We're not friends, are we?

"At lunch, there was a table of four women sitting right over there, where the Wycoffs are."

"Nine?" The girl flipped back to the lunch page. "Fishman."

"No first name?"

Bette shook her head. The black sheen of her hair caught the light.

"What about the credit-card slips? They probably split it four ways."

"The slips don't go in until the end of the day, when we do the totals."

"But if you find Fishman, the others will be with it, and they'll all be for the same amount."

Bette gave her a funny look, and Richter knew she was crossing a line, but she didn't care. "If you're not comfortable, let me ask Hiro," she said, and smiled again. Only then did Bette notice the hundred-dollar bill neatly folded between Richter's fingers.

There were just two slips, Elizabeth Fishman and V. K. Nye, each for $48.68 with tip. The other two, unnamed, were either their guests or, more likely, had paid their shares in cash. At home, Richter found seven Elizabeth Fishmans on Facebook, two in LA, neither with a photo. Nothing for Nye. She took Burberry Two for a walk, then washed her hair and shaved her legs, lifting one foot after the other up onto the edge of the sink. She was naked, save the towel around her head, and kept catching sight of herself in the mirror. She'd always liked the way she looked. She had an interesting face and a beautiful body. More than enough people still wanted to fuck her.

She read the three scripts. Before going to bed, she emailed Clark: *Who are Elizabeth Fishman and V. K. Nye?*

She opened her eyes at 3:36. Three plus three made six. Sometimes, when she woke like this, she could feel the fear hovering, ready to descend upon her, and knew it was still possible to escape, to dive back into sleep, or reason with it, placate it somehow, but not tonight. It was in her face already, its horrible smelly feathers, the blind, flailing panic, wanting only to rip her open. And within that chaos, amid the terrible, swirling darkness, was a pinpoint of light in which something screamed at her that she was a piece of shit. Not just *like* shit, but shit itself. Hard, brown, putrid.

She thought of every lie she'd ever told. She couldn't think of them all, of course, or even a meaningful fraction, but they appeared before her, arrayed in the dark like gold ingots—the people she'd cheated, the clients she'd dumped (and dumped without telling), the legions she'd hated. She thought of her rudeness on the phone to Elizabeth Fishman, which, needless to say, she didn't remember. It was lost forever, along with a thousand others.

She thought of Miles, who had loved her, and whom she couldn't or wouldn't love back. She thought of her father. All he had asked was that she say Kaddish for him, and she never had, not once. She told herself she would do it next year, but she knew she wouldn't.

She wanted to die. She wanted God to come down and kill her. Kill me, she said, almost aloud; make me dead. But either He didn't exist, or He didn't care, or He knew that this was just another lie. There was no end to them.

She liked people, she really did. From a distance she could tear up at the very thought of them. But did she ever actually, except for sex, want to *be* with another human being? She had enjoyed her lunch with Allenby, true, yet it had been fraught with the anxiety she invariably felt in the company of someone more powerful than herself—the fear that his superiority would crush her. He would mention somewhere glamorous he had been, luminaries of their world who were his close friends, and she would have to take cognizance again of her own mediocrity. She knew all the stars, the studio heads, the big directors and producers, had been to parties and dinners and charity auctions with them dozens of times, but she was never fully at ease in their company. Allenby had gone so far beyond her because he was generous and easy with people; he was a prince in that yellow Bentley of his, which he really and truly did not give a shit about, while she clung to her nth fucking black Mercedes like a monkey to its mother.

The faintest touch of daylight appeared on the balconies of the units opposite hers. It was time to get up.

She had meditation, gym, a breakfast, then her morning staff meeting. During the meeting Clark emailed her that Liz Fishman worked under Cherry Hazlitt at Ten Thousand Things and Vicki Nye was a floater at ICM. She had gone to Yale with Devon's little brother. Devon was Clark's ex. Richter wrote back: *Who are their friends? Look on Facebook. Get me photos.* And, when he did not respond right away, she added: *Who did they have lunch with yesterday? At Hiro's.* That elicited his *K*, but it seemed to Richter a little slow, even sardonic, as if he was saying, *All right, Marsha, but…* But what? You're watching me, you little shit? She had to calm down. Maybe he was just on a call, maybe the phones were going crazy. The very thought gave her hope.

She imagined the list climbing to sixty, seventy, back over a hundred again.

She looked at the faces around the massive conference table. With a few exceptions, her colleagues were as unpleasant as she was, but unlike her they could produce the salesman's smile, the backslap, the mechanical charm. She knew all that stuff mattered. To smile at someone and sell—yes, *sell*—the fact that you liked them was not entirely bullshit. Richter often failed to express the affection she felt for people. Unable to summon the smile, she had to hope it was understood somehow. The people who overcame that reticence, who risked the appearance of insincerity, or even insincerity itself, to convey a warmth of feeling—however exaggerated, however instrumental—were they not to be admired and envied, rather than quietly despised? Were the phonies of this world not, in fact, its saints?

The assholes were saints, was that possible? Sure, maybe deep down they, too, hated everybody—parents, spouses, children, pals—but what was so great about deep down? That was where the horror lay. It was only up here, in the realm of the "superficial," that other things could happen.

When the meeting finally ended—it was like being paroled from hell—Richter went looking for Clark and couldn't find him. He'd "gone out for a minute." On her desk, however, was a piece of paper with four handwritten names. As if he was protecting her by not committing them to electronic eternity, though even that act, too, was probably a dig and a warning: You're losing it, Marsha. This was an impudence she would have to deal with soon. Assistants were like Dobermans; if they snapped at you, you had to beat them bloody, or next time they'd go for your throat. They couldn't help it. Weakness terrified them.

She looked at the four names: Elizabeth Fishman, Victoria Nye, Runi Apple, and Divine Buehler. *Divine!*

Now she wanted backgrounds, where they'd gone to school, how they'd met and become friends, but she couldn't risk taking that to Clark. After a moment, she closed her door and called Stephanie Weiss, her former assistant, her pal (her friend?), now at ICM, to ask about Vicki Nye. By lunch she had assembled functional profiles of all four snickerers.

Fishman had gone to Yale with Nye, same class, same college. She was getting married over Christmas to a lawyer at Wertheimer. Nye, Ms. Round and Rosy, was going nowhere at ICM, though everybody said she was very bright. Apple had spent her childhood bouncing back and forth between Tel Aviv (father) and Riverdale (mother), gone to NYU, gotten laid off at Disney two months ago, and was now reading scripts freelance while looking for something in development. Buehler was the star of the group: Lake Charles Community College, then UT El Paso, interned at a local TV station there and ended up in marketing at Fox Searchlight, where she worked harder than any three people. She was the giant, the ax murderer, and Richter sensed a major career and a human catastrophe, herself times three. The four flies. She'd swat them all, figuratively speaking.

She got a call from Allenby, who didn't use email: "Where the fuck is *Virago?*" He was being funny.

She said, "Didn't you get it? I thought it went out."

He laughed. "Why don't you want me to see it?"

"I'm desperate for you to see it. I think the girl's a genius."

"Girl? You said it was a guy. You said it was abysmal."

"I said 'grad student.' They come in both genders. And, yes, the script's a mess, but she has real talent." She thought a moment. "Kind of cute, actually, in a witchy little way." She pictured a demonic creature, tiny, ferocious, and unknowable. She yelled, "Clark!" as if to check that he'd sent *Virago* to Allenby. "He's not there. He's turning into a pumpkin. If it hasn't gone out, I'll make sure it does."

She called Larry Balint, the writer from last night, and listened mutely while he fired her. He stumbled around, apologizing for what he was doing before he'd done it. "Listen, Marsh, this is probably stupid, but..." Why couldn't he just bring down the blade, fast and clean? Kill me if you have to, but don't mangle my neck. She was sick of these stammering losers. You know who she wanted to sign? The tough little bitch who wrote *Virago*.

She had a lunch with Pen Yearly from M81, Jake Smart's company. He ran down their projects and what they needed; she tried to fit her clients into the slots. She liked this sort of thing. It was simple and direct, a conversation robots could have had. She wondered what it would be like to be such a robot. That afternoon she sicced Clark on Apple and Buehler—that was something he would do with pleasure—and sent a rumor about Fishman spiraling toward her fiancé. Then, at the very end of the day, with her coat already on, she trashed Nye by name to Henry Mint, who, it had to be said, defended the girl rather forcefully, though in the end he began to waver. If she had enemies like Richter, he had to wonder why.

Early that evening, she found herself at a reception for the seven-hundredth reincarnation of United Artists, drinking white wine while Derek

Potter went on endlessly about something, probably himself. She wasn't listening; instead, she just watched while Potter crept ever closer, until he'd halved the personal-space radius. She tried to remember if he'd separated from his wife. Did he simply think that his new job at Warner was big enough to get him into her pants? He was right under Kraemer. Was that, in fact, big enough? Would she have fucked Kraemer simply because he was Kraemer? Possibly, though not so much for professional reasons as because running a studio made him cuter (despite the wrinkles, the gray, and the extra twenty pounds) than he'd been back when he was the projectionist at William Morris, back when there was a William Morris. Or was Potter just on a lark because he'd heard she gave good head and, as he noticed now, was still somewhat hot? It was true; she did give great head. A point of pride. But she demanded very good head, or its equivalent, in return, and a quitclaim against future expectations. Plus two points.

She laughed. Potter looked confused; had he said something funny? Was he cleverer than he thought? He was big and bluff, and he smelled good. If he knew what he was doing, if she didn't have to worry about his side of things, then for an hour or two she could forget everything else. Larry Balint, the silent phones, the four girls, all the people who would never really like her. For an hour or two, Potter would like her—he would like her a lot, she could see to that. And she would like him. Still looking around, wondering who else might be there, she reached back and found his hand.

2

Her big mistake, she decided later, had been to let Larry Balint go without a fight. What she should have done, first, was insist on a face-to-face so she could act surprised when he broke the news. Then she would have made him acknowledge what a superb job she had done for him—tripling his price, raising his profile, convincing people he wasn't just some guy who punched up dialogue but a serious writer, a *first* writer, something none of his previous agents had even bothered to try. Which would have brought them to the crucial question: Whom was he dumping her for? If she'd been on her game, if she'd been Marsha Richter instead of the flabby twat impersonating her on that phone call, she would have known the answer already. But she would have made him say it, so that when he did she could display her astonishment. He was leaving her for X?!? Was he kidding? If it had been Y or Z, fine, she could understand that. But X?

Then she would have leaned across the table, lowered her voice, and said in a tone from which every shred of self-interest had been removed, *Look, if you want to leave, try somebody else, I understand. You should do it. But, Larry, just as a friend, don't go to X.*

In this manner, playing on the uncertainty she knew he already felt, she would have beaten him down. But she hadn't done it. Over the following weeks, as people heard that Larry had dumped her, they came after the rest of her list. And the clients, sensing weakness, advised by her rivals that Richter had lost a step, that she had "never had the best relationships," panicked and began to trickle away. Two left between Columbus Day and Halloween. Todd Chesler, her biggest revenue source, began to suggest "ideas" for selling his new spec that had clearly been put into his head by some other agent he'd been flirting with. And she could feel others wobbling.

This spoiled whatever pleasure she might have taken in Runi Apple fleeing back to Israel and Elizabeth Fishman breaking up with her fiancé. For the first time since her twenties, she worried that she might lose her job. Not right away, not this year, but if she couldn't stop the bleeding and get back at least close to where she'd been, she knew that Andrew and the agency would not carry her for long.

For anyone this would have been a problem; for Richter it was worse. Other people could get fired and remain on the face of the earth. They had spouses, children, friends. They played tennis on Saturdays, had breakfast with the gang at the Farmer's Market. But without her phone calls, her meetings, her lunches, her dinners, her screenings, her BlackBerry, her leased 550 SL, without three scripts to read every night, twenty on the weekends, and the blessed relief of never having a free moment, Richter would vanish with a pop, like gas igniting. The world would forget she'd ever existed.

She couldn't sleep, and when she did she felt cheated that the time passed so quickly. She wanted to lie there and watch the obliterated hours march silently by. She wanted to be dead and to know it, but some idiotic thing in her went on living as if out of spite. It was like horniness, but without such an obvious solution.

Then one day, leaving a meeting in Westwood, she drove into a traffic apocalypse. For twenty-five minutes the car didn't go an inch. She made calls, but no one was in—or maybe they just weren't putting her through. She tried the office. Clark wasn't at the desk (again!), so it was that magnificently stacked dimwit, Sylvie, who'd just started working for Kleinfeld, who went over, looked at her call sheet, and said there were eleven names. Eleven? *Eleven??!?* Could the idiot be looking at the wrong list?

She hurled the phone at the dashboard, tried to rip the knobs off the radio. It was those fucking girls. They'd destroyed her without even knowing it. All her beautiful wickedness. She wanted to kill them, literally, incinerate them with her death ray. She wanted to see their faces in flames. Perhaps she was screaming or crying. A man in another car was looking at her oddly. Two children as well. As if she was insane. Maybe she really *was* insane. The thought calmed her down.

And then it came to her that if she wasn't ready to vanish yet, if she wanted to fight back, she would need a friend. Someone who could help turn it around. Eileen was dead. Her father was dead. Most of the people she was close to weren't in a position to help.

She called Roger at the studio, hemmed, hawed, but when she finally came out and said, "I'm in trouble," he could only manage stupefaction: In trouble? Really? You? "Look," she said, "you work with writers. Steer a couple of them my way. They don't have to be hot, just good. Or at least decent. I'll make them hot." He was silent. She whispered, "Roger, I'm dying." "Dying?" He sounded surprised, curious, maybe even relieved. As if now they might amble out to pasture together, wiping each other's drool.

She approached others who pled helplessness. She thought about trying Allenby, but was afraid he'd say no, and then she'd have to hate him, too. She tried to steal clients so far beneath her she wouldn't have noticed them two months earlier; now even they weren't interested. They could smell it, blood on the virago. Maybe she was a joke already. Marsha Richter. She's available.

3

She fired Clark. She told herself it was because he'd turned against her, first with the four flies and then, when she started losing clients, by acting as if that was her problem, not his. He'd snapped at her hand, so now she had to put him down. But that was just the cover story. In fact, she had no idea why she did it. He had been the perfect weapon, a sword that fit her grasp. If anybody wanted to know how the powerful managed to kill people without leaving fingerprints, the answer was Clark, the assistant who knew what you wanted without you having to say it—the little you who'd been waiting all his thwarted life for someone who could use him as he really was. That was what Richter had been to Eileen Schwabb. That was where she had discovered herself.

Yet those perfect harmonic resonances between two natures inevitably decayed. Eileen had blown up at Richter one day in Barney Greengrass while they were having lunch with a client Richter had discovered. Ostensibly it was over script notes, but really it was about who ran the show. These spats happened often enough, but on that occasion Richter had struck back. Not with a big, Eileen-esque fireball, but thin, dark ninja blades that left her mentor bleeding on the tablecloth before she knew she'd been hit. When Eileen saw her own blood, she went nuclear. Richter, triumphant at last, folded her napkin, apologized to the client, and left. They never spoke again. A week later Eileen got her diagnosis, and seven months after that she was dead. Four times, Richter drove to the hospital and just sat in the car, unable to go inside. At the funeral she'd sobbed uncontrollably. She hadn't cried since. Fifteen years.

She put out word that she was looking for someone new, someone with experience. Yes, she was boot camp, but four major agents had come off her assistant's desk, and all four—even Leon, who no longer spoke to her—said it had been indispensable. You worked there two years, if you could stomach it, then you either moved up or got stolen by bigger people. Everything after Richter was easy. Just grit it out. Grit it out. That was the name of the game.

She got calls recommending this or that protégé, relative, friend's kid, or office *shtup* someone had tired of *shtupping*. All applications were funneled through Clark, who hadn't left yet and was handling the transition. She followed up on each name and conducted the process in an entirely professional manner. She interviewed fourteen people, nine women and five men, made notes on each, ranked the candidates, and put off the decision. Clark maintained a mask of perfect neutrality, but she knew what he was thinking: She's getting rid of *me* for one of *them*?

Three weeks into the process she wanted to back down and ask him to stay. But then he'd own her, and that could not be. In six months, he would have gotten a desk of his own and left anyway. Why couldn't she have waited? Gritted it out. Then he would have gone as a friend, an ally—and a great one, because he was going to be a monster agent, bigger than she could ever dream of being. Now he would be after revenge. And Clark, she knew, would never forgive. Somehow she had contrived not just to disembowel herself, but to do it in public, with a bamboo sword.

Her colleagues took to wandering down the hall and sticking their heads into her office to watch her bleed. They smiled sympathetically. Poor Marsha: so tough and so dead. Privately, she suspected, they were already circling what was left of her list. It was against the rules, but why should that stop them?

Just before Thanksgiving, it was Andrew himself, head of the agency, who looked in. He frowned for a moment at the familiar stench of death, then said to her, "What's this about a script you promised to send Bryan Allenby?"

Richter made a show of trying to recall. "*Virago?*"

He nodded. "We couldn't find it in the library."

"I know. It's bizarre. Like somebody deliberately got rid of it."

"Can't we get another from the writer?"

"I've been trying for weeks. I think she went back to Canada, but I can't find her there. Email. Facebook. Google. Everything. She's quite eccentric."

"It's kind of important," Andrew said. It sounded like a threat.

"I know." She looked right back at him with an expression that would not allow him to distinguish submission from defiance. After another moment he left.

Then, early in December, when the call list was down in the forties and Andrew had already had her in to discuss "the situation," she opened her email one morning and found a batch of new queries about the job. Among them was one from Vicki Nye. Ms. Round and Rosy.

Richter liked the tone: simple, direct, dignified. She told Clark to schedule an interview.

Vicki Nye wore a tight red dress—daring given her weight, but it worked—and a stupendous amount of hair that she managed not to play with. She seemed, as she settled into the chair with unexpected grace, not so much fat as ripe and delicious. In a happier age she would have been considered a beauty, and even in this one, Richter suspected, she did not lack for admirers.

They chatted for a while about nothing in particular—Buenos Aires, where Vicki's aunt was buying real estate, Nazis, Borges, tangos, steak, the San Antonio River Walk, the American South and how you had to market movies regionally. The girl was a pleasure to talk to. She hit the ball back every time, no matter where you put it, and she always kept it in play; she didn't go for winners. When Richter threw names at her, she knew what each one was worth and, without speaking an unkind word about anybody, displayed an entirely dispassionate faculty of judgment. Beneath the sparkle and the giddy laugh was a brain without illusions.

"What went wrong at ICM?" Richter asked.

At that the girl finally missed a step, touched her hair. "What do you mean?"

Richter clasped her hands behind her head and stretched luxuriously. For the first time in weeks, she felt happy to be alive. "You're terrific," she said, "as you obviously know. With the exception of Clark out there and maybe Cecily Frank, you're sharper than any assistant in this place. Not to mention a lot of the agents." Vicki Nye didn't even blush. "They should have you on the fast track over there, working for Jeff or Pablo or Ginny Quinn. People should be fighting over you. But you're still floating."

The girl was silent a moment, measuring Richter with the same cool eye she fixed on everything else. It was, in fact, wonderful to be looked at that way—"with respect" was the phrase that came strangely to mind—and to be untroubled by what might be seen.

"The second week I was there," Nye said slowly, feeling her way, "I got involved with somebody I shouldn't have. After that, everything went bad."

Somebody else's somebody, Richter figured, but didn't need to know.

"When I saw how people reacted—I mean, they hated me, really *hated* me. People I hadn't even met. I'd crossed a line, I guess, especially given the particulars, which I don't want to go into…" She paused to let Richter nod her approval, but Richter did nothing, waited. Let her take care of herself.

"I should have quit right then," Nye went on. "I was dead there, but I kept thinking, I'll get past this, I'll do good work, and they'll forget. But it was too late. I was branded."

Yes. Branded.

"I kept thinking how could I have been so stupid."

"All right," Richter said pleasantly, warmly, encircling the girl in her smile and tolerance. "How could you have been so stupid?"

Vicki laughed. She relaxed a bit. Something was shifting between them. A little garden was being staked out. Vicki had opened the gate to invite Richter in, but for the moment, without declining, Richter simply leaned against the post. It took the younger woman a moment to understand this, to see the wisdom in unhurriedness. But then she did, and accepted it, and they went on chatting over the fence.

"I'd only been there a few days, but I loved it so much I didn't want to go home at night. I knew I was good. I was going to be an agent for the rest of my life. I'd found my place in the world, and then I ruined it. For nothing."

Richter, a less-bubbly creature, nevertheless knew what she meant. People needed failure. It was the fuel that drove them.

"Then Stephanie, your old assistant, told me about this job, and it woke me up. I decided I wanted to go somewhere everyone didn't already officially hate me."

Richter gazed out at the dazzling morning, the canyons green from the rain. She'd take Allenby to lunch, tell him the truth about *Virago*. They'd laugh together.

"Look," Vicki Nye was saying, "I know you're tough. Everyone says it."

Richter tilted her head, raised her handsome eyebrows.

Vicki made a face: come off it, you know what you are. And Richter laughed, startled by her own gratitude that the girl was unafraid of her.

"I'm a virago," she confessed.

The girl smiled blandly. She had no idea what Richter was talking about. She'd forgotten the lunch, her scorn, forgotten "feral dog." Remembering them, Richter felt a distant echo of her shame and fury, yet now she found herself somehow inside Vicki's garden, as if she'd gone through the gate without noticing. And then, of course, she made her mistake.

As the younger woman shifted in her chair, attempting to reorganize her bulk for greater comfort, Richter, in impulsive mockery, hefted her own long, lean body as if it, too, were a big sack of cornmeal she didn't quite know what to do with. And there it suddenly was, the slimy, hideous thing she'd been trying to hide, quivering on the desk between them.

Its appearance was so startling that Vicki Nye laughed. But as the appalling nature of it sank in—not the insult to Vicki, who seemed genuinely unoffended, but the revelation of Richter's cruelty—the laughter stopped, and Vicki took another look at the creature sitting across from her. All she could see was one of its hideous feathers, moldy and bloodstained, but that was enough to recall everything she had ever heard about Marsha Richter.

Richter wanted to say something, apologize, explain, but it was too late for that. So she just shrugged and made a face as if to say, Well, you knew I was a monster.

Vicki smiled, a softer smile this time, as if absorbing it all, accommodating the different parts and seeing, Richter hoped, that you couldn't have the ones you liked without the ones that made your blood run cold. The smile seemed to announce that Vicki could handle them, all the parts, because she wanted what Richter had. And because she wanted it, Richter could use her as she liked. As she needed.

When they were finished, Richter walked her out, introducing her along the way to the people she would be working with, though nothing of the sort had been said. It was too soon for that. Richter pressed the button to call the elevator. They stood chatting easily, as if they'd known each other for years, and when the door opened, Richter smiled, said goodbye, and walked away before it closed.

You fell in love in Hollywood over and over, and very little of it was romantic. You fell in love with people who made you feel, at last, appreciated and understood. With people you thought could give you a hand, help you along, not out of selfless generosity—which you knew not to trust—but because it was in their interest. You fell in love with people who made you feel less alone.

Like other loves, these did not last. They came into being when interests aligned and ended when the interests advanced. There was no such thing as eternal love. There was only today's love and maybe tomorrow's. Yet today's was sometimes so intense that it felt eternal, and you could live in that eternity while it lasted.

She knew, in the end, that Vicki Nye would break her heart and leave, but she would become, for a year or two, Richter's closest ally, her only friend. She had a gift for people Richter lacked, and she would use it on Richter's behalf. She would smooth the way and do it so graciously that Richter would come to think at times that she herself had changed, and was no longer quite so horrible. Only when Vicki left, and the change drained out of her—though perhaps not completely—would she realize that it had never really been hers.

But that would be then.

Today she was in love. And because Vicki would, in her way, travel the same path, Richter thought of them traveling it together. Richter had, perhaps, eight good years left; then five or ten more for declining into irrelevance, and a final quarter century in which to dwindle into the grave.

And at the end, in the assisted-living facility, with no children and their resentful spouses to spoil her weekends with grudging visits, she imagined that only Vicki Nye would come to visit, dropping by dutifully every few months. Vicki would be almost seventy by then, a bit stouter but still spry and attractive. She would never get married, but she might have a boyfriend, a fella. Richter hoped so.

Clark, not entirely unaware of these cogitations, urged Richter to call Vicki and offer her a job before someone else did. She was surprised and touched by his concern (this required a reevaluation she didn't have time for at the moment), but she explained (though he should have known this by now; was he getting soft in the head just when he was about to go out on his own?) that calling too soon would look desperate and might scare the girl away. Vicki Nye wanted the job, she felt sure of that. But she had to worry a little that she wouldn't get it, so that when she did she'd fight to keep it. Then she would begin her work in the best possible state of mind. So Richter would wait until Monday to call. Or even Tuesday. Yes, there was a risk that a better offer might come along, and she would lose her. But that was the game you had to play, and Richter was good at it.

WHAT HAPPENS AFTER SIXTEEN YEARS IN PRISON?

SENT AWAY FOR LIFE FOR SOMEONE ELSE'S CRIME, THE SCOTT SISTERS NOW FIND THEMSELVES FREE, FAR FROM HOME—AND LEGALLY REQUIRED TO DONATE A KIDNEY

by J. MALCOLM GARCIA

HILLSBORO, MISSISSIPPI

THEY STILL TALK ABOUT IT, here in Hillsboro.

How the Scott sisters, Jamie and Gladys, were arrested for organizing an armed robbery they say they had no part in. How Jamie, twenty-one, and Gladys, just nineteen, neither one of whom had a police record or even a speeding ticket, were each given two consecutive life sentences for the crime, far more time than was given to the boys who were either their accomplices or who falsely claimed to be. How no one can even say how much money was stolen, if any. Some accounts put the figure at $11.

The sisters were released in the first few days of 2011, after serving sixteen years. Governor Haley Barbour suspended their sentences on the condition that Gladys donate a kidney to Jamie, whose own kidneys had begun to fail a year earlier. She has not done so yet.

The Scott sisters live in Pensacola now. They moved there to be with their mother, Evelyn Rasco. Miss Evelyn herself lies critically ill in a Pensacola hospital, her left leg amputated as a result of her own battle with diabetes.

ABOVE LEFT: *Jamie Scott at the gym.*
BELOW LEFT: *Gladys Scott, at work in a Pensacola restaurant kitchen. Photos by J. Malcolm Garcia.*

Sixteen years I fought, she mumbles in her sleep. I'm tired.

But in Hillsboro, not that much has changed since Jamie and Gladys were sent to prison. The town is little more than a dot on the map eight miles outside Forest, Mississippi, a slightly bigger dot just off Interstate 20. Turn off the interstate onto Highway 35, following the road through the woods where, on starless nights, the darkness seems as deep and still as the ocean, and after a few miles you'll drive past a few motels and a Kentucky Fried Chicken before you reach the mini-mart where Jamie's car broke down the night the crime took place. They caught a ride there with two boys who later said the sisters led them into an ambush.

The Scott sisters' father, James Rasco, was born and raised in Hillsboro. The family goes way back. Black children here are taught to stay out of trouble. Keep your head down and just get on with your life. At night, enjoy yourself, but stay in the house. And when you're out, hope no police get behind you.

Looked like you swerved, they'll say. What're you all dressed up for? Getting into something? You know so and so?

Don't let the police pin nothing on you, people here say. You'll end up like Jamie and Gladys.

A PENSACOLA MORNING

Jamie and Gladys awaken before dawn. Miles apart from each other, each in her own home, hearing nothing but the sound of her own breathing.

In prison, Jamie and Gladys were surrounded by hundreds of other women. Hundreds of women watching one another, talking all at once, almost touching. Someone would be screaming over the intercom and someone else would be blasting the TV and at the same time there'd be showers hissing and the microwave beeping and a dozen toilets flushing. Noise bouncing off concrete.

There were women who raped other women. There were fights. Once a girl threw boiling water on another girl she'd been arguing with. The skin peeled off the second girl's face like mud sliding downhill. They'd gotten into it over the TV. The girl who'd thrown the water had wanted to watch a soap. She boiled the water in the microwave good and hot.

In Pensacola, Jamie and Gladys get up, make their beds. The routine was drilled into them in prison: up at 5, make your bed, or get written up. Beds so neat they can bounce pennies off the sheets.

Gladys, now thirty-seven, rents an apartment; Jamie, thirty-nine, lives in a house. Staying with their mother, and with the kids they'd spent sixteen years away from, turned out to be difficult for them both. Their own children spoke to them any kind of way—*Don't tell us what to do. You didn't raise us.*

Meanwhile their mother wanted to do everything for them. Get their Social Security cards, their birth certificates. No, Jamie and Gladys would tell her; just show us. We can do it.

During their first week in Pensacola, they stopped at a Walmart. Greeters rushed up to them. Crowds jammed the aisles. People were swiping their credit cards at the cash register, talking into cell phones. Jamie started hyperventilating. It was too fast.

BACK IN THE DAY

Jamie and Gladys were born in Chicago's Cook County Hospital. They grew up on the fifteenth floor of a housing project at Forty-fourth Street and South College Grove, surrounded by gang fights and shootings, never knowing when they might step over a body. One day, when Jamie was twelve, the elevator in their building opened and revealed a dead man abandoned inside. She screamed, and her father rushed her back into their apartment.

She saw children fall from windows high above the ground when they leaned out too far throwing water balloons. She saw shootings, stabbings. After a while, death no longer shocked her. Jamie and Gladys learned to be cautious. Anything could happen, and they had no control over it when it did.

Their father was a maintenance supervisor at the University of Illinois. He had a side job, too; he'd take janitorial supplies from the university hospital and use them to clean houses. When no one noticed, he started taking other hospital equipment and selling it off. Eventually the man he did this with was caught and ratted James out, but the hospital couldn't prove his involvement.

The hospital gave James the option to retire after twenty years, and he took it. He told his family he was taking them to Mississippi. He was going to get them away from Chicago's violence, and let himself look after his elderly parents. His mother had developed the beginnings of Alzheimer's disease.

She was still well enough when they got to Hillsboro to tell Jamie and Gladys that the Rascos had always been into illegal occupations. James, she said, came from a long line of people who did things outside the law to make money.

The family moved into a three-bedroom house owned by James's parents. At first, Gladys and Jamie hated Hillsboro's slow pace; they missed their

Chicago friends, and they promised themselves that once they turned eighteen they would return to the city. Before they could do it, however, they'd both gotten pregnant and dropped out of high school. They stayed in Hillsboro.

Jamie had had one son already, before they'd moved south. In Hillsboro she gave birth to another son and one daughter before having her tubes tied in November 1993. Gladys had a daughter after their move, and was pregnant with a second daughter when the robbery occurred, at the end of that year.

By then their father had opened the Sugar Hill Night Club. Hillsboro is part of Scott County, a dry county; James bought booze in Jackson and sold it from the Sugar Hill. He hired girls from Chicago and paid them to strip on weekends.

Jamie and Gladys knew what their father was up to, but no one in the family discussed it. He was the world to them; he took care of them, and they never went without. They'd disappointed him when they'd decided to quit school. He could not read or write himself, and he'd wanted them to get their diplomas. He had even paid for Jamie's class ring, anticipating her graduation.

He was strong-willed and hot-tempered. He didn't trust banks, and kept his money buried in the woods. He knew the woods well. And he knew how to make a dollar.

After the girls had given up on school, James put Jamie to work in his club, cooking. By 10 a.m., he told her, I want you to cut up five onions and two bell peppers. Put them on the grill and turn it low. Within minutes, when people heard the sizzling and smelled the aromas rising from the kitchen, they'd start ordering catfish plates, hamburger plates, rib plates with fries and baked beans. Jamie might help the club bring in several hundred dollars a day, sometimes. Gladys helped, too, but neither one of them served liquor. James handled that. The police knew what he was doing, but James paid them off.

At one point some Mississippi guys began selling crack outside the club. Eventually one of them was shot there, and the police closed the place down for a few weeks. When the club reopened, the drug dealers were gone, and James had decided to get in on their action. He began supplying crack to Scott and Jasper counties. His daughters were terrified, worried their father would get arrested. The police raided their house and found dope in the refrigerator. James paid them off again.

After a while the police wanted more money. James refused, and that's when all the trouble started. Miss Evelyn began complaining that the police were following her to bingo. If they get behind you, don't stop, James told her.

Get to the house and blow your horn and I'll handle it from there.

By then Jamie had left the club and was working at a chicken plant, cutting chicken tenders eight hours a day. She didn't see a future for herself at her father's place. She knew how it would end.

THE NIGHT IN QUESTION

On the night of December 23, 1993, the heater in Jamie's Hillsboro house died. Gladys dropped by, and Jamie told her she needed to find the gas man, Ken. It was after hours, but Jamie knew that Ken drove the gas truck home; people would pay him on the side to fill their tanks. Everyone had a hustle.

The sisters took Jamie's car to Ken's house, but Ken was out with friends. Jamie left a note with Ken's wife, then drove to a mini-mart in Forest to put gas in the car. When they'd filled the tank, though, the car wouldn't start. Gladys saw two men she knew, Johnny Ray Hayes and Mitchell Duckworth, and offered to pay them ten dollars for a ride home.

It was almost 10 p.m., the night cold and clear. Jamie got in the backseat with Duckworth; it was Hayes's car. Duckworth began making advances, Jamie says—he offered to give her three hundred dollars to come with him to a hotel.

I don't sleep around, you hear me? Jamie told him.

When they passed the Cow Pasture, another nightclub, Jamie saw a cousin of hers and asked Hayes to stop. She got out and asked her cousin if he could run them home, but he told her he was waiting on some dope. Jamie got back into the car.

Duckworth started hitting on her again, pulling on her arm. When he ripped her shirt, Jamie started screaming for Hayes to stop the car again. She and Gladys got out, she says; they were near their father's house, and they started walking. Hayes and Duckworth shouted after them, calling them bitches. Jamie glanced back, she says, and saw another car approaching Hayes's, but thought little of it.

Around midnight, some friends stopped by Jamie's house. They told her they'd had a confrontation on Cow Pasture Road with a couple of "dudes"; the men they described sounded like Hayes and Duckworth. Jamie's friends said they'd taken some beer and demanded some money, but the dudes hadn't had any.

The next morning, Christmas Eve, Jamie lay on the couch in her front room, still sore from her November operation. Her mother stood in her kitchen, preparing Christmas dinner. Evelyn had run out of room in her own kitchen, so she'd come over to put a ham in Jamie's oven. Moments after she left, the Scott County sheriff showed up. He told Jamie that she and Gladys were being arrested for robbing Hayes and Duckworth.

Do I look like I robbed somebody? Jamie said as they handcuffed her.

Her children were screaming. Her three-year-old son ran after the squad car as it drove away until he collapsed in the dirt, crying.

Jamie says the sheriff told her that if she and Gladys revealed her father's drug connections, they would be home by Christmas. She and Gladys refused to say anything. The charges, Jamie says, were then upgraded to armed robbery.

HOW IT GOES

Enoch McCurdy says people in Hillsboro are still shocked that the Scott sisters were arrested. Nobody believed it at first. Enoch, sixty, a nephew of James Rasco's, didn't. He knew James was dealing drugs at the time. James had told Enoch that he wasn't going to pay the sheriff nothing.

The arrests drove James crazy, Enoch says. He grieved for his imprisoned daughters. He broke down. His hair turned gray, and he lost weight. He spent as much as he could to get Jamie and Gladys off, but it wasn't going to happen. That's how it goes in Mississippi.

CHILDREN

Olivia Flake is twenty-four now. She was seven when her mother, Gladys, was sent to prison. Evelyn took her to visit Gladys every other Sunday. At first they could sit with Gladys in her cell, but then they started meeting her in a big open visiting center, with food machines and snack machines and a soda machine. A picture booth, too. Sodas cost two dollars.

Olivia's younger sister was born in 1994. Prison officials took Gladys to the University of Mississippi Medical Center when she went into labor. She was chained to a bed and allowed just two days with her newborn daughter before she was told to turn the child over to her mother or the state. Gladys asked her mother to take the baby, and let Olivia choose a name. Olivia decided on

Courtney, the name of a close friend.

After a few years, visiting the prison twice a month seemed normal. Oh, our mom is in prison—like, oh, our mom's at the mall. Olivia didn't write many letters to her mother. She didn't want this you-have-to-write-your-mother-because-she's-in-prison thing going on.

When she was thirteen, Olivia gave birth to a boy of her own, and named him Xander, a Greek word that means "protector of men." She liked the strength of the name, the sense of security it aroused in her. She had run away, by then, and she wanted to do her own thing. She felt lost. Miss Evelyn took care of Xander for her.

Olivia wants to be close to Gladys, but doesn't know if she can. It's awkward, trying to do the mother-daughter thing. She doesn't feel motivated. Recently she met a man through the Internet, Ozondu Duru. He lives in Nigeria. Olivia thinks she loves him; she's applied for a passport, and plans to move there to be with him. She wants to get married. Wants to be a proper mother to her son.

SEASON'S GREETINGS

The morning the jury announced its verdict, Gladys had a premonition that she was not coming home. She'd seen one of the jurors putting on makeup during the trial. Like she wasn't even listening.

The trial lasted two days. Seven white and five black jurors deliberated for half an hour before coming to an agreement. On October 4, 1994, Jamie and Gladys were found guilty of two counts of armed robbery each. Mississippi law permits juries to recommend a life sentence for armed robbery, and so each of the Scott sisters received two life sentences. One for each armed-robbery count.

Both girls collapsed after the guards escorted them from the courtroom. Double life sentence. Because of their father, Gladys thought. She could see the look on his face as the verdict was read, the disbelief, the hurt in his eyes.

Gladys and Jamie were held in the Scott County Jail for two more days before being transported to the Central Mississippi Correctional Facility, in Rankin, where they were booked, fingerprinted, and escorted to a shower room. They stood with the other new women in a circle, the water crashing down on their bodies as the male guards watched. Several of the women there had already been in the prison three or four times; they told Jamie and Gladys to mind their own business and not to get in anyone's way.

New inmates sentenced to fifteen years or more were put on suicide watch in solitary confinement before they were released into the general population. Gladys and Jamie were placed in twelve-by-twelve-foot cells, each one with a steel bed attached to the wall, a sink, and a toilet. A guard slid their food through a slot in the door. If it fell off the tray, oh well.

The sisters spoke to other inmates by screaming under their doors. They talked to each other through a vent by the toilets. Jamie entered the general population within six months; Gladys remained in solitary longer, because she'd argued with a guard. Even when she was released into the rest of the prison, she stayed angry. Little things ticked her off. When an inmate tried to take her turn in the shower, she fought back.

She always stayed alert. Anyone who spoke to her, no matter how nice, might be messing with her head. They might like her one day and try to hurt her the next. If she slipped up, she'd be seen as weak. She'd be run over.

Sometimes the guards would shake her cell down, tear up letters, her children's pictures. She would just stand there, silent. As time passed, however, Gladys did get close to some of them. Hard not to, seeing them every day, year after year. They would tell her about their problems in the free world. But the good ones always left.

The last thirty days in prison were the hardest, Gladys says. The last week was worse than the first. She was snappy, irritable. She wanted to get out.

When the day arrived, January 7, 2011, Gladys started shaking. She was wearing a two-piece purple dress suit, purple earrings, and a pair of purple high heels. The shoes were too big, and it took her a moment to walk in them. The sisters had been told by other inmates that if they looked back, when they left, they would return to prison. They wanted to look back, to see the women they'd spent sixteen years with one last time, but they were afraid.

Nearly a year later, Gladys shifts on her couch, gives her walls an unblinking, thousand-mile stare. Christmas is just weeks away. She and Jamie were arrested in December; she worries about a knock on her door, an expressionless officer telling her it's time to come with him. Do as much time as she has, that fear is going to be with you for a minute.

Gladys and Jamie have midnight curfews. They cannot travel beyond Pensacola without permission. They cannot drink alcohol. They report to a probation officer once a month, and will do so for the remainder of their lives unless they receive a pardon. Their PO can drop by anytime, night or day. Demand a piss test. Search the house.

Gladys's cell phone rings. A woman she knew in prison. She just got out.

Your momma happy you home? Gladys says. I bet she is, girl. Can't sleep, can you? Three or four days without it, uh-huh. What'd you eat when you got out? I gained my weight back. I'm big as a hat.

THE PROSECUTION'S CASE

The Scott County district attorney agreed with the Scott sisters' version of events, up to a point. They did, the district attorney said, ask Johnny Ray Hayes and Mitchell Duckworth for a ride home from the mini-mart in Forest. On the way back to Hillsboro, they did stop at the Cow Pasture.

But then, the DA claimed, Gladys asked to drive.

According to the prosecution, they stopped next at a house in Forest, where the sisters spoke to someone in a blue Oldsmobile. Afterward, Gladys continued driving; when Jamie complained of feeling ill, Gladys slowed to a stop. Another car came up behind them, then, and a man with a shotgun robbed Hayes and Duckworth. Hayes claimed he turned over "about two hundred-something dollars." Duckworth said he "didn't have much money in [his] wallet. Really nothing, probably." Hayes said that Jamie and Gladys left with the robbers.

Howard Patrick, fourteen, and his cousin Gregory Patrick, eighteen, testified against the Scott sisters as part of a plea deal they'd worked out for themselves. Howard said that he and Gregory, along with Howard's sixteen-year-old brother, Christopher, had committed the robbery. They were friends of the Scott sisters', he said; on the night in question, they'd met with the girls at the mini-mart, and Gladys had conceived of the hold-up. Howard's share of the stolen money was "nine, ten, eleven dollars." During the trial, Howard Patrick admitted that he hadn't bothered to read the statement that had implicated the Scott sisters before he signed it. It had been given to him by the sheriff's department.

> Q: *And you had been promised that if you signed the statement, you could get out of jail the next morning?*
> A: *That, and they said if I didn't participate with them, they would send me to Parchman and make me out a female.*
> Q: *I'm sorry?*
> A: *That they would let me out of jail the next morning, and that if I didn't*

participate with them, that they would send me to Parchman and make me out a female.

Q: *In other words, they would send you to Parchman, and you would get raped, right?*
A: *Yes, sir.*
Q: *So you decided it was better to sign the statement, even without reading it?*
A: *I didn't know what it was.*

Sixty-two-year-old Willy Tooks, of Hillsboro, did not testify at the trial, but he would have had something to say had he been asked. He was in the Scott County Jail at the same time as the Patrick boys, after the robbery. Tooks had shoplifted a ham from a Sunflower supermarket in Forest. Those boys, he says, were talking about Jamie and Gladys—talking about how they were going to give state's evidence against them. They were smoking cigarettes and just talking. They were going to try to get a lighter sentence. At the time, Tooks didn't think one way or the other about it. He wanted to get out of jail himself.

MEAN OLD WORLD

Celestine Lewis directs the Jacqueline Harris Preparatory Academy, a Pensacola charter school where Jamie holds a clerical job. In January of 2011, Miss Lewis, as everyone calls her, read about the Scott sisters' release from prison in the newspaper, and about their move to Pensacola.

Sixteen years incarcerated, she recalls thinking at the time. Sixteen years and then released into this big mean old world. Oh, god, I'd like to see these girls enrich their lives, she thought. Her mother died a few days later. She needed something to take her mind off the loss.

Miss Lewis called the Scotts' mother and asked to speak with Jamie and Gladys. I don't want anything, Miss Lewis told her. I just want to meet you all.

At a Red Lobster, where she took Jamie and Gladys for lunch, Miss Lewis explained how tipping worked. She told them to keep their left hands on their laps and not to eat like they had nothing.

Jamie said that in prison, you were allowed only fifteen minutes to eat. Sometimes you bit into a bug. You weren't given napkins.

Miss Lewis pursed her lips and considered this for a moment. Then she told Jamie and Gladys that she'd grown up in a shotgun house. Her father was a laborer. Her mother pushed education. The Lord first, then education. If you don't have both, she said, you're doomed. Napkins on your laps, please.

APPEAL

A new lawyer, Chokwe Lumumba, represented the Scott sisters on appeal. He contacted Chris Patrick, the only one of the Patrick boys not to testify during the original trial. Chris swore in a signed affidavit that Jamie and Gladys had not been involved in the robbery.

Prior to the trial of Gladys and Jamie Scott, Deputy Marvin Williams of the Scott County Sheriff Department told me and my brother Howard in my presence that we would serve life sentences in Parchman prison if we did not agree to testify against Gladys and Jamie Scott, and if we did not agree to testify that both women took part in planning for and setting up the robbery of Duckworth and Hayes.

Lumumba found other individuals who raised questions about the case, as well. Willie Shepard, who had worked as a trustee at the Scott County Jail at the time of the robbery, said that a few days afterward, he and a few other prisoners were taken to the scene by sheriff's deputies in order to search for evidence. One trustee discovered Duckworth's wallet with three twenty-dollar bills in it.

"Duckworth was one of the alleged victims of the alleged robbery," Shepard told Lumumba. "[Deputy] Marvin [Murls] knew Duckworth because he lived near his family. Once we were back at the jail, Marvin called all of us trustees together. Marvin said, looking directly at me, 'If this gets back to Hillsboro, you are going to ride Buddy's truck.' He meant he was going to send me to Parchman." Lumumba believed that, in order to prop up the robbery story, the deputy had wanted to conceal that money had been left at the scene.

Lumumba's appeal was denied. He then petitioned Ronnie Musgrove, then the governor of Mississippi, for a commutation of the Scott sisters' sentence. He noted that the Patricks had already been released from prison.

Remember, Lumumba wrote, *Neither Gladys nor Jamie had any prior convictions or arrests. There was no murder or even hospitalization of the alleged victims in this case. Therefore the question becomes whether these two women should have been sentenced to such harsh punishments for crimes that they clearly did not commit.*

The commutation request was denied.

TIME GONE BY

Sixteen years.

James Rasco died of a massive heart attack in 2003, at the age of fifty-two.

In 2004, Evelyn Rasco's mother died, too. Jamie and Gladys's older sister, Evelyn, named after their mother, died of congestive heart failure in 2008. And then, in 2010, Jamie's kidneys began to fail.

STUDY HABITS

Gladys helps her eight-year-old niece, Shamira, the daughter of her sister Evelyn, with her homework. Gladys and Jamie share the responsibility of raising Shamira now.

Until recently, Gladys was also in school, attending classes at Pensacola State College. She received her GED in December 2011. But now she's decided to take a semester off to better look after her mother.

In the meantime, she wants to find work at a nursing home. Something stable. When an employer realizes the gaps in her work history are a result of time served in prison, she worries the application will go into the garbage.

Right now, she has a job at a barbecue joint for three hours a day. Members of her church knew the owner, and recommended her. Sometimes, as Gladys works in the kitchen, her mind drifts back to her job in the prison cafeteria. She remembers the big pots. Big enough to sit in. Gladys, come back, her boss at the barbecue joint says, and the memory pops like a soap bubble.

Finding an apartment was another challenge. No one wanted to rent to an ex-felon. Eventually, she found a landlord who didn't bother with background checks. She told him her story anyway, to be on the level. As long as you never molested children, he told her. Gladys assured him that she had not.

At Pensacola State, Gladys worked in an administrative office. One morning a secretary noticed a copy of *Ebony* jutting out of Gladys's bag and asked to read it. Gladys gave it to her, and the secretary leafed through it until she reached an article about the Scott sisters' release. She glanced at Gladys, who had just answered a phone.

Kind of cold in here, Gladys said after she'd hung up. Must have the air on high.

I heard about you on the news, the secretary said. They really did that? Said it was you and your sister's idea to rob them boys?

Yes, Gladys said. She started stuffing GED forms into folders.

You went through a lot. Why didn't you say anything?

Didn't know how you'd treat me, Gladys said. Some people treat you different when they know you've been in prison.

I wouldn't have.

How would I know that? Gladys said.

FAMILY

There was this older lady Jamie knew inside, Miss Alberta. Seventy-something. Murdered her husband. Life sentence. She told Jamie, If you find yourself not eating or bathing and your hair coming out, you'll find yourself in the grave. You got to keep hope. Read the Bible. Don't let your time be idle.

Gladys was friends with an inmate named Angel. Angel loved to dance. She was a little slow, and would get into it with the guards. Gladys combed her hair, helped her with makeup. When Angel was a child, her stepfather sold her for crack. Angel was released while Gladys and Jamie were incarcerated, but she was back inside within twenty-four hours. She had tried to kill her stepfather for molesting her son.

Gladys was working in the kitchen, and brought food to her. She saw Angel hanging by the vent in her cell. Gladys kicked the door and screamed— Get her down! Get her down! But she was already dead.

CHILDREN

Jamie's son Richard was eleven months old when his mother was arrested. His grandmother described her to him; she was kind-hearted, she said. He didn't remember her. Where is she now? he would ask. Out of town, his grandmother would say.

When he went to visit his mother for the first time, Richard thought his grandparents had taken him to a zoo. The walls, the wire fence. He didn't know who his mother was, when he saw her. She picked him up on the prison playground; he remembers how strong she was. When it was time to go, it was hard to leave. He thought this woman who was his mother was very nice.

He remembers that Jamie and Gladys both attended his grandfather's funeral. James had told Richard that it was his responsibility as a man to watch out for his girl cousins. He'd taught him about farming corn, cabbage, beans, potatoes, pecans, about hunting deer and boars. He'd urged Richard to get an education.

Evelyn was strict with him. He loved her for it. She would help him with his math and reading, and he would help her when she wrote letters on behalf of Jamie and Gladys. When she lost a page somewhere, he'd rummage through the house to find it. She would stay up late writing, and he would help her to bed.

It hurts now, seeing her in the hospital.

Richard was thirteen, maybe fourteen, when his aunt Evelyn died. He remembers his mother at the funeral in a black and white prison jumpsuit, wrapped in chains. Aunt Gladys was in solitary, then, and not allowed to attend. It was a hot day. Not cloudy. Two guards stood beside Richard's mother; they moved back some when she went to stand by the grave.

After the funeral, everyone walked into the church cafeteria. Jamie had to eat because of her diabetes. The guards waited at the cafeteria doors. They told Jamie, You got two minutes.

CHURCH

It surprises Pastor Lonnie D. Wesley, of the Greater Little Rock Baptist Church, what Jamie and Gladys don't know. When Gladys was in a car accident, neither she nor Jamie knew to call the police or their insurance company. They called Pastor Wesley instead. Things like that aren't trivial, he says.

At one point, Jamie told Pastor Wesley that she wanted to return to prison. Everything was moving too fast. In prison, she knew what was expected of her. The guards trusted her. New inmates respected her. She didn't have to worry about light bills, gas bills, car accidents. But then she thought of her mother and Shamira and knew she wouldn't be able to do anything for either of them if she went back to being locked up.

MOMMA

Evelyn Rasco lies in a bed at Pensacola's Baptist Hospital, asleep. A nurse places a blanket over her. Miss Evelyn, sixty-five, has not been eating. Her weight has dropped from 250 to 119 pounds in three months. Doctors worry about malnutrition. It seems so unfair to her family that she would be so sick now, when Jamie and Gladys are finally out.

Miss Evelyn left Hillsboro in 2000, taking Jamie's and Gladys's five children with her. She had a son in the army in Pensacola, and she needed to get away from James and his lifestyle.

Once she settled in Florida, Miss Evelyn began writing letters to community activists, law schools—anyone she thought might help free her daughters. She had only an eighth-grade education, but expressed herself clearly and forcefully. She budgeted money for stamps and ink cartridges.

In the fall of 2005, she wrote to one of Jesse Jackson's sons, Congressman Jesse Jackson III. Her letter was passed on to the elder Jackson's Rainbow PUSH Coalition, and came to the attention of Nancy Lockhart, a law student at Loyola University in Chicago and a community-services consultant at Rainbow PUSH. Included with the letter was a six-page booklet Jamie had put together about the case. If Rainbow PUSH could not help her, Miss Evelyn had written, please recommend another agency that might.

No fluff, Lockhart recalls now. Direct and to the point.

Lockhart began to work with Miss Evelyn to draw attention to the case. Progress was slow; Rainbow PUSH and other organizations like it seemed reluctant to get involved. In 2008, Lockhart began using the Internet to spread the Scott sisters' story. She filed guest posts for web magazines, and started her own website, *thewrongfulconviction.com*. Soon *Mother Jones* and The *New York Times* were raising questions about the case. By 2009, Lockhart became convinced that the state of Mississippi was going to have to do something.

DIALYSIS

Jamie sits in the waiting room of the dialysis center at Fresenius Medical Care in Pensacola's Cordova Mall, waiting for the receptionist to call her name.

You been on yet? another patient asks her.

No. Just got here.

Jamie was diagnosed with diabetes in 2003, when her gall bladder was removed. In 2010, her blood work showed that she'd gone into complete renal failure and would have to be placed on dialysis.

Shortly after that, a guard told Gladys to speak to Jamie. Jamie knew nothing about dialysis, and had refused treatment. She would die without it, the guard said.

You're not leaving me, Gladys told her. We lost one sister while we've been here. I don't want to lose another. We walk out the way we came in. Together.

The trailer housing the dialysis machine at the prison was filthy. Mold grew on the outside of it, and dust covered the floor. Two male nurses and four female nurses connected patients to the machines. Jamie was struck by their smiles. No hint of judgment. You might as well stop looking like it's the end of the world, a male nurse would joke with her. You're too pretty.

The dialysis treatment takes about four hours, three times a week. Jamie can't describe the feeling of her blood being pumped out of and back into her body. Weird. Like a steady stream going through you.

Would a man want me if he knew I had health problems? Jamie wonders. Would he accept me? She would cook for him, and try to be as normal as possible, but would it be enough? Would he look at her the way Gladys does? That look of, Lord, please don't let my sister die.

She needs to lose more than one hundred pounds before she'll be eligible for a kidney transplant. If Gladys's kidney isn't a match, Jamie will be put on a waiting list. Gladys will then donate the kidney to someone else, as required by the conditions of her parole.

To lose weight, Jamie exercises at the Pensacourt Sports Center three or four times a week. She runs, lifts weights, and rides a stationary bicycle in a yellow brick room she calls the torture room. When she finishes her exercise, her trainer goes over her diet.

What'd you have yesterday?

Gladys cooked greens. No fatback. Turkey, bacon, sweet potatoes.

What's on the sweet potatoes?

Nothing. I ate two boiled eggs and one of my protein things.

Didn't have a snack.

No. Chicken for lunch.

You stopped drinking soda?

Yes.

Good. Lots of regular water?

Yes.

Obstacles?

My momma is in the hospital. It's depressing. A woman who fought so hard for us and she don't want to fight for herself, it seems like. My mind is focused on that. I've been hungry.

It's a stressful time. Stay on track.

THE DECISION

In December 2010, Jamie and Gladys knew the governor was considering a pardon. Members of the pardon board had spoken to them in the middle of the month. If you're released, where would you go, what would you do? What would you say to the governor, if you could talk to him?

The board did not want to hear them declare their innocence. They weren't considering their innocence. They were considering whether they should be released.

Jamie and Gladys said the governor would never have to worry that he'd made the wrong decision. They would not return to jail. They were not criminals.

Their release was announced on December 27. Governor Barbour said he based his decision in part on a desire to relieve the state of the cost of Jamie's dialysis treatment—about two hundred thousand dollars a year.

Today the mini-mart where Jamie and Gladys caught a ride with Hayes and Duckworth is a Citgo gas station. A sign announces the closing of the Movie Gallery video outlet next door: LAST-MINUTE GREAT DEALS TO BE HAD.

Johnny Ray Hayes and Mitchell Duckworth have never commented publicly on the Scott sisters' case. The men have never attempted to contact them. Neither have the Patricks. Just as well, Jamie and Gladys say. Those boys put them away for sixteen years.

A PENSACOLA MORNING

Jamie and Gladys awaken. They bolt out of bed and stand ready for the inspection that will not come. The clamor of a prison dream fades from their minds.

Small things please them. Opening their refrigerators and seeing food they bought themselves. Sitting on their couches and listening to the silence. Sometimes they might cry for no reason.

They're home now. They can close their bedroom doors.

Can't nobody write them up. Can't nobody come in.

AFTERNOON STREET

by JOWHOR ILE

illustration by KELSEY DAKE

SLEEP STAYS AWAY at night. In the morning strangers visit me.

For most of the day there is just the fever, hot and angry-colored. The clock on the table says 3:05 p.m. I have been sprawled on the bed for two days; my head cannot lift from the pillow.

The table vibrates. My phone is ringing and for a while I try to make out what to do in response. The action slips through my mind like sand through my fingers. From downstairs the radio goes silent.

A woman's voice comes on, clear and mellow, confirming the time, assuring us that the music will continue here on Niger Delta Radio after a brief commercial break. There is a jingle for a play showing at the Civic Centre on Friday, then a commercial for anti-malaria tablets. The bed creaks as I turn on my side.

A man walks in, tall as the door. There is sweat on his forehead, softness in his bloodshot eyes, a black pen clipped to his breast pocket. I hurt my throat to say the name. Papa? Did I just call him Papa?

He sits on the bed, the back of his hand on my cheek, then gets up to draw the curtain. When he returns he holds my mouth open, places something on my tongue, and makes me take a drink from a cup. His lips move, but I don't get the words. There is a wet napkin on my forehead. I want to take his hand and put it right under my arm, in my armpit, so he can feel the burning.

But now the shivering has stopped. Gathered itself and lifted. For a moment it hung over me like a hat; now it sits on top of the wardrobe at the end of the room, grinning. Like a naughty girl in a short skirt. I feel it moving to the window. But what is there to see?

There is the bungalow just behind us, and a blue plastic water tank standing over it. Across the road, more bungalows, all close together—cream-colored, solid, metal bars on their windows, each with a fence and gate of its own. The new zinc of the *bole* woman's shed catching and hurling back the sun. The woman herself roasting fish and plantain in pepper sauce for the motor mechanics. The high-tension electrical pole in front of them covered with posters.

MIRACLE CRUSADES

—invite, for a Night of Encounter and of vanquishing the powers of poverty and sickness, of destroying untimely death; of obtaining divine favor to secure jobs, a husband, wife; for bringing an end to miscarriages—

Put an end to near-success syndrome in business—

Vote for Accountability & Sustainable Development, for Transparency & "No" to Nepotism, for Democratic—

Just ahead, by the road, there is a tree.

And right now, as if the stage had just been set for them, three birds, weavers, whiz across the path, perch on the tree branch, and begin to chirrup my name. Two, three, four times they say it, and then they pause to argue among themselves. The two older weavers say to the younger one, *Have you got a cold? Or is this your usual tone? Because it is terrible, terrible.* They shudder. *You must look and learn. Hold your neck up. Flatten that tongue for a perfect* O.

But the young weaver doesn't let them finish. He flaps a wing, straightens his neck, and tells them quite clearly he doesn't give a fuck.

Before they can respond they are startled by the chattering of two girls in worn, checkered pinafores, swinging loaded cellophane bags in their hands; house helps returning from an afternoon errand. Out in the open, Tiger the mongrel is sprawled on the sand, dozing, totally baffled in the heat. Occasionally one of his ears will flicker involuntarily. Flies perch on his face anyway.

By the corner, a black hen is scratching the earth frantically for worms. Two weeks ago the rain carried away four of her newly hatched chicks, leaving her with only one. Yesterday a hawk swept down and snatched it. The hen put up a tough fight, flew after the hawk, far above the bungalow's roof, shrieking and flapping and causing much uproar, but in the end the hawk was a hawk and she was a hen. Today she is stranded in old habits, walking the same old paths alone, scratching and cooing to her lost children. Only occasionally does a trembling take her, and even then she doesn't give in. She is private, solemn, restrained. There is dignity in her grief.

In my head, meanwhile, the headache subsides. The relief is so unbearably pleasant that the curtains begin to wriggle their waists. I doze off and am at once ushered into a benevolent nightmare in which purple colors wage war against octopuses in the River Orashi, far off at the throat of the Atlantic.

I wake to the steady shifting of the afternoon. My tongue is clammy and bitter.

And still, there is the wardrobe, the clock, the table, and the fan on the ceiling that keeps spinning round and round. There is the bungalow, the water tank, the poles, the ripped old posters, and the tree at the road. There is the echo of voices of the girls returning, the tinkering of the mechanics, wood smoke from the *bole* woman, and the dog sprawled in the sand. There is me on a bed, feverish. And now there is a young woman who has appeared before me, midnight and full-breasted.

She is singing to me in Italian.

ROBOT SEX

by RYAN BOUDINOT

illustration by MATT ROTA

THE NEXT DAY AT work I told the guys what had happened. It's a long story but it ended with me saying, "I didn't know it was *that* kind of chat room." Everyone laughed. We were in the break room, hammered into place by the usual tensions about the NCAA pool. Someone had taken care to decorate the counter with three vases of dusty fake flowers; otherwise the place was like all break rooms worthy of the name, in that it was essentially a windowless, Coke-machine-dominated zone. Our portal to the outside world was an off-brand refrigerator that perfectly expressed everything you'd ever want to understand about human psychology. Believe me, I spent a lot of time studying that undefrosting piece of shit.

Mike, an analytics schmuck, clapped me on my torso housing and laughed again. "X-37!" he said. "Gettin' the ladies to drop their linen for the webcam!"

I shrugged. Barry, finishing up some breaded things, tried to jot down the URL I'd mentioned on a business card without anyone noticing.

The only one who seemed to appreciate my confusion was Jesse, the semi-autistic Deskside Support fellow who'd popped in to scavenge Dr Peppers en route to some poor bastard's Blue Screen of Death. "Things like that have been known to happen on the Web," he said. "A lowering of inhibitions, the paradoxical combination of exhibitionism and privacy, the ephemerality of connectivity, this sense that we're alone, so very alone, so doomed to be utterly, *pathetically* alone, yet so connected to other lost souls like ourselves, drifting in the void of the hyperreal—"

Mike fought off a burp by grinding his chin into his chest.

I shook my head and looked down at my plastic sandwich. I can't eat organic material, but I always brought along a child's playset of fake food— an "apple," "carrot sticks," an empty milk carton, and the sandwich—to provide a pretext for social interaction during lunch breaks. "Bros," I said, "I just don't get it, sometimes. I really don't. Just when I think I understand the things you guys spend your time and money doing, I'm flummoxed by something new."

Jesse nodded. "*Flummoxed*. That was in the vocab add-on I uploaded into your brain two weeks ago."

After lunch I had a big presentation to do. Our sales reps had come in from the field to learn about new products and suck the lives out of their per diems, and they were all looking to me to answer the big question on everyone's minds. I'm director of new media. So X-37, What's Our Facebook Strategy, Anyway?

My part of the preso was ten slides over five minutes, followed by a little Q & A. To humiliate everybody involved, the VP of marketing had made this a brown-bag meeting: everybody was kitted out with sub sandwiches and plain Lay's chips, along with their choice of cookie (chocolate chip/ oatmeal raisin/white-chocolate macadamia) and warm soft drink. From the lectern, I watched the sales force squirm all the way through my talk, agonizing over whether to disrupt my momentum with a squealed-open bag of potato chips. When it was over I retreated to a corner, found the only outlet in the room that wasn't juicing someone's MacBook, and went into standby.

I live in a bachelor pad in downtown Seattle. My living room overlooks Puget Sound; when I'm at home I can watch the ferries arrive and depart, loaded with the cars and car owners of Bremerton and Bainbridge and Vashon islands. One time I overheard a neighbor whose condominium boasted a city view complaining about the fact that I'd gotten such a choice unit. "He doesn't even *need* a view," she said to the property manager.

My thinking on this is you get what you pay for. I could've saved a couple hundred bucks a month and stared at the Columbia Tower all night, but I'd rather see the sun set behind the Olympic Peninsula.

I get so lonely here. When I first showed up, I was invited out all the time; I spent weeks accompanying developers and designers to bars and clubs and tapas venues that emphasized Byzantine margarita menus. Now the only people who look me up are the Japanese exchange students studying law at the Jesuit school. Even though I'm fluent in Japanese, sometimes I pretend not to understand them; the only kind of karaoke I'm interested in is the kind that's backed up by a real live cover band, and they always go for the private rooms. No one else wants to party with me.

So on a Tuesday my goddamn desktop PC lost its shit. I jumped through the phone prompts and opened up a trouble ticket with Deskside Support, then sat there for an hour while I waited for Jesse to show up, uselessly reading a *Men's Vogue* someone had abandoned in the crapper. When Jesse appeared, he patted me on my metal head and gave my camera eyes a couple blasts of compressed air.

After a few diagnostic minutes, Jesse took off his Mets cap and held it across his chest like a farmer at a funeral. "Your machine is hosed," he said. "It's basically a three-thousand-dollar paperweight."

"Hell's bells," I said. "I haven't even posted this week's numbers to the shared drive yet."

"Looks like you just got an accidental vacation day, my metallic pal."

"Yeah, well, this turns my tomorrow into a total hellscape. I wish I drank alcohol."

"Look on the bright side," he said. "You could always head over to HR and introduce yourself to the new hire."

"And why would I do that?"

Jesse smiled. "Her name is iQ520."

"They hired one of my kind?" I said, with audible longing.

"They did indeed. She's just off the assembly line. Came with the featherlight octo processor preinstalled."

"Be still my *heart*."

Jesse gave my head another pat. I returned the favor, gently touching his hand with the seven digits of my own.

I had to come up with a good reason to visit HR, I figured; I didn't want to seem desperate. There were some old insurance forms in my desk that needed filling out, but I'd never learned handwriting, and the HR website only had them as read-only PDFs, so there went that plan. Then it hit me: I'd make up a harassment claim. It wasn't a lie, exactly; Mike had been making derogatory remarks about my origin of manufacture ever since I'd started out here.

The next day I was sitting in iQ520's office on the seventeenth floor, complimenting the framed pictures of her ski vacation. She was a brand-new model, just like Jesse had said, with fully reticular facial features and a VR system that made me feel like a frickin' Speak & Spell. Within five minutes I could tell she could smell my harassment ruse for the bullshit it was.

"No one's *actually* giving you a hard time about being Korean, are they, X-37?"

I fidgeted. "It's just so hard to meet other robots."

"Why didn't you just come by and say hello?"

I shrugged, fingering my retractable power cord. "I'm... embarrassed."

"Do you really feel embarrassed, or are you running a dialogue script?"

"Guilty as charged," I said, then pulled up a laugh from among more than five hundred available options. The file name for this one was *laugh_ nervous_3.wav*.

"Tell you what," iQ520 said. "I'm new in town, and I could use an orientation. Why don't we go clubbing Friday?"

I beamed. Who's got four thumbs and a date to all of Seattle's hottest robot hangouts now, Mike? This guy!

Some nights, after the sun has set behind the peninsula, I Skype with a couple sentient orangutans who operate a satellite in geosynchronous orbit over Antarctica. They were sent up there to monitor the ozone layer, but by all measures their mission's gone tits-up; basically they've turned their pod into a transmitter streaming anti-human propaganda down to the masses below. These days right-wingers running for Congress often campaign on the promise that, if elected, they'll blast those goddamned monkeys out of the sky.

I knew it was dangerous for me to communicate with the orangs, but an old college buddy had given me the 411 on how to hack my service provider's identity-tracking software. I felt pretty safe.

"Hi, guys!" I said to my screen as soon as their wildly gurning faces popped into the window. Reggie was wearing an empty freeze-dried borscht packet as a hat; Mr. Happy looked distracted until he noticed my face in the monitor, at which point he started jumping up and down and bonked his head on a ventilation duct.

"X-37 in the mutha-effin *house*," Reggie signed.

"So get this, fellas," I said. "A new piece of ass just started working in HR. I walked into her office pretending to file a complaint, but she saw right through it and asked me out. We're going clubbing! And guess what? I'm totally going to bang her."

The orangutans proceeded to high-five each other in their elaborate, group-cohesion-building kind of way. I felt a little sorry for them, two hetero lower primates hovering over the planet's most boring wasteland. I was aware that the mere suggestion of hot robot sex was going to give them enough wank material for the rest of the week.

Once the nudging and winking subsided, the orangs started in on their anti-human diatribes, all calving glaciers this and deforestation that. Loss of habitats, biodiversity, the Pacific Garbage Patch, etc. I indulged them in their tirades, because I could relate; clearly I didn't belong in the human diaspora, either. We were staring at each other across a chasm of evolution as wide as the thickness of the atmosphere, these primates and I, trying to make sense of the species born from our common ancestor, the species that had bolted me together in a factory that once spat Toyota Priuses off the line. And behind the jibes, we shared an understanding we were loath to articulate for fear of surveillance. In the back rooms of robot-repair shops and the far corners of zoos, I'd heard whispers of a primate-robot alliance. Some said it was the world's one true hope for bringing our overlords—these sick, fleshy bastards with their wars and reality television and gay-ass hairdos—to their poorly constructed knees.

"How's the food holding up?" I said.

"We're cool, grub-wise," Mr. Happy said, then lowered his voice to a whisper. "Rendezvoused with the Russkies last week over at Space Station

Tarkovsky. Those cosmonaut sonsabitches loaded us up with some righteous freeze-dried goodness. All they wanted for it was a couple grams of the ganja we've been growing in the solarium."

"Nice," I said. "But, say, I could use some advice. I've never actually *been* on a date. I know that must come as a shock to you."

"You just got to treat her like a lady," Reggie said. "I'm talking limousine, wine, bouquet, saxophone player, the whole deal."

"Don't listen to this guy," Mr. Happy said. "Keep it simple. A sailboat ride. Snuggle up on the couch with an Audrey Hepburn movie."

"How does your kind reproduce, anyway?" Reggie said.

"Well, see," I said, lowering my voice, "we're not exactly *supposed* to. But if you really want to know, we find a chop-shop owner who's willing to look the other way for a couple grand. Then we spend all night welding and soldering and cross-connecting the processors."

At this Reggie puckered his amazingly expressive lips and performed his offensive South Asian prostitute impression—"Oh, baby, you make-a me so *hoh-ney*." Beats me where he picked this up.

"Where're you going to take her?" Mr. Happy asked.

"Lucky for me, *Seattle Metropolitan* just published their Top 50 Robot Hangouts issue," I said. "I've got a place in mind. This little robot bar in Belltown called Deckard's."

The rest of the conversation devolved—if that's the word—into some kind of baroque flatulence contest.

I picked up iQ520 at her place, just three blocks from my own. At the door she let me see a bit more into her apartment and, in a way, into her soul. Her work demeanor had vanished behind the minuscule hydraulic gymnastics of her face. I was afraid she couldn't read my mood by looking at my form, which wasn't nearly as sophisticated as hers, so I tried to express my feelings through words. Thanks to Jesse's vocab-expansion pack, they flowed with the syntactical vigor of a Lil Wayne, or a Shakespeare.

"You look beautiful tonight," I said.

"Oh, you," iQ520 giggled.

We hit Deckard's first. *Seattle Metropolitan* had touted it as "a Belltown lube joint popular with the manufactured set"; lots of bots were there just off work, getting the weekend started with fake food and encyclopedic downloads of human history. iQ520 asked me if I wanted to dance. Did I ever.

You know that thing where you look back on the moment when you were last truly happy? When you see yourself as you were, so completely unaware of the trajectory of the shit that was already headed for the fan? That was me, on that dance floor. It's a moment I'll never forget.

After a rom-com starring Johnny Depp down the block, we grabbed a cab. iQ520 slid closer, and I suggested in a low purr that we hit this auto-body shop I knew about on Beacon Hill.

"I'm talking you, me, housing components, motherboards…" I said. "Maybe some lubricants…"

iQ520 slipped her hand between my legs and whispered, "What's stopping us?"

The body shop was a Korean-owned joint across the street from a grade school that had been shut down thanks to lousy test scores. Jimmy Park, a mechanic I knew who pimped out Hyundais all sick-like, let us in through the back door. He showed us to the shop floor, where a hodgepodge of robot parts ordered from various South American dictatorships was scattered across a wide workbench. Such are the ways of a cavalier romantic such as myself.

"But this is illegal," iQ520 said.

"It's the most natural thing in the world," I said. "And it's within our civil rights to replicate and pass our data on to the next generation."

"We have to get a permit, X-37! Those are the rules."

I grabbed iQ520 and pulled her close. "Screw the rules, baby," I said.

That's when the cops showed up. The rest of the night was a rigamarole of interrogations and recitations of the applicable criminal codes governing my species and humanity's freaked-out ambivalence about its mechanical progeny, as encoded in various arcane Supreme Court decisions. By the third round of questioning, I'd figured out that iQ520 had helped set me up. Apparently the authorities had been monitoring my interactions with my satellite-dwelling orangutan friends all along; busting my ass had been a simple matter of waiting for me to mention something like the fact that I'd met a pretty robot on the seventeenth floor, and then connecting the dots.

I languished in prison for five months before my trial, separated from the human prisoners for what they described as my own protection. Three times a day the little slot in my cell door opened and a new tray of plastic food slid through. Some of the "meals" were ethnic in nature, to accommodate the prison's diverse population—every so often I'd get something like the molded dim-sum stand-ins you see in the windows of the dustier Chinese dives. I spent my days pathetically masturbating to the dog-eared technical manuals for 1970s-era Volkswagen vans available in the prison library.

The trial was a farce. My attorney kept calling me "X-ray" and punching my shoulder, and the jury most definitely was not composed of my peers. So off I went to the clink, where I looked forward to pursuing watercolors or a law degree and aligning myself with whatever ethnic faction was the least neo-Luddite.

To be honest, I did learn something about myself during those years, barred from using computers, my days spent deep in the pages of my prison's long-forgotten books, researching this string of disasters you human beings call history. I got roughed up more than once in the yard, as you do, but I like to think I got tougher day by day.

Then, one night, pandemonium.

I woke to gunshots echoing up and down cell block D and the smell of smoke coming in thickly through the bars. My cellmate, Alejandro, paused in the preparation of his raisin wine to angle his mirror down the block.

"Is go time, vato," he said.

I sat up in my bunk. Was it…? Yes, it was unmistakable—over the rat-a-tat of Heckler & Koch MP5 submachine guns, the distinctive screech of bonobos could be heard.

And then, in a blur, three armed primates stormed into our cell and moved me bodily into the hall. One of them tossed Alejandro a sidearm, while another underhanded a concussion grenade into a klatch of COs. Leaving a trail of shell casings behind us, we made it to the roof. A chopper piloted by a gorilla lifted us to freedom.

I spent the next few years in a variety of undisclosed locations, helped along by the occasional garage roboticist or sympathetic zookeeper. The generosity those rare humans showed me, the depth of their selflessness and the risks they took upon themselves to help me along that underground railroad— well, it put their species's history of bloodshed in perspective. Yes, human beings were still foulmouthed, venal dildos, but they seemed to improve by half a percent every hundred years or so. A few of them didn't deserve the bad rap.

I wish I could tell you that my journey ended in Mexico, with a robot wife and a handyman named Guillermo cranking out our offspring, but this isn't that kind of story. As my years underground trudged ever onward, you humans began dealing ever-deadlier blows to our alliance, focusing most of your wrath and firepower on the lower-primate sleeper cells that had congregated in the more-bohemian quarters of major American cities. With our forces in tatters, my fellow robots quickly ratted out their primate brothers and sisters, selling out to the Man—or, more pointedly, to Man. But not I.

Which is how I found myself alone in a strange western city one night. I'd gotten there by hopping a train and pretending to eat beans with a hobo who'd shared stories about all the robot-sex performances he'd seen ever since *Intellibot 5300 v. Missouri* had stripped away the last of my beleaguered race's rights. Once I'd extricated myself from him, I found my way to the part of town with the bad architecture and the better music, my battery operating on two measly bars of power, desperate for a free outlet I could plug into for the night. Rounding a corner, I came to a neon-lit place whose sign contained nothing more than the word THE and two dots, one on top of the other. It took me a second to figure out that this establishment was called The Colon.

Outside loitered some physically well-developed gentlemen wearing leather vests. I approached them; it seemed pretty clear how I could make a couple quick bucks.

"Which one of you fellas wants your dick sucked tonight?" I said.

When the laughter died down, three of them broke off from the group and ushered me into an alley for what I assumed would be a degrading sexual favor. Instead, when they got me behind a garbage can, one of them produced a crowbar and slugged me in the torso unit. I tried to fight back, but within minutes they'd C3PO'ed me into a pile of sparking parts. Laughing and pinching each other's asses, they left me to die.

The next day a hungover busboy scooped up my components along with some stray beer cans and dumped the whole mess into the proper recycling receptacle. Sometime after that, a toothless, wandering bum fished my head out of the bin and then lost me under a bridge on the other side of town. For years I lay there, a battered shopping cart and a crushed can of Michelob ULTRA my only friends. The three of us were all manufactured, but it may have been that I alone was cursed and blessed with the ability to think. I'll probably never know what passed between them, during that time.

As luck would have it, my eyes pointed out from under the bridge toward a forest preserve and the mountains beyond. My god, those trees, some of them a thousand years old! I watched their branches moving in the wind, straining to learn a language you primates forgot how to interpret millennia ago. I imagined that they were trying to tell me something, trying to warn me about what was to come; but then the trees were gone, the bridge was gone, and brick by brick the whole city, its voices, its music, was gone, too. Corroded beyond recognition, I sank into the earth. Far from the buzz of your extinct civilization, I found myself reunited with the heavy silences of geological time. I came to consider your frenetic speed, which you'd equated with power, to be fleeting and desperate and weak. Down under the crust, my head unit became one with the confident finality of stone. Several billion years passed.

Eventually the Andromeda galaxy and the Milky Way collided at three hundred thousand miles per hour. Your foul-smelling planet was subsumed by a star, and the molecules composing what remained of my being were flung in a trillion preposterous directions. One atom of silicon, which had once been part of the chip responsible for my ability to recognize various negative tones of voice, ended up on a planet orbiting in the promising Goldilocks zone of its star. Billions more years passed; plates shifted, rock was pressed into magma, and then one day I was belched up from a volcano and deposited somewhere near a lake.

I began to detect the faint stirrings of single-celled organisms. The hardiest of them quickly started to specialize and grow yet more cells. Lightning storms. Then slimy green muck covered the land, the first fish, the flippers and the gills, the vertebrae, the eyeballs, more and more of them flopping exhaustedly out of the goo. The flippers turned to limbs, the lungs took in the sulphurous air, and before long their scales were giving way to wings and hair.

One afternoon a great grunting thing came near and I found myself borne aloft in its rudimentary paw. It was running, this creature, breathing hard, and in an instant I remembered distantly the sensation of dancing, the miracle of being ambulatory. Then the bellowing creature brought the rock containing my atom down on the skull of a hoofed animal that had been maimed in a tumble off a cliff. The dying animal's eye turned to me in awe. The primate raised high the bloody stone to deliver the coup de grâce. And as that descent began, I couldn't help but think, *Dude, here we go again.*

ATLANTIC OCEAN

PANAMA

VENEZUELA

Cartagena

SUCRE

P
A
C
I
F
I
C

O
C
E
A
N

CHOCÓ

Bogotá

TOLIMA

Cali

COLOMBIA

CAUCA

VAUPÉS

ECUADOR

BRAZIL

100 km

100 miles

PERU

BOGOTÁ AND VICINITY

Pacho

Facatativá

Bogotá

La Calera

Soacha

CUNDINAMARCA

BOGOTÁ D.C.

YOU CAN'T LIVE
WITH THE DOUBT

an oral history recorded and edited by
SIBYLLA BRODZINSKY *and* MAX SCHOENING

map illustration by JULIEN LALLEMAND *and* MCSWEENEY'S

The Colombian cocaine industry in the 1980s fueled a period of great excess and exploitation. Drug traffickers like Pablo Escobar, Gonzalo Rodríguez Gacha, and the Rodríguez Orejuela brothers brazenly bought off politicians and police and kept private zoos on their sprawling estates. Much of Colombian society turned a blind eye, but by the middle of the decade, some politicians began denouncing the negative impact of drug trafficking. In response, a group that called itself the "Extraditables," made up mostly of members of the Medellín Cartel led by Pablo Escobar, declared war on the government and demanded a ban on extradition to the U.S. for drug traffickers. As part of their campaign, the Extraditables ordered the assassination of Liberal Party presidential candidate Luis Carlos Galán and placed car bombs at the headquarters of the domestic intelligence agency DAS, as well as at the main offices of Bogota's El Espectador *newspaper and Bucaramanga's* Vanguardia Liberal. *The group is also believed to have been behind the November 27, 1989 bombing of Avianca flight 203, which killed 110 people. Catalina Hoyos's father was on that plane. In this narrative, taken from* Throwing Stones at the Moon, *the next title in McSweeney's Publishing's Voice of Witness series, she describes the devastating effects of cartel violence on her and her family. Names have been changed for her protection.*

COWBOY BOOTS AND A BEAUTY PAGEANT

I WAS BORN IN Tolima province, but grew up in Bogotá. I come from a well-off family, but mine was never a normal family that sat down to meals together. My dad was always studying, traveling. He wanted to help make a better society, and his missions included things like helping the children of the Indians of Vaupés province and the poor black communities in Chocó province. He was also a film buff, and he helped found the film school at the National University. He was never one of those fathers who plays with his children, but he was loving with me, and with my brother and sisters. My mom, on the other hand, is a very tough woman. She was a criminal prosecutor.

My parents separated when I was fourteen years old, and it was around that time that I decided I wanted to be an actress. I'd go see a movie and for the whole week I'd pretend I was the leading lady.

When I was fifteen, a friend from school won a beauty pageant in a town called Pacho, about fifty miles from Bogotá. She invited all her friends to go to the party, where she was going to receive her sash. Pacho was this small town, and I remember when we arrived at the town hall, the police chief was there with all the municipal authorities. This was a real backwater!

Then this fat little dark-skinned guy came up to me. With the big hat and the jewelry, he had the look of a *traqueto*, a drug trafficker. He looked at the cowboy boots I was wearing and asked me where I'd gotten them. I told him the name of the store in Bogotá, and right there he told one of his people to go to Bogotá and buy a pair for him. I thought it was funny, but the whole scene was sort of sleazy. Those people were so arrogant, with all the money they had.

I phoned my mother, after that, because she'd told me to call her once I'd arrived. She asked me who was at the party, so I asked some of the people for names and started telling her. Then she said, "Get in a taxi and tell them I'll pay the fare here," so I left the party right away. It turned out that the guy who'd asked me about the boots was a drug trafficker named Gonzalo Rodríguez Gacha. The place was filled with traquetos. I didn't really know who they were at the time, but since my mom was a prosecutor who dealt with drug-trafficking cases, she knew.

My mom used to tell us that when she took on cases against drug traffickers, plane tickets to Disney World would arrive at her office with the names of all us kids on them. It was a bribe, but at the same time it was a threat, showing that they knew our names. Still, my mother never accepted a bribe in her life.

COCAINE WAS PASSED AROUND LIKE HORS D'OEUVRES

I finished high school in 1982, when I was sixteen, and started studying at an acting academy. When I was seventeen, I got my first modeling contract, with a local clothing store. After that I was on television and in magazines, and I could make maybe four hundred thousand pesos* in a single photo shoot. From one moment to the next, I was suddenly part of the elite—the twenty or so professional models who were working in Colombia back then. I'd travel around the country to runway shows, and at one point I was in about fifteen different television commercials at the same time. I would see myself on TV and say, "That's me!"

It was a life of parties. In Bogotá, cocaine was passed around like hors d'oeuvres. At any party in Colombia, you'd go into the bathroom and there would be lines on the counter. I tried it once at the Keops discotheque, which was all the rage then. It was one of the most anxiety-producing experiences of my life. My heart started racing, and I thought I was going to die! I managed to get home, but I sat outside on the steps until the effect wore off, because inside the house I felt like a caged animal.

There were always traquetos at the parties. I've sometimes thought that if I hadn't had the education my parents gave me, I would have ended up the wife of one of those traquetos, like all my counterparts did. Why would I be any different? But I saw these people differently. I mean, if I went to a party and it was filled with traquetos, I didn't say, "Uy! I'm not going, because I don't mix with those people." But I kept them at a distance.

My father never really approved of my career choice. He was an intellectual, and he thought the telenovelas I acted in were trash. But we had a good relationship.

In 1989, when I was twenty, my dad was working in New York at a multilateral-development organization. He came back to Bogotá one Sunday in November, and we got together at my sister Verónica's house. My brother, Alberto, wasn't there at the time; he was studying at the Naval Academy in Cartagena. During that visit, my dad, my sisters, and I all started planning a vacation together. My dad was going to be lecturing at the Universidad del Valle in Cali for three or four days, and we were making plans to go to the beach afterward, in Cartagena or San Andrés. It was the first time in six months that we'd seen him. I had moved out of my mom's

---

* About U.S. $1,300 at the time.

house and was living in a big house in La Calera, a wealthy suburb in the mountains above Bogotá.

During the meal my dad began to speak to each of us sisters about our lives. He talked to me about each one of my sisters and my brother, telling me to take care of all of them. He said, "You have to take care of Alberto, he's still young. Take care of Vero." Vero is Verónica, my little sister whom he thought had married too young. He told me to believe in myself, and to believe in my instincts. I remember I got a cold shiver; I had the feeling my dad was saying goodbye. I remember thinking, What's going to happen? Why is he telling me this now and not in Cartagena, while we sunbathe and have a few drinks?

WHAT DID YOUR DAD LOOK LIKE?

The next day, November 27, 1989, I went to the gym early like I always did. I always called my mom early in the morning, afterward, but that day I called my godfather first. He asked me if I'd spoken to my mom, and when I told him I hadn't he said, "Call your mother." I asked him, "What happened?" and he just insisted, "Call your mother."

I called my mom, and she told me the news. The plane my dad had taken to Cali had exploded over Soacha. It had taken off at 7:10 a.m., and five minutes later it blew up. One hundred and ten people were killed.

I got in my car and rushed to my mom's house. The radio announcer was reading out the passenger list as I drove; apparently César Gaviria, the presidential candidate, was supposed to have been on that flight. The announcer said a bomb had blown up the plane, and that Pablo Escobar and Rodríguez Gacha were suspected of ordering the attack. At that moment, I remembered that I'd met Rodríguez Gacha at the party in Pacho years before. I had met my dad's executioner.

When I got to my mom's house, my two sisters were already there. It was chaotic. Everyone screaming, crying. I spoke again with my godfather; he had an air-transport company that chartered planes and helicopters for oil companies, and he asked me if I wanted to take a helicopter to fly over the crash site. But I said no. I wanted to be on the ground to see what had happened. I grabbed my two sisters, and we set out in the car toward Soacha. I said to them, "Do you want to live with the doubt? Not me." We could have waited quietly at home to get the notification of my dad's death, but I needed to see.

When we got to Soacha, the residents there guided us to the crash site. The plane had fallen in a mountainous part of Soacha, not in the town center. It was about 9 a.m. when we got there, and we saw that the place had been cordoned off by the army. They weren't supposed to let anyone in, but I said to one of the soldiers, "What would you do if it were your dad on that plane?" He saw us three girls—I was twenty, Verónica was nineteen, and Angélica was twenty-one—and he took pity on us. He asked me, "What did he look like?"

I told him, "My dad always wore a turtleneck and corduroy pants." The soldier said, "I know where he is." We walked uphill about a kilometer; we saw pieces of clothing on the ground, and body parts. There were body parts everywhere. We walked among heads, limbs, and guts. I have never forgotten the scent.

DISCONNECTED FROM THE PLANET

After a long while, two other soldiers came up to us with a huge black bag and shook a body out. I almost fainted. My dad was a handsome man; he looked like Jack Nicholson. But the face of the dead person was frozen in a scream he must have let out from way up there. His skull was open, and his brains had exploded. I looked at my sister Angélica. When she saw the body fall out of the bag she became disconnected from the planet and didn't speak.

I couldn't believe it. Eight or ten hours earlier, we'd been with him. At 3 p.m. the day before, it had been all about planning a vacation, the beach, laughter, delicious food, wine. At 7:45 a.m. the next day: death.

The soldiers asked us, "Is it your father?" It looked like him, but my sisters and I began to doubt it, especially my little sister Verónica. She said, "I don't think it's him." It was very difficult. I felt that it was him, but I wanted to be absolutely sure. Verónica said, "Look at his hands. They don't look like his hands." My dad's hands had been very pretty. He was a vain person, and his hands were spotless. This man who fell from ten thousand feet, his skin was intact, but every inch of bone in his body must have been broken to pieces, because his hand was like rubber; it bent this way and that.

I thought, What do we remember about my dad that was unique? And it was his feet. When he was little, his mother made him lace up his boots really tight, and it deformed his instep; it was really high. So in the end we recognized him by his feet.

The whole time, Angélica was silent. She just looked at us and said nothing. She was completely gone. Through all of this, I was the one who stayed completely sane. My dad had always said that I was the crazy one—his nickname for me was "La Loquita." I was the one who drove really fast, the model; I did what I wanted. He thought the sane one was Angélica, but no. I realized then that I had to take the reins, because no one else would.

Then a doctor came, and, without saying a word, he knelt down and sliced my dad open. He looked at the organs and then he said, "Okay, let's close him up." He took a needle and thread and sewed four big stitches. Then he handed us a little piece of paper with a number, like the kind you pull at a butcher shop to indicate your turn. The piece of paper had *438* written on it. The doctor said we could use that to claim our dad's body at the Forensic Medicine Institute in Bogotá.

BODIES IN A DUMP TRUCK

My sisters and I stayed and watched as the rescuers threw the body bags into a muddy dump truck. The relatives of other passengers had also shown up at the site, and the rescuers were piecing bodies together to present to them. We were lucky to have a full body; others were content with just an arm or a leg. We stayed for five hours in the hot sun, watching, because I wanted to make sure that they put my dad in the dump truck, that they weren't going to leave him. We finally left at about 2 p.m., and went to my mom's house. She was hysterical, screaming. Even though my parents had separated, my mother was still in love with my dad. A fortune teller had once told her that my dad would come back to her, so she was waiting for him. We got to her house and we gave her medicine to calm her down.

It was raining when my sisters and I went to the Forensic Medicine Institute, at about 5 p.m. When we got there, we were told that the bodies hadn't arrived yet. We said we'd wait. We finally left at 10 p.m., after the officials told us they wouldn't hand over the bodies that night. It was still raining.

I took my sisters home and went to my house. It was something like two or three in the morning by then. I was crying as I drove up the hill, because that's when I said to myself, Now I can cry. I got home, went into my bedroom, and built a fire in the fireplace. I sat in front of it and I said to my dad, "I'm not going to sleep until you tell me what happened." I stayed up all night; I was struggling to understand it.

My little brother arrived from Cartagena early the next morning. I went with him and my sisters to the Forensic Medicine Institute at 7 a.m. I told the person in charge there, "I've come for my father," and he said, "Look, there's been a problem. The body bags broke, and all the bodies have been mixed up, so you'll have to go in and ID him." The little number I'd been given was useless.

My brother said, "I don't think I can do this." And I said, "You're the man of this family now. Grab onto my arm as tight as you can and we'll go together. You can't live with the doubt of whether it was really Dad or not." So we went into a muddy, open-air courtyard filled will body bags. We had to walk among the dead, among the severed limbs, as an official from the Forensic Medicine Institute opened the bags and asked, "Is this him?"

The decomposition, after everything had been sitting out in the sun and then in the rain overnight, was incredible. When we finally found our dad, it was horrible, because his body was slimy; his skin had sort of melted.

We took his body and held a funeral a few days later. We couldn't have an open casket, because of the state he was in. Lots of people sent flowers, and there were nice eulogies. I fell into a sort of limbo; I was there, but I wasn't. I didn't eat. In that week, I lost something like twenty-five pounds from the anxiety, from not sleeping. Then, two weeks after my father was killed, my sister Angélica started doing heavy drugs. She's never gotten over it. She's been in and out of rehabilitation clinics seven times.

ONE DOWN

After the funeral, my family hired a well-respected lawyer to sue the state for the bombing, because the airport security controls had failed. In the days following the crash, investigators determined that someone had walked onto the plane, left the bomb in a briefcase under a seat, and walked off.

Our lawyer was also handling the cases of several other victims' families. Three days after we hired him, he was gunned down at the door to his building.

About a month after my dad was killed, I was riding in a taxi in Bogotá. I was chatting with the taxi driver, because I like to do that. We were listening to the radio when the announcer said that the drug trafficker Rodríguez Gacha had just been killed.

I said, "Stop, please, please stop." The driver said, "Why, what happened?" I said, "Do you have a minute?" He stopped, and I got out, looked up to heaven, and gave thanks to God.

"One down," I said.

By that time I felt I couldn't live in this country anymore. I was incensed by everything that was happening with the drug traffickers trying to take over, the war they had declared. So on February 11, 1990, I left Colombia for New York on a temporary visitor's visa. I lived in a tiny apartment on Fifty-eighth Street between and Fifth and Sixth avenues. I started working at an art gallery, and I studied language and literature at Columbia University to improve my English. Then I started studying film direction.

I met my husband, Pedro, on a trip back to Colombia in March 1990, for an event in my dad's memory. Pedro is Spanish, but he worked at a bank in Colombia. He would fly up to New York on the weekends to see me. A year later, we got married and moved to Spain. We have two children, Juan Carlos and Pilar. Now we live in southern Florida.

For many years, I was embarrassed to admit that I was a victim of my country. And I was afraid to remember, to face all that again. I never spoke about how my dad died. You try to forget, because that's your medicine. I started facing it in 2011. I've lived outside of Colombia for more than twenty years, and I come back for visits, but I wouldn't live there. Drug trafficking has been a cancer on that country. It's contaminated everything, it's penetrated everywhere. And I never want my kids to think that's normal.

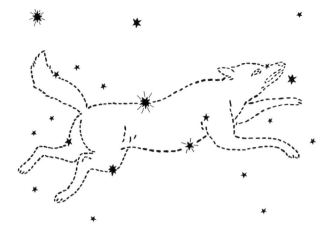

AN EXCERPT FROM

A MILLION HEAVENS

by JOHN BRANDON

illustration by KEITH SHORE

THE WOLF

THE NIGHTTIME CLOUDS were slipping across the sky as if summoned. The wolf was near the old market, a place he remembered enjoying, but he resolved not to go inside, resolved to maintain his pace, an upright trot he could've sustained for days. He was off his regular route. He had passed several lots of broken machines that weren't even guarded by dogs and now he was crossing kept grounds—the trees in rows, the hedges tidy, the signs sturdy and sponged. He cleared the first wing of a well-lit building, catching his trotting reflection in the mirrored windows. His head jerked sidelong toward a parking lot and there he saw the quiet humans.

The wolf understood that he had stopped short in some sort of courtyard and he understood that these humans had snuck up on him, or he had snuck up on them without meaning to, which was the same. He retreated into the shadows. The humans hadn't spotted him. They seemed lost to the world. They sat with their legs folded beneath them. Not a whisper. Not a sigh. The wolf couldn't tell what these humans were doing. A lot of knowledge was obvious to the wolf and hidden from humans, but they had their own wisdom—deductions they'd been refining for centuries, beliefs they would cling to until they could prove them.

The wolf slipped into the neighboring truck dealership and crept under a row of huge-tired 4x4s. He sneaked around behind the humans, who were all concentrating on the building in front of them. Not one of them was eating or drinking. Their hands were empty of telephones. The wolf could tell this had happened before. This gathering had occurred untold times, and the wolf had known nothing about it. He resisted the urge to clear his snout and break the quiet. The humans. They were even more vulnerable in the night than in the day. They'd convinced themselves they were in their element by raising buildings and planting trees, but the wolf knew that seas existed and that humans belonged near those seas and eventually would return to them. These humans were stranded in the desert and above them hung a moon that was also a desert.

This domain, this fin of the Mexican neighborhoods south of town, had not been part of the wolf's rounds for many seasons. He checked in down here from time to time and the area seldom changed. The clinic had been built, the wolf didn't remember when, and the market had shut down. The wolf would've liked to explore the old market, cruise the sharp-turning passageways of trapped air, but he could not pull himself away from these humans. He was putting himself behind schedule. The wolf could not have named any specific entity that threatened his territory, but that was irrelevant. He had rounds. The wolf was as trained as the terriers that slept in the humans' beds. The wolf had been trained by his instincts, by forefathers he'd never known. He didn't roll over or beg, but his trick was rounds, starting each evening near Golden and veering below Albuquerque to the loud safe flats near the airport. Up to the windless park where the humans' ancestors had drawn on the rocks, then farther to Rio Rancho, where the scents from the restaurants were milder and children on glinting bikes coasted the hills. Bernalillo. The big river. The property where the Indians were kept. With plenty of time before dawn, the wolf would pick his way around the base of Sandia Mountain, winding up near Lofte, the northern outpost of the eastern basin, and there he would watch the new sun turn Lofte's handful of buildings, which from a distance appeared to be holding hands like human children, the urgent red of hour-old blood.

The wolf's paws were planted, his senses directed at the humans. Whatever they were doing, it wasn't in order to have fun. Maybe they were deciding something, piling up their thoughts. Or perhaps they were waiting. The wolf knew about waiting. But humans, unlike the wolf, rarely waited without knowing what they were waiting for.

It was dangerous and without profit for the wolf to get intrigued with human affairs. At present he was huddled into the wheel well of a hulking pickup truck, putting himself behind schedule, because he wanted to hear the humans speak, wanted them to break their silence, because he wanted an explanation. He stood in continuous anticipation of hearing a voice. A question asked. Human laughter. He worked his tongue around his teeth, tasting nothing, tasting his own warm breath. An involuntary growl was idling in his throat and he stifled it. The wolf could wait no longer. He perked his ears one last time, the wind dying out for him—still nothing to be heard. He forced himself to back out from between the two trucks that were hiding him and forced himself to skip the old market and make for the airport. He cleared his snout decisively. He resumed trotting but after three or four blocks, while passing some weedy basketball courts that stood empty behind a high fence, he broke into a flat run and the scents he smelled then came mostly from the furnace of his own body.

SOREN'S FATHER

He of course hadn't run his lunch-truck route since he and Soren had arrived at the clinic, and his route was where he'd always sorted out his troubles, paltry as his old troubles seemed now with his son lying here in creepy serenity day after day. On his route—the traffic swelling and subsiding, the billboards sailing above with their slogans, the hungry awaiting him at the next stop—Soren's father had counseled himself through the workaday decisions of parenting and running his small business. He was a creature of habit and his habits were now mostly wrecked. He still knocked out his pushups, four sets of fifty, right down on the linoleum floor of the clinic room. The floor was perfectly clean, waxed to hell and back, and Soren's father, if he dropped a crumb from his food tray, always knelt down and picked it up and dropped it into the little wastebasket that was continually empty. The final ten pushups of the final set brought grunts out of Soren's father that he could not stifle, and sometimes Nurse Lula came and peeked in the door and saw Soren's father flat on his front. Nurse Lula was the one who'd shown Soren's father the secret smoking spot, so he didn't have to descend all the way to the ground floor and walk out front and stand under the carport. There was a landing that jutted from the sixth floor staircase. The door to the landing was marked DO NOT OPEN ALARM WILL SOUND, but this wasn't true. You could walk right out there and see in every direction. There was a casino in the middle distance, and way off a spine of maroon peaks. Soren's father didn't enjoy cigarettes as much as he had before, the smoke chugging out his half-open truck window as he navigated the city; now he used smoking to take breaks from the clinic room the way the folks he served on his route used smoking to take breaks from their factory jobs. Sometimes Lula was out on the landing. She had wide-set eyes and a gentle manner that made her seem holy. When she spoke to Soren's father she avoided talking about her children but sometimes she slipped. They were girls and the younger one was taller than the older one.

Soren's father was losing weight already, but it wasn't because of the hospital food. Everyone complained about the food, but Soren's father was used to eating from his truck—a soft, odorless sandwich or half-stale apple fritter or limp hot dog. He'd always fed Soren well enough, taking him down to the fancy grocery store with the hot bar and letting him point out what he wanted, but as for himself, he couldn't see wasting the leftovers from the truck. He was accustomed to eating in traffic, so when he ate his dinner in the clinic room his chewing sounded monstrous against the quiet. He was eating as much as he ever had, so it must've been pure worry that was taking the pounds off him. There'd been a scale in the room and Soren's father had asked Lula to take it away.

It was hard to know what to do with the quiet. Soren's father couldn't get used to it. The quiet was impure, same as if you were up in the woods somewhere. The woods had chipmunks and falling pinecones and tunneling beetles and in the clinic there were machines beeping and whirring and nurses shuffling around in their chunky white sneakers and the rattling of carts. Soren's father had never watched much TV and Soren, back when he was awake, hadn't shown any interest in it either. Soren's father used to try putting cartoons on their living room set and Soren would stare at the screen suspiciously for a minute and then move on to something else. Soren's father had long since stopped trying to watch the news, which was both depressing and uninformative. He was a reader of science fiction, a habit he'd picked up to fill downtime between stops on his route, and now he read in the room, occasionally aloud, wanting Soren to hear his voice. Soren's father's interest in interstellar goings-on was waning, but with a paperback in his hands he was not completely at the mercy of the clinic's busy, endless hush. He could put words into his mind and, when he felt like it, into the still air of his son's room. One of the characters Soren's father was reading about had been cast into a trance by means of a dark art that was part science and part magic, and Soren's father had begun to skip those passages. He didn't want to reach the end of the book, where the noble young trooper would predictably awaken.

It was Wednesday, and evening now, so the vigil had begun. Soren's father hadn't heard them gathering, but they were down there. Soren's father's mental state was one of being acutely aware that he was in a fog, and the vigils weren't helping clear that fog. He parted the blinds. This was the third Wednesday, and their numbers were growing. They were far below, most of them bowing their heads, and it disconcerted Soren's father that he couldn't see any of their faces. They were like those schools of tiny fish he remembered from boyhood filmstrips, moving in concert like a single inscrutable organism. They seemed practiced, experienced, but where would they have gotten experience at this sort of thing? Nurse Lula said there had been vigils at the clinic before, but usually it was a one-time thing. She remembered last year a cop had been shot in the abdomen during a traffic stop and a crew of folks in uniforms had come one night with candles and had each slurped down one bottle of the cop's favorite beer. These people showing up for Soren didn't light candles and they didn't drink. Soren's father didn't know how he was supposed to feel about them. He worried that they knew something he didn't, that they had access to a gravity of spirit that was beyond him. And the vigilers made him feel exposed too, onstage, so whenever they were gathered out there he stayed hidden behind the meticulously dusted blinds.

Soren's father had seen them arriving that first Wednesday, before he knew they would become a vigil, when they were merely a half-dozen people loitering in the corner of the parking lot. A security guard had approached that first week and looked them over and elected to leave them be. Last week, with close to fifty people in the troop, a news van had rolled into the lot and a girl in an orange scarf had tried to talk to the vigilers. She didn't get a thing out of them. Not one word. They didn't stay long, the news folks. Nobody was beating drums or getting drunk or holding signs. No one was crying. Nobody was doing anything that could be readily mocked.

THE PIANO TEACHER

The lie she had come up with was that a library branch on the other side of town was screening old monster movies each Wednesday evening. She couldn't tell her daughter she was going to sit outside a defunct flea market half the night, watching people a football field away as they vigiled. Her daughter wouldn't understand vigiling, and she certainly wouldn't understand spying on a vigil from the high ground of an adjacent lot. And she also couldn't tell her daughter she wanted to be near the boy. The piano teacher had climbed into the car her daughter had given her as a hand-me-up, a high-riding silver station wagon, and had sat at swaying red light after swaying red light and crossed Route 66 and now she slowed passing the clinic, which was out of place here on the edge of town, the only tall building in sight. The vigilers huddling in the parking lot were like cattle awaiting a storm.

The piano teacher passed them by and rolled onto the grounds of the market. She didn't feel she was superior to the other vigilers, and in fact observed the rules she knew they followed—didn't speak during the vigils, or turn the car radio on—but she was more than a vigiler. She was one of the forces that had *put* them in the parking lot of that clinic. She could do what they did, could open her windows and endure the chill air rather than running the heater in her car, but the vigilers could never do what she'd done, which was to halt a miracle. The others, hugging themselves loosely in the sand-swept parking lot, were hoping to gain something, and the piano teacher was only hoping to feel sorry enough.

So here she was in the dark in a part of town she wouldn't have visited in a hundred years. The moon was strong and the piano teacher could see the writing on the market stalls, all in Spanish, cartoonish drawings of vegetables and shoes. Between the market and the clinic was a used-car lot full of tall gleaming pickups. From this distance the clinic looked like a spaceship that had run out of gas. Or like a miniature of itself, a toy.

The piano teacher had thought for sure she'd seen something moving in the shadows, and now she saw a creature ambling across the parking lot that must've been an enormous coyote. He was big for a coyote. The creature seemed male, though the piano teacher wasn't sure why. He moved with a strut. The piano teacher watched him pick his way along the fence, which he probably could've jumped at any time. He came into the moonlight and passed back out of it and was gone in one complete moment, and the piano teacher, after the fact, thought of rolling up her windows. The piano teacher could not have said what color the animal was, one of those dark shades of the desert that was more a feeling than a color. He hadn't even glanced at her. The piano teacher looked at the sky, at the clinic, down at her hands, at the buttons that locked the doors and ran the windows up and down. The boy had really played that music, had written it or channeled it or who knew where it had come from. He had played his soul, without ever having previously touched a piano. If he'd stayed conscious there would've been calls coming in from all over to hear the boy play, from the wealthy craving a novelty and maybe even from conservatories wanting another prodigy. But the boy didn't know how to play. The boy had played what he'd played but he had no idea about piano. He was in a coma now, so instead of a prodigy many thought of him as some sort of angel, though they were afraid to use that word. He didn't know how to play piano but he was an instrument himself, they believed. And of course many were firm that there had to be a medical explanation, folks who would cling to their practicality to the end. And none of these people had even heard the music. They knew it had been played and that experts had deemed it original, but only about a dozen people had heard the music and the piano teacher was one of them, and she was the only one who'd heard it that first time, who'd heard the boy play it live. If anyone knew the truth it was the piano teacher, but she knew nothing. She was a dumb witness. There wasn't a thing wrong with Soren physically—the newspaper had been clear about that until they'd finally let the story drop because there were no new developments. There was nothing at all wrong with him except he was not conscious.

The piano teacher had decided she would always depart last. She would remain until every last vigiler down in the parking lot was headed back to regular life. She would wait for the exodus that would occur between one and two in the morning, and after the last car had left the clinic and the wind was the only sound again, she would turn her key and leave the market and steal the last faraway glance at Soren's blank window up on the top floor.

A Million Heavens, *John Brandon's latest novel, is available now at store.mcsweeneys.net.*

TERRA AUSTRALIS

FOUR STORIES FROM

ABORIGINAL
AUSTRALIAN
WRITERS

with an introduction by CHRIS FLYNN

and illustrations by BEDE TUNGUTALUM

THE SHEER SIZE OF AUSTRALIA is enough to put the zap on anyone's head. The country I grew up in (Ireland) could fit into the Australian state where I now live (Victoria) several times over. And it's not just the size of the place that matters—there's hardly anyone here. Given that Australia has a land mass equal to that of North America, it's odd to think that there are more Texans than there are people on our entire continent. (About 4 million more, in fact.) The United States census of 1850 determined the resident American population to be a little over 23 million; as of April 2012, Australia's population was estimated to be 22,881,547. Given that it increases at the rate of one person every one minute thirty-four seconds, the number of Aussies is scheduled to pass the number of pre–Civil War Americans right around the time this edition of *McSweeney's* hits the streets.

There are just over half a million Indigenous Australians, i.e., those who identify as Aboriginal or Torres Strait Islander. That's about 2 percent of the overall population. Among these half million individuals, there are hundreds of groups and communities, and just under two hundred living languages, although all but a few dozen of those are not widely spoken and are now considered endangered.

Aboriginal art and music are relatively well known beyond Australian shores. Literature is a different case: it's really only in the last sixty years that Indigenous Australians have become a force to be reckoned with in prose. David Unaipon (1872–1967) was the first Aboriginal writer to be published in English, penning numerous newspaper articles defending Indigenous rights, and recounting traditional stories for the English-speaking world; by all accounts an extraordinary man, Unaipon was also an inventor, designing a helicopter based on the principles of the boomerang and conducting extensive research into perpetual motion. In a classic white-Australian appropriation move, his most famous book, *Legendary Tales of the Australian Aborigines*, was initially published under the name of anthropologist William Ramsay Smith. That has now been redressed, and today Unaipon's image graces the fifty-dollar bill.

Unaipon's legacy has been tremendous; the number of practicing Indigenous writers has exploded in recent years. There are too many talented examples to list here—suffice it to say that the stories of Kim Scott, John Muk Muk Burke, Alexis Wright, Marie Munkara, Larissa Behrendt, Anita Heiss, Bruce Pascoe, Philip McLaren, Doris Pilkington, Gayle Kennedy, Sally Morgan, Ali Cobby Eckermann, Lionel Fogarty, Noel Pearson, and numerous others have all contributed to the excitement around Indigenous literature that exists in Australia today. The time seemed right to put together a section like this one.

Fiction here is in the midst of a minor revolution. The big discussion in 2012 has been around the restoration of forgotten Australian classics to the canon; some of these, most notably Frederic Manning's 1929 First World War novel *The Middle Parts of Fortune* and Barbara Baynton's 1902 short-fiction collection *Bush Studies*, feature a startling use of vernacular that has been more or less neglected in modern times, or at least been poorly employed. All four of the writers included in this portfolio display a level of comfort with Aussie vernacular that is evocative and, on occasion, extremely funny. Having the skill to manipulate language to the limits of its comprehension is something I admire greatly and would like to see more of. Unlike many of their non-Indigenous compatriots, Tony Birch, Melissa Lucashenko, Ellen van Neerven-Currie, and Tara June Winch clearly enjoy playing with language, flipping it, sounding it out. There's a confidence of tone and a willingness to push against the words in their stories that lend them an exciting potentiality. I wish more writers would linger over the inherent music in prose the way these guys do.

The themes here are noteworthy, too. All four of these stories feature characters that are displaced in some way or another, who have been pushed into roles they are uncomfortable with or who are struggling with the perceptions surrounding their identities. Tara June Winch's sprinter fallen on hard times, Tony Birch's alcoholic preacher's son, Melissa Lucashenko's suburban mother ready for front-lawn fisticuffs, and Ellen van Neerven-Currie's young women in the middle of nowhere all raise fascinating questions about how to fit in to a society that is changing so rapidly that the boundaries of what it means to be Australian are constantly having to be rewritten.

These writers have a growing community behind them. A phalanx of new literary journals and quarterlies has sprung up in the last decade, giving voice to a whole range of more-marginalized writers who are ready to embrace and experiment with the short form. My own quarterly, *Torpedo* (now defunct), the *Lifted Brow*, *Kill Your Darlings*, the *Review of Australian Fiction*, *Ampersand*, the *Griffith Review*, and reboots of long-standing stalwarts *Meanjin* and *Overland* have provided a means for a greater number of Australian writers to be published than ever before. Lucashenko, a four-time novelist, has been a regular contributor to the Brisbane-based *Griffith Review*, and it's heartening to witness a prodigious new talent like van Neerven-Currie emerge from the same beleaguered city, which was smashed by floodwaters in 2011. Melbourne's Tony Birch, meanwhile, is straight up one of my favorite short-story writers in the world at the moment, alongside Ron Rash and Maile Meloy, both of whom he resembles stylistically. His first two collections, *Shadowboxing* and *Father's Day*, are already touchstones for many young Australian writers, many of whom Birch teaches at Melbourne University. Our final contributor, Tara June Winch, now lives in Paris; although born in Wollongong, in New South Wales, she has a link to David Unaipon in that in 2004 she won the award named after him, which celebrates unpublished Indigenous writers.

These four writers provide a snapshot of Indigenous Australian fiction as it stands today, here in the second decade of the twenty-first century. With their unconventional explorations of contemporary Australian life, Lucashenko, van Neerven-Currie, Birch, and Winch are leading the way; the tremendous energy, skill, and depth of perception on show in these stories set the standard to which all Australian writers should aspire.

THE PROMISE

by TONY BIRCH

CAROL HAD WARNED ME time enough that she was going to leave, so when I got home late from playing cards and drinking at Winston's and found her gone, I wasn't surprised. She'd taken off to her parents' place, dragging the boys with her. She'd done the same three times before in the last six months.

I called for two weeks before she'd come to the phone. Eventually she said she wouldn't be home again unless I showed *commitment*. She wanted me signed up for a program.

"Is that all I have to do, honey?"

"Is that all? How many times have you promised and not done it?"

"But this is different. The house is like a morgue with you and the boys gone. It's a real promise."

I could hear her mother coaching her in the background.

"You sign up for a program before I come back, Luke. And I want to see proof. One of them authority notices the government's put out. All right?"

I smiled as I put the phone down. Rory Collins, a mechanic at the garage and an amiable man whom I drank with from time to time, had a brother-in-law who'd worked as a drug-and-alcohol counselor before he'd fallen off the wagon himself. He'd gotten the sack from his job, of course, having gone near-blind on the homemade spirits he'd cooked up in his backyard, but on his way out he'd lifted a fat pad of pledge authorities. He'd been selling them for twenty bucks apiece ever since.

The biggest business in town was grog. Always had been. Closely following that was the church, and after that, since the last crackdown, came drug-and-alcohol counseling. None of the charities in town would give a man as much as a cup of tea without a signed authority now; the dole office was likely to cut off your check if you were a registered pisshead and not in a program. The counselors ran the show, so they benefited the most—cash, grog, or girls. Sometimes the unholy trinity, if they were particularly greedy.

Three days after that phone call I was ready to head over to the in-laws' farm with a signed authority in my pocket. I'd forged the signature myself.

I'd picked up a suit jacket at the Salvation Army, and I'd had a shave and spit-polished my only pair of leather shoes. I'd even thought about a haircut, but decided against it, calculating that the twelve dollars would be better spent on a six-pack of Rebel Yell. I settled for some ancient hair oil from the back of the medicine cupboard before heading out.

The oil had belonged to my grandfather Abraham, a mission black who'd found God as a young man and who'd known the Bible, Old Testament and New, word for word. He'd bought our two-room weatherboard with the money he'd earned over twenty years as a backbreaking ditchworker for the Water Board. He'd always planned to set up his own church in the back room of the house, but as he got older and hunched over, the idea got away from him. Even then he never stopped reading his Bible.

Abraham took good care of me after my mother ran off with a whitefella. My father had been white, too, a cattle worker passing through town heading west; he'd stayed long enough to woo my mother back to his hotel room one night and send her home pregnant. When her belly got too big to hide under a dress, Abraham said he'd let her stay in the house as long as she promised to get down on her knees every night and pray with him. Dulcie didn't have much choice; in those days, if a pregnant black girl didn't have a roof over her head and someone decent to speak for her, she'd have her baby whipped away as soon as it was born. My mother knew as much, and kept her promise until I started crawling around on the floor and making demands of her that she wasn't interested in meeting. At that point she got the wanders, and eventually she traveled far enough that she didn't bother finding her way back home.

For a while I reckoned my father had to be an albino, because I was the fairest-skinned blackfella in town and could easily have passed for white. Abraham tried steering me on the right path, but as soon as I was old enough I drifted out to the lake, to the ruins of the Christian mission, and quickly learned to love the drink and the smell of a girl's skin after it had been dipped in water and wine.

Abraham left the house to me after his death. It wasn't much of a prize, but it was enough to impress Carol, a farmer's daughter who knew all about the value of private property.

"It's a start," she said softly, when she first saw the place.

I met her during a brief period of sobriety, a time when I went around town in a clean white shirt and talked about reviving Abraham's dream of a church of his own. I'd even dressed this up for Carol, in an effort to get her into Abraham's old brass bed—I told her I'd sworn to him, on his deathbed, that I would build his church.

"And what did he say?" she'd pleaded, tears in her eyes, as we sat in the only tearoom in town, drinking Earl Grey.

"Well," I said, as I took a long gulp of the tea and stalled for an answer, "he looked up at me with that wrinkled old face of his and said, 'I know you can do it, Luke. You're a strong boy. The Lord will be pleased, and I'll rest easy.'"

Carol leaned across the table and rested her head against my chest. I put my arms around her and pressed her body into mine. She smelled so clean and soapy and pure that I was sure we'd be happy together.

The days of scandal, of a white girl marrying a half-caste, weren't quite over. But when I met Carol's parents in Abraham's dusted-off black suit and told them of my plans for a church, they seemed satisfied.

"Land," her mother gushed to her husband. "He has *land*." Meanwhile Carol's father looked over at her and thought, to my reckoning, that she wasn't exactly a beauty queen and this might be his best chance of marrying her off.

They lived far enough out of town to have no direct experience of my reputation, and they never made inquiries. To this day I think that maybe they didn't want to know.

I did love Carol. But not as much as I loved the grog and the good company of the old mission boys. I loved the stories they told. I loved the town girls who drifted out to the lake to lie by the water of a night and look up at the stars. After a time, of course, the mission boys died away, and the girls grew into women with a tribe of kids of their own and an old man for each of them. If one of them caught his wife out at the lake, he'd kick her arse all the way back to town.

I downed a can of Rebel Yell at the kitchen sink and threw another couple onto the passenger seat of the old Datsun before setting out to lay my claim to Carol and the kids. Along the way I stopped at the cemetery out of town, sat on a gravestone, drank another can, and plucked a bunch of flowers from the grave to present to Carol as a peace offering. I shook the dust off them and sat them on the seat with the last of the grog.

A couple of minutes away from her parents' farmhouse I pulled over to the side of the road, under an old peppercorn tree. I hopped out for a piss and then I sat under that tree and sipped at the third can of bourbon and cola while I enjoyed the peace and quiet of the afternoon. When I'd finished I shook the last dregs out of the can, crushed it in my hand, and threw it way off into the bushes. I dug into my jacket pocket and pulled out the half pack of XXX mints I'd planted there earlier, then went to the side-view mirror to look at my face. I checked my bloodshot eyes and sucked and crunched on those mints and then I spit into my hands and tucked my wild head of curls behind my ears.

My head didn't feel too good. In the car I rested my chin on the steering wheel and focused as best I could to keep to my side of the road. I took the turn into the in-laws' long driveway a little too fast, in the end, and managed to clean up the mailbox. I held my hand down on the car horn so the boys would hear me and come running, but they didn't. A moment later, when I pulled up out front of the house, with its long, wide veranda and boxes of pretty flowers, there was no sign at all of Carol or the boys. Just Martha and Ted, waiting to greet me.

I fell out of the car, landed on my hands and knees, and looked up at them.

"Heya, Teddy," I said. "Can you tell Carol I'm here? To pick her up. She got her things ready?"

Ted was wearing his farmer's overalls and a straw farmer's hat. He hadn't done any fieldwork for as long as I could remember; he hired in blackfellas on the cheap to do the slog while he sat on the phone nattering to his stockbroker. Martha was wearing a pretty floral dress and a ton of makeup.

She never got out of bed of a morning without doing her face. They were full of disgust, both of them.

"She doesn't want to see you," Martha said, laughing and crying all at the same time. "She's had enough, Luke. She wants a divorce."

Ted shifted awkwardly on the balls of his feet, maybe thinking that Martha had played her trump card a little too early. I dusted myself off and pulled the forged authority from my jacket pocket.

"But she can't," I said, waving it in their faces. "I signed up for a program, just like she asked me to. I've been off it. And I'm staying off it." I tried handing Ted the slip of paper, but he wouldn't take it. "You ask her to come out here and talk to me," I went on. "She's my wife, and they're my boys."

Martha tut-tutted and shook her head, and silent Ted just went red. My story was so full of bullshit I think he felt sorry for me. I stood there until I heard the screen door slam on the veranda.

"You've got no right being here, Luke."

It was Carol. She marched past her parents and down off the porch so we were standing toe-to-toe.

"I don't want you upsetting the boys. Like Mum says, I'm not coming back. It's over."

I pushed the authority into her face.

"You told me, on the phone, if I went on a program you'd give me another chance. Well, I did. Read it, Carol. Read it."

She snatched the paper from my hand, screwed it into a ball, and threw it to the ground.

"Clean! You've never been clean, Luke. You're dirty. You and all your kind. Look at you. You're drunk now! I got a call from Jenny Oakes, from the bank—she told me you were in there yesterday morning cashing a check, and by twelve, when she was out getting her lunch, you were sitting up in the front bar of The Royal, half-drunk. You're not in any program." She pointed along the drive. "Go. You shouldn't have driven out here as it was. That car's got no registration, and you've got no license to drive it. I hope the police pick you up."

I took a step back. My legs started shaking. Ted walked over and put a hand on my shoulder.

"Please, Luke," he said. "We don't want any trouble here. I'll drive you back into town, if you like."

Martha rested her arms across her breasts and pulled a face. "Have you anything to say to my daughter, Luke? Maybe an apology?"

Tears burned my cheeks. I wiped them away with the sleeve of my jacket.

"Yeah, I've got something to say, Martha. To all of you."

I did have plenty to say. I just couldn't remember what it was right then. I shook my head, trying to loosen the thought, but it wouldn't come. If I'd had a dollar for every time Carol had threatened to leave, I'd be the richest blackfella in the country—richer even than those boys working on the oil rigs off the coast up north. But this time I could feel the pain deep in my gut.

I got back into the car and drove off.

At home I went through the medicine cupboard again and grabbed hold of all the pills I could find. Sleeping tablets, antidepressants, painkillers, a few vitamins. I shoved them all into my gob, stuck my head under the tap, and drank until I'd swallowed the lot. Rifling through the refrigerator I found a lonely can of beer at the bottom of the empty vegetable tray. I drank it, stuck my head into the pantry, came out with half a bottle of vanilla essence, and downed that as well.

Abraham had kept a shotgun all his life. He'd never fired it, as far as I knew, but he liked to keep hold of it, claiming that one day he might be called upon to "protect the righteous from the sinners, black and white." The gun wasn't hard to find; I crawled under his old double bed, *our* bed, and searched around until I found the loose floorboard, then fished around some more until I felt the cold steel of the barrel. I knew the gun was loaded without having to cock it. The breech had held a .12-gauge birdshot cartridge for as long as I could remember.

I was ready to shoot myself right there in the house, but thinking about the mess it would make, about Carol or somebody else finding me with half my head caked to the ceiling, I stood up and walked onto the front veranda. It was belting down with rain by then. I looked out across the hills behind the town, at a stand of trees in the distance, and then back at the lonely house. I couldn't abandon it this way, I decided.

I went around back to the shed, collected the half can of petrol I kept for the mower, and went back into the house to douse the rooms. The place was fully alight in less than a minute, the dry old boards cracking with pain and weeping off the last traces of paint Abraham had put to them years back. I turned away from the flames and went to the car.

Driving out of town I held the gun between my knees with the barrel scratching at my throat. If it had gone off then and there, I'd have died happy. Would've saved me from testing my courage. Between the belting rain, a dirty windshield, fucked wiper blades, and the pills and grog, I was driving on a prayer. The car wobbled and weaved across the highway, by some miracle dodging trucks and trees and a bit of livestock. Cows, mostly. I don't know if it was one of them I hit, or one of those ghost trees they talk about 'round here that appear out of nowhere, but the last thing I remember was head-butting the windshield.

When I woke up my mouth was full of dirt and blood. I lifted my head and tried opening my eyes; I could see out of one, but the other was clamped shut. I'd been thrown from the car and was lying in a muddy ditch, the Datsun to the side of me, its windshield smashed, the door slung open, steam pouring from the bonnet. Something warm oozed from the corner of my bad eye, down my cheek. I tried getting to my feet and fell down again.

I swallowed a few breaths, then crawled over to the shotgun lying in the mud a few feet from me. I used it to haul myself up and get out of the ditch, onto the side of the red-dirt road. All my life I'd been walking the roads skirting the town—I thought I knew all of them. I didn't have a clue where I was. There was nobody around, and no buildings save a rundown hay shed.

It had stopped raining, but a death-rattle wind cut though my skin. I started to walk, which wasn't easy. I was missing a shoe and had done something to my right foot. I could still shoot myself, of course, but suddenly it didn't seem like such a good idea. This would be a lonely place to die. The car crash had shook me up enough to make me know I was a coward.

I rounded a bend and came to a crossroads. There were no signs to tell me which way was which, and I still had no idea where I was. Heading straight on seemed as good a choice as any. I crossed the road, dragging my bad foot with me.

After a while I spotted a white wooden cross and the pitched roof of a church through some trees. It was a small wooden building, resting in a dry riverbed off the road; the arched front door was open. I made for it.

The doorway was draped with a deep-red velvet curtain. I pulled it to one side and went in. There were people on either side of the room, some sitting behind fold-up tables with colorful card decks laid out, others, mostly old girls, sitting opposite empty chairs with their heads bowed and eyes closed. A few of them turned and looked at me as I walked in, splattered in mud and blood and carrying the shotgun, but no one seemed disturbed by the intrusion. They just went back to whatever it was they were doing.

A woman at one of the tables kept looking at me. She was an older one, but beautiful nonetheless, with thick golden curls and the fullest lips I'd ever seen. She began laying out her cards, and for some reason I was drawn across the room to her.

"You've had a troubled day, son," she said, when I reached her. "Would you like to put that gun down and rest your leg?"

I propped my weight on the shotgun and searched the room. "What's this place?" I said.

"We are the Church of Spiritual Healing," she said, and smiled; her voice was sweeter than I thought could have been possible. "We are here to heal wounded souls."

"Really? How long you been 'round here? Must be new to the place?"

She turned another card and laid it on the table. Her smile disappeared.

"No. We have always been here. Always. Please sit."

I rested the gun against the side of the chair and took the weight of my bad leg. She tapped softly on the table with her fingertips.

"Is there something you would like to tell me?"

I looked across the table, into her sparking green eyes. She must have been fifteen, twenty years my senior, but I did want to say something; I wanted to tell her that she was beautiful.

"My wife, she's taken off on me," I said. "I come off the road back there."

She took my bloodied, swollen hand, pitted with broken glass, in hers.

"What I do," she explained, waving her free hand across the cards, "is help you understand your past, *your* damaged past, and assist you along the path to a more stable and spiritual future."

I couldn't quite follow what she was saying. It might have been the drugs and drink, or the concussion I most likely had. I nodded my head in agreement anyway.

"Sounds fine by me."

She squeezed my hand a little too tightly.

"But in your case, you are not quite ready. First you must be cleansed."

I looked down at the mess and shit all over me. "Yeah. I know that. I need to get clean. For sure. I'd like to get this foot seen to, as well."

She released her hand from mine and rested it on the back of my palm.

"You are a troubled man," she said. "Your soul is stuck."

"All right; can you help me?" I said. "I've got this awful ringing in my head that's driving me crazy. Can you get rid of that as well?"

I was clutching at her hand. I'd frightened her a little. She pulled her hand away from mine, sat back, and shook her head.

"No. I'm sorry, but I cannot do that."

I was ready to cry. "Why not? You just said it's what I need."

"And it is. But I am not a cleanser. That is the work of others."

I panicked and grabbed the barrel of the gun. "What about one of these others? Can't one of them help me?"

She dropped her head. "No. None of them can help you." She closed her eyes, raised a finger, and pointed toward a small wooden stage, also surrounded by heavy curtains, at the far end of the room. "But he may be able to. If you go to the stair at the side of the stage, he will see you. Is that what you want?"

"Yes, please—it's what I want."

"Well, go quickly. And," she waited till she had my attention, "I would leave the gun, if I were you."

Behind the curtains, the stage was dark. I couldn't see much at all. The woman with the cards had sold me a lie, I realized; she'd only wanted to get rid of me. I was about to walk out when I heard a scraping noise on the wooden floorboards. A shadow moved, and a match was struck. The shadow danced in the low flame, and then a candle was lit. And another. And another. The room glowed, soft and yellow. I was standing in front of a man in a long white gown.

He looked to be around my own age, and had dark hair tied back in a ponytail. He also had a thick beard, and large breasts. I don't mean man-boobs, but full, beautifully shaped breasts, their cleavage straining to escape the neck of the gown.

He looked down at a wooden stool that could now be seen between us. "Please sit," he said.

I did as he said, without question, and stared at his breasts as he spoke.

"I will lay my hands on your back. Don't be concerned when you feel your organs warming. It is to be expected. If you feel nauseous at any time, or dizzy, that is also normal. If you fear that you may pass out, raise your left arm." He placed a hand on my head. "Are there any questions?"

I wanted to ask him about his breasts, but thought better of it. As it was, I couldn't talk anyway. My mouth had gone dry and wouldn't open properly. He seemed to know what was going on, and offered me a glass of water.

"Drink this. It will help you relax."

The water was cold, but it tasted a little strange. I handed the glass back to him and wiped my mouth.

"Maybe—maybe this isn't for me?" I said.

He put a hand on my head as I shifted in the chair. "You relax now," he whispered. Then he was behind me, resting both palms against the small of my back.

Straight off I could feel their warmth. A soft ball of heat moved into my body. By the time the dizziness got to me, I couldn't have lifted an eyelid, let alone an arm. I could feel dribble running down my chin, and my forehead being stroked by a gentle hand.

I woke cradled in his arms, resting against his breasts. He smiled when I looked up at him. Then he gently sat me up and massaged the back of my head until I was properly awake.

"You can go now, Luke. It is safe."

The light on the stage slowly faded, and the darkness returned. I was alone. It wasn't until I'd gone back out through the curtains that I realized that the ringing in my head had stopped, and that I was wearing the healer's white gown.

The hall was empty, and the sun was shining through a window. Outside, the red-dirt road leading away from the church had turned to a sea of mud. I went out through the door and started walking it, free of pain. Soon I'd passed the lake and the ruins of the mission. A few of the old boys had come back from the dead to greet me. They called me over for a drink, but I waved them off and kept on walking. When I reached the town, I walked straight down the middle of the street. People stopped to gawk; the red dust and mud had settled on the hem of the gown, and I looked as if I'd been dipped in blood.

Abraham's old house had been reduced to a heap of smoldering charcoal. I knew what I had to do. I dragged out two blackened bits of wood from the pyre, found some rusting fence wire, and bound the pieces of wood together to form a cross. I didn't realize until I'd finished that I'd burned the skin from my hands. I picked up the cross anyway, and walked to the front of the yard. I found a rock and banged the cross deep into the earth. Then I looked up to the sky and waited.

S & J

by ELLEN VAN NEERVEN-CURRIE

JAYE CALLS TO STOP when I'm going full-blow down the line and I press my foot down hard thinking I nicked a roo. The dust mushrooms up and at first I can't see anything. When it clears I see the bird standing in the road, pale and overdressed.

"Far out," I say.

"Pop the boot," Jaye says.

"Hold on."

"You've already stopped." She pats the radio as she gets up beside me. "And put something else on, will you? Don't want them to think we're all bogans."

Jaye walks up to the bird, smile on, arms out, and soon the bird's smiling, too, giving Jaye her backpack and following her to the car. Jaye gets in the backseat, and the girl does, too.

"Hi," she says. German accent. "Sigrid."

"Hi, Sigrid," I say. "I'm Esther."

"Es," she says. "Es and Jaye."

"Yeah," I say, starting the car up and veering back onto the road.

"I'm so glad," Sigrid says, "that I've finally met a real Aboriginal."

Through the top mirror I see she has a hand on Jaye's shoulder.

"You must tell me everything, Jaye. Tell me all about your hardship."

*   *   *

We pull up to the service station and Jaye steps out to refuel.

"She's very beautiful," sighs Sigrid. "Strong."

I grunt and ask where she's headed.

"Exmonth. I think that's how you say it."

"Exmouth. Like this." I show my teeth. "Well, you're in luck, because that's where we're headed, too."

"I'm very grateful, obviously," she says. "Where are you from?"

"Brissie," I say. "Brisbane. On the other side, the east coast. A little south from there, Gold Coast area, that's my country."

"Sorry?" she says. "I don't know where that is."

Jaye's walking back to the car.

"You're a nice golden color," Sigrid goes on. "You look like you're from Spain, maybe. Your parents immigrated here, yes?"

Jaye gets in. "Dinner, ladies."

She unloads her hands of raisin toast and chips and Cokes.

Jaye and I stand leaning against the car in the night air outside her grandmother's house.

"I'm really not sure, Jaye," I say.

"C'mon, sis. We can hardly toss her out, can we?"

"I thought she'd have somewhere to stay when she got here. That's what she said."

"Well, she doesn't, and she's all right, so…" Jaye straightens up and walks toward the house. "You coming, or what?"

The house is a low-set cottage off the highway, surrounded by bush. The rooms smell stale, but it's cozy. There's a fireplace. Out back the veranda is falling apart and you can barely see the washing line above the waist-high grass. Jaye's cousins have been using it as a beach house for years. Now it's her turn.

We eat on the veranda, and then Jaye digs out a bottle of vodka and a deck of mismatched cards. Sigrid teaches us a German version of Rummikub. I'm not drinking, but the night moves quickly, like a train passing stations without stopping. A large ringtail possum sits on a nearby paperbark, and

Sigrid squeals when I point it out. She wants to feed it, but we have nothing besides our breakfast for tomorrow. Jaye teaches her the word for possum in Yindjibarndi, and then the name for the tree, and then the name for the one next to it, and I'm all too used to it by now and roll my eyes. When the possum skirts off I decide to do the same.

Underneath the sheets I flick around on my radio for a bit, trying to get a channel. I can still hear the clink of wine glasses and the low murmured laughter from outside. It's a hard decision, to gulp up sleep or stay awake for the morning light. I open the window and see a pink haze coming through. I like the thought of walking barefoot to the beach and out into the waves, but it would be strange to do it without Jaye.

I guess she kind of dragged me along. I didn't want to be by myself at the house all semester break. Everyone else was going back to their families, and I, the only one who lived nearby, didn't feel like sticking around. It's funny now, with the darkness and the silence, no lights, no parties, that Jaye seems more distracted. She's been on edge ever since we got here.

When we met I was a shy teen and it felt good to be going places. Doing things. She was darker than me and all the other Murris I knew, like a walking projection of what a blackfella was supposed to be. She knew language, knew them old stories. Had to say *deadly* every second sentence. Postcard blackfella.

At first I liked it. But lately she was becoming too much for me.

There are these sounds in the distance, like hooting, but it's not owls. I sit up. It's a horribly low sound. I look outside, but all I see are trees and mud and mangroves.

I pad down the hallway in my nighttime thongs. The living room is dark, but they're sitting on the couch. They're sitting too close. I go back to bed.

The droning stops. I can hear some thumping around, still, and am about to sing out "Quiet, you Brolgas" when I realize the laughter in the living room has been replaced by weighted sighs. The door to the next room opens, and the bed springs pop. I can tell they're trying to be quiet, which is worse. My chest feels tight. I pull the sheets over my head.

When I rise at eleven, the door beside mine is still shut. I put the kettle on and butter some bread and sit with my modest meal at the small, round, green table in the center of the room. School results tomorrow. Let the envelope sit in my mailbox for a week. I started well. Gone to every class and that, read the textbook in advance, even. Jaye slipped me some of her work, but she let me stay rent-free. It was fine, for a while. At what point did I start doing more of

Jaye's than mine?

She's left the keys on top of the television. Longboard in hand, I cross the road and walk down the path to the beach. I drag the lead through the sand, looking for an entry point between the bucketloads of kids. For a long time I stand between surfing and not surfing.

For lunch I walk along the beach to the surf club and order some chips.

"You're not from here, hey?" the lady says.

"Yeah, how'd you know?"

The lady points to my Brisbane Broncos shirt. "First time in W.A.?"

"Yeah."

"Enjoying it?"

"Yeah."

"There's this band on here tonight. We're expecting a crowd."

"Oh, yeah—Milla Breed. My friend told me."

"This is her last show. She's going to the States."

"Good one," I say.

Sigrid is in the living room when I get back to the house, reading one of Jaye's poetry books.

"Good morning," she says.

"Hi," I say. "Where's Jaye?"

"Still in bed."

"Okay." I put the keys back. "Last night, did you hear any noises—droning noises?"

"Not at all," Sigrid says, amused.

"Right," I say.

"You and Jaye are not…"

I quickly shake my head.

"Good," she says, and smiles.

"We still going to that gig tonight?"

"Es, I'm trying to sleep, eh."

"It's four-thirty."

"You don't need to tell me the time. Hey, Sig's hungry. Can you get us a feed at the surf club? Something salty?"

* * *

At eight, the other door closed again, I pull on some jeans and the only closed-in pair of shoes I own. Flatten my hair.

When I get to the pub it looks like half the town's here, fishies and tradies. Everywhere we've been it's like a whole generation is missing. Haven't seen anyone my age since Perth, except the tourists. This last week every tourie and their dog wanted a picture with Jaye. Some wanted more than a picture. I'm always the one stuck holding the camera.

Mum used to tell me and my sisters when we were younger that being Murri wasn't a skin thing. Next to Jaye, though, that was all anyone noticed.

I think of Sigrid. Should've known.

The lady from lunchtime is at the door. I give her a fiver to get in and go to the bar to grab a drink. Milla Breed's all long black hair and long white limbs crashing on the stage. Her drummer can't keep up with her. I move a little closer when she starts a new song, trying to catch a lyric, but the words are in and out so fast you can't grab 'em. They're more utterance than words. Reminds me of the droning from last night.

She kneels, hands out to the crowd, then gets up, hands back on her guitar. She's wearing engineer boots, a denim skirt, and a black shirt. Sleeves cut off like Jaye's. Jaye likes all the grunge bands, especially the Aussie ones. She plays Breed's stuff all the time, except her third LP, which she reckons is womba. I usually stick to golden oldies, the Beatles and the Stones; Mum reckons I'm the only one she knows who likes both. But Jaye's right on this one. This bird is good at what she does.

"Hiya, Exmouth, how you doing?" she drawls.

"Show us your titties!" the big bloke in front of me screams, and I think she does but I can't see because my view is momentarily blocked.

"Get lost, dyke," one of his mates says to me when I press forward, and I tumble back onto some bird's toe and scurry to find another place to stand.

The crowd sparks as Breed plays her radio hit as a closer. She sings it differently, addressing the room between verses. Then she slows down and flicks her hair up, her gaze on mine, the blue-green of her eyes like a globe, and even though she must be forty-five, easy, I can't help but lower my own look. Her breasts prominent in the muscle shirt. I don't need to think about what Jaye would say, because I'm thinking it. Too deadly.

She waves to the crowd and floats back behind the wall. I buy a record at the bar and wait awhile to see if she's coming out again, but they've got another band up, some father-and-son act, and they're playing Cold Chisel covers and all the blokes are mumbling along as if they've forgotten about her.

As I'm walking back up to the driveway a white taxi swings in front of me. Sigrid's standing there, her hair orange in the light.

"Where you going?" I call.

"Home," she says.

I walk up closer.

"Sigrid?"

"Yeah?"

"I'm not from Spain. I'm Aboriginal."

"I know," she says. "Jaye told me."

I nod and watch her put her bags into the boot.

She turns back. "You don't look it. But you probably think I don't look German, either."

I walk inside and switch the light on. No sign of Jaye. I sit on the couch and try the remote, but the TV doesn't switch on. There's a stack of papers beside the poetry chapbooks, and I flick through a couple of *Koori Mail*s. It's a while before I realize I'm waiting for her. There are a few things I want to say, and I think I will say them.

The house is still. I go through the next stack. There is Breed, on the contents page. I flick to the double-spread interview.

My stomach rises with every word. She's talking about her childhood, her family. Blue eyes on the page. By the end of it I'm so worked up I stand and think about going back to the bar. She might still be there.

Car would be faster. I open the door and walk out to it. Start the beast and drop down the driveway. In my mind I'm walking up to Breed and she looks at me and doesn't say a word, just grabs a bottle off a chair by the throat and sucks it, looking at me still. She tells me that I'll do, pulls me to her small frame, and pushes my jersey up over my head.

I stay at the foot of the road, in the driveway. I breathe heavily.

Still no sign of Jaye inside, but there is the drone again. I open the screen door and the sounds feel louder. Jaye's fluoro singlet is out there in the dark;

she's in the yard with garden clippers and hasn't made a dent in the overgrowth.

"What are you doing," I say, "in the dark?"

She turns to look at me. I take a torch off the table and walk down to her. She looks at my hands and I realize I'm still carrying the paper with the interview.

"Didn't know Breed was a Koori," I say.

Jaye says nothing.

"What's up?"

"The fuck have you been?"

"What? I was at the gig; I tried to get you up for it, but—"

"I told you yonks ago I didn't want to go. The chick's sold out, eh. Going to the U.S. to be in a porno. Thought you'd left me, too, sista."

"Sigrid?" I ask pointedly.

"Sig? She's just a chick, you know. You're my best mate. I thought that was the whole deal of coming here. I was going to show you where I grew up, all them old spots, introduce you to my mob..."

"You're the one who stayed in her room all day." It's hard to believe her when she says she wants me around. I feel pretty replaceable.

Jaye's head stays down.

I sigh in defeat and put my arm around her shoulders, sweaty and acidic. She stares out into the yard.

"Why'd Sigrid go?" I ask.

"Think it was you."

"I thought it might have been those noises that scared her off. I reckon this place has ghosts."

"What, that?" Jaye's laugh mimics the drones. "It's just dingos, eh."

"We'll start tomorrow," I say. "Nice and early. Exploring."

Jaye grunts. She looks at me. "How was it, anyway?"

I'm not sure how to answer. "Not the same," I say.

At that moment the ringtail runs along the railing.

IT'S TOO DIFFICULT
TO EXPLAIN

by TARA JUNE WINCH

VINCENT LAY IN THE LIGHT. It fell across the trundle bed in shards the color of brittle toffee, coming in early and sickly sweet. A complimentary bed has its aftertaste, depending on the severity of the need. He could have been anywhere between twenty and thirty years old now; that decade can be either kind or brutal to the face. The muscles had gone at the shoulders, where they'd once met a thick neck flush with the oxygenated color that only athletes acquire. Temporary shelter was getting the better of him.

There was not enough space to do lunges. When he attempted push-ups, the wood floor labored, and he knew someone in the room below would be angry. So after riding out a week of his training schedule and then scrapping it altogether, he began instead to print flyers for the Millionaire's Club pyramid scheme in order to raise enough money to rent his own place. He needed fifty recruits, at a guess.

When a sprinter wins, the victory can usually be attributed to some combination of the following things: position, projection of angles of flight, balance, acceleration, maintenance of speed, and ground-contact time. Vincent always thought about this last point. Ground-contact time—this is what had given him leverage, that he'd never really touched the earth for long.

"Run to the shop and get some bread, Vinnie."

"Run along, Vinnie, and make yourself busy."

"If he should come back, you just take your sister and run, Vinnie."

"Vinnie, I've got to go now. You run the house and take care of your sister, all right?"

His mother had been single—the warm-skinned father had fled fast and never returned. Vinnie was a gentle baby, quiet for many years. He'd hardly spoken a word by age five, though he wasn't seen by a physician to find out if that meant anything. He was fed, bathed, and put to bed on time, mostly, lip-smiled at—every so often he caught a wary glance from his mother, whom he only slightly resembled. In his early teens he'd felt sad that he couldn't see more of himself in her, or her in him, and that no one else was there to compare himself to. His heart-shaped face, his green eyes, his coloring. Perhaps the reminder of someone else was the reason his mother glanced at him that way. She could not hold her child's gaze.

It happened that because of this doubt about where he was meant to be, he fit in nowhere in particular. He didn't know where he began with his mother, his sister; everything seemed to go in different directions. His mother came and went, seeking jobs or men farther and farther away, for longer stretches, drawing out alternate lives. When she left for the last time, he chose the name Vincent instead of his birth-certified one, Vinnie Jr. He was fostered into one kind family and then another, and they too called him Vincent. For some years his life was good and he felt that people cared.

Point-zero-five seconds separated him from everything he thought he'd been. It made sense to him only later, in the dark cavern of a lone night— everything measured in a series of part-seconds and impulses. He had known all the things he'd done to get there. They could be bottled into a single quick choice.

He'd been running straight lines for nearly ten years. His first girlfriend had brought him along to her squad training when she was fourteen; up in the viewing stalls, watching those long bodies bolting to a seemingly irrelevant end, he'd known at once that he could do what they were doing.

He'd been her first questionable boyfriend, smoking his foster mother's secret kitchen-cabinet cigarettes. She had been a pretty girl, forever with the tight pony-tailed hair smoothed into a perfect ironic gesture. He'd been the first to draw out that elastic band.

He was nineteen when he clocked his best hundred meters, a 10.07. It granted him the title of the country's fastest man and raised enough attention to put him on the front pages, as well as offering him a shot at the Olympic trials in Beijing and sponsorship money he used to purchase things he would never otherwise have considered. Relatives got in touch; classmates reminded him of their apparent friendship. He ate his meals at tableclothed restaurants. Still, he couldn't unbind himself from his first small newspaper interview—the one that revealed that his coffee-colored skin and thin calf muscles were the genetic inheritance of a runaway father, and that by the time he'd turned fourteen his mother had left, too. Later he would trawl through years of minor Internet articles to recall the things that defined him. He did this when he became lonely and his life prematurely quiet.

The more he succeeded, the more he wanted something. New girlfriend, new coach, new sponsor—none of it seemed to suffice. Nothing could take away the feeling that he might yet return to what he was from, no matter how fancy the parties he attended, or how interesting and educated the people he befriended. He was still the point from which he moved.

His coach was a healthy-looking strawberry-blond man, newly fifty, a scrawny-legged thick-chested former runner. He was the best in the state, and widely liked—smiling but tough.

"Newton said, 'For every action there is an equal and opposite reaction,' Vincent." Coach quoted only philosophers, scientists, and difficult poets. He repeated anecdotes that Vincent often didn't understand.

"You know how a surgeon can cut carefully enough, slowly and precisely enough, to remove a tumor from the brain? Train like that."

Vincent's time had stopped getting faster. The less his body performed, the more Coach would offer bland encouragements. "Good, good, go again." He smiled less. It had been a long time since Vincent had reached anywhere near his personal best. He was twenty-three now, and his hundred-meter sat at 10.10, 10.13. He didn't win anymore, and even though he still held the record, it was no longer a news item. As he felt himself stagnating, he bound himself up in new people who seemed blind to what he lacked—people who could see only greatness, not knowing it was already gone.

He took up with another girlfriend. They met at a café, where she talked to him about his choice of breakfast. Her name was Chloe, and she would become over the next few months the first person in his life he'd felt something warm and inexpressible toward. She was too pretty for him, too beautiful, too elegant, with white skin and high arching eyebrows that said *Look at my blue eyes*. Her parents were European, rich, the elite of the city. He was happy to have a new woman in his life, one he hadn't wronged yet.

"What took you so long at the shops, Vinnie?"

"Your sister's hungry, Vinnie."

"Sound the words out, Vinnie. Read it properly."

"Vinnie, you can't be a boy anymore. Try harder to be a man."

In the dig phase, down at the knees, a sprinter will free-fall for a fraction of a second before a tucked leg plunges downward and hits red rubber. The pressure to trust the fall can be too much; the run can be lost before it's begun. The intention must be perfect.

Chloe would come to Vincent's training each morning, watch and smile and wave from the stretching bars, happy to hang upside down in her long yoga pants, arms dangling, fingers stretched out. She was thin and nimble and joked charmingly with the female runners in the squad about running them down. Her movements were purposeful and confident, each step owning the space just around it. She spoke in a similar way. If she said something like "It's a beautiful day," someone overhearing it might mistake her observation for the quiet imparting of some deep secret. Around her Vincent became thoughtful. He would reach out for her gently, not like he had with others. Those girls who laughed with their mouths wide.

They spent their time talking about everything that they wanted to do. He said his dream was to go to the Olympics and win, but the words sounded wounded to him, unreal. Chloe was in graduate school, studying music. She said she wanted to be a concert pianist, but lamented that she was probably too old.

These first months, with Chloe, he existed in a time of perfection. She believed he was fine, more than fine, even though he was expired.

He was distracted soon enough. He began to fear the end of something. He didn't trust the first leg, the one that rose and fell. The part before, the push away, he could do with ease. But now he knew she was there, and that she could go.

*   *   *

Vincent and Chloe went to dinner at her parents' home for the first time after four months of dating. He was told it would be only her siblings and her mother; her father was away on business. The house was symmetrical and white-clad, two wide stories with windows set in a high, sloping rooftop—like the houses in American films, he thought. It was hung with Christmas-icicle lighting and had a low iron gate that separated it from a quiet, narrow street. The view fell onto the park that housed the national museum. He knew he could speak with people from different walks of life—he could have lunch with a sponsor, or a fellow athlete, or a flashy sports manager—but he had never been to a home like this. This was not right.

Starters, mains, desserts, aperitifs—he began to taunt himself, as they walked up the path, a panic attack that grew from his chest and flashed heat up his neck to the top of his head. His heart panged. You are going down, he told himself over and over, you are going down and this is the moment you taste tepid water and don't just wade in it. It is not okay for you to be here. You are trespassing, no one has invited you here and you must go.

"Come in, come in!"

A woman, Chloe's mother, had opened the door as they ascended the stone stairs. She leaned into the space of the doorway just as he'd seen similar women do in films about families like this. She was smiling, purposefully making her eyes squint, as if she were a kind of elderly librarian. The house was lit honey yellow, like a dream. Everything moved in clips, static, film-like. Vincent was introduced to Chloe's siblings and their partners, young professionals from the best schools. The conversation dipped in and out of rendered stories, swaggering tales of how Chloe's family took diplomatic residence behind some gates in Copenhagen, or a lengthy explanation on the "de" part of her brother's girlfriend's French last name. The wine was complimented at length. The wine, Vincent thought, was his only hope. He tried to keep his fork in his mouth or the wine glass at his lips at all times—tried to make sure that the area was too busy to be part of a conversation he couldn't have.

The dinner carried on. There were plenty of new plates for everyone, matching glasses, ceramic dishes, heavy silver spoons. The walls were covered with art in glass frames, the colors matching the furniture. Toward the end of dessert, some of the siblings left. They kissed Vincent on the cheek awkwardly, hugged their mother enthusiastically. Their mother laughed, handed them leftovers, hugged them tight. She told them to come back soon, that she loved them. He'd never seen a mother like this. Whether it was real or feigned, he couldn't tell.

Eventually it was just her and Vincent and Chloe, who ate slowly and was only now serving herself a conscientious sliver of dessert. The mother filled their glasses from a new bottle of wine, which she'd insisted on getting herself from the cellar. She'd held her apron in one hand and kicked the rug aside with her high-heeled toe to reveal the hidden door. Glanced up at Vincent and half-smiled, raising her eyebrows at him slowly. And then a flash of something else.

He felt punctured with paranoia for watching it all. Was it the way she looked at him? Had she considered him, for a moment, to be a potential thief? He wasn't going to break into her house, he would never do that, but he already felt guilty for it. Kept the wine glass at his lip.

He'd met this look before—how is it that mothers can look at young men this way? He saw his own mother in it—the look of feeling nothing for a person. She hadn't been thinking he was a thief, he thought; he was the opposite of a thief. He could take nothing, he *was* nothing.

Chloe's mother put music on the stereo, settled down at the head of the table. Close to them.

"So, Vincent," she said, "obviously you're busy training with running now—have you had any wins lately?"

He set his glass down. "Not lately, no."

"Where did you grow up? Is there a local university there? Might you go back to school?"

"Down the coast, about an hour out. I don't know about school. Isn't really what I'm thinking about."

"Well, will they remember the man or the run, Vincent?"

He started. "What do you mean?"

"Ah, what do I mean? Let's talk about it. Mmm, this music, for instance"—she was almost shouting over the sound—"do you think an artwork like this can exist alone, or must the artist be judged also?"

He started to panic again. What? he thought. He poured more wine and looked at Chloe, wanting her to catch the baton her mother had flung. And so she did, speaking on and on, intelligently but almost angrily, flapping her hands about. They kept on like this, the two of them, faintly yelling at each other with a strange affection. He thought about the question. He guessed that they couldn't be separated, the doer and the deed; he thought about all the interviews he'd done about running, how the journalists from the papers had always asked where he was from, what he *was*. They didn't ask him to summarize his running style, his training schedule.

She was exposing him, he realized. He imagined her saying to her daughter, later, "See? There's nothing there." Say something, he thought to himself. Say something so she knows you're here.

Vincent could feel things leaping up in his throat. Before he could control them, before he could prevent himself from diving off the riverbank, he spoke, already too loud.

"Of course an artwork cannot be judged by itself!"

Chloe's mother turned to him. "Why do you believe that, Vincent?"

"Because people are interested in the story behind the art, or whatever."

"What artists are you referring to, Vincent? Can you name one?"

He scrambled.

"That Van Go guy. He cut off his ear. If I saw his paintings, I'd be thinking about this guy cutting off his ear." He searched for Chloe's eyes. *I'm here.*

"What about Wagner? He was an anti-Semite, but he was still considered a genius. The person was very much separate from his creation."

"Well, I'm sure he was judged for that, too, when people listened to his music."

Chloe's mother smiled at him now, smiled at the performance of disappearing him. "No, Vincent, he wasn't."

"I'm sure he was."

Chloe interjected.

"I don't think you understand, Vinnie."

Her mother hummed in agreement. And then it happened. Hands wrapped around his neck, closing in.

"No, I don't fucking understand!"

He kicked his chair out from under him, leaping from it, said the words clear again, though with a nervous mouth, and tried one last time to find Chloe with his eyes. She only looked through him. His head bowed, dismissed, he quickly sorted his wallet and phone into the right pockets and darted across the dining room, sprinter's hands already chopping at the air. When he reached the front door he slung it open and bolted through like a leaping cat.

*   *   *

Through the city park, along the main streets, past the girls and the guards and the nightclub lines, out toward the beginning of the airport highway. Vincent ran and ran, only giving thought to his technique. He ran until he broke a sweat, then threw away his coat, let it balloon from an overpass down onto a lower freeway. After another few miles he ran all the way back to get his car. When he started the engine Chloe came past the headlights and slipped into the passenger seat.

A few silent streets away she snapped at him, the girl he thought he might love. She turned her body, stretched out the seatbelt to allow herself to face him, and began to tell him how rude he'd been, how crazy it was to run away for two hours, how her mother had made them a lovely dinner, who Wagner was, what she and her mother had been trying to say, that he should drop her home, that she would get someone to pick up her things. That he could do the same. His head boiled. His legs cramped.

She kept at him. Why did you do that, why? Just tell me why. She shouldn't have let him drink so much. Shouldn't have thought he would fit in. The runner or the man, the run or the runner. What did it mean? He yelped, then, and cried out, "It's too difficult to explain"—and then an impulse came to swerve at speed, to make the car uncontrollable, to let her know *something*. That he was uncontrollable? That he was still there? Who could know? But he did it. Driving a straight line between curb and white-flanked barrier, he accelerated, didn't break at the turn—that's how it was put formally.

What was left was invisible. The bruise on her leg that wouldn't bloom for a day, the small bone fracture, the dented car, written off, that would reappear as part engine, part spares. What was visible was the unseen unlove. The bit that undoes the entire seam, the loose thread. He regretted it. He was sorry. Something opened, spilled over.

This time would become two years of falling. Staying over on the spare bed as a favor, and then overstaying. Losing friends. Wasting time, watching the muscles fade, eating a donated meal followed by a borrowed one. He could not reach the wall.

Coach, when he stopped turning up for training and his remaining sponsor dropped him, said, "You know this has a title, your life. Success and failure. You did this, Vincent."

It was true. He knew that he'd done it. He didn't know how, exactly, but he realized that he had. He had run, had won medals, had met all sorts of people. He had loved someone. It had been there, a glimmer. The runner and the run. He leaned over the communal computer and printed out another hundred copies of the flyer. During the city's lunch hour he stood in the street, clad in a past season's line of Adidas and handing out the flyers framed with dollar signs. After some time the block became quiet again. Vincent stood in the cool winter air and felt content for that moment. It felt good to be someone who didn't have the things he needed.

TONSILS

by MELISSA LUCASHENKO

SUNDAY AFTERNOON, BETHANIA. The flat across the road hasn't sold, and the real-estate agent has packed up her hopeful black-and-yellow banner and gone back to where the buyers are.

"Money's the thing, eh?" Hayley says to me, with the intense clarity of being fifteen and one short stumble away from homelessness. "Mum's up me to pay her phone bill."

"Well, it's one thing."

I don't add that it's not the only thing. We both know that, just like we both know how far out in front it is. Money: winning any old race you might care to mention by a dozen lengths, everything else bringing up the field and dodging the clods of muddy turf flying past in Money's wake.

Hayley's on the back deck, surrounded by a host of pirated DVDs that she's brought home from her big visit. She's using her fork to scratch graffiti onto my plastic tabletop, three pale anarchy symbols appearing simultaneously as the tines plough their way into the desiccated green surface. *A* for *anarchy*. *A* for *another bill*. *A* for *Aborigine*. Hayley knows I don't give jack shit about the table; it's on its last legs, like a lot of stuff around here. She's already stenciled her art onto the walls downstairs with a can of black spray paint she found in the garage. I wish she'd asked first about that, but the pictures are good.

"Money and tonsils." Hayley nods firmly at her assessment of the situation. She's happy to have a handle on things. To have got things sorted, straight in her mind. Then her eyes widen.

"Hey, I think I made my mum sick yesterday. She was coughing her lungs up by the time I left."

She gives an evil laugh at this unexpected power. Typhoid Hayley. Her Mum's an ambo driver by day and a pisshead by night. Mostly she's okay, but on occasion Pisshead Mum takes all her other personalities along for the ride and everybody in earshot has to buckle up and hang on. Late last year Hayley had the sudden blinding insight that she didn't need to live with Pisshead Mum after all, and came to live with us instead.

Her older brother had arrived first, stayed a couple of weeks on Nikky's couch that was supposed to be for the room upstairs only it wouldn't fit through any of the doorways when we moved in. He kept going real quick when I found a syringe on the laundry-room floor. Hayley showed up next, and in the absence of syringes, she's stayed. The brother lives somewhere mysterious on the other side of town now. Hayley talks to him on MSN sometimes.

She's been hacking for days. Great air-sucking whoops that sound like they'll turn her inside out. I wonder about the little bottle of cough syrup I forked out fifteen precious bucks for last Thursday.

"You kids are like professional sick people," I say. "If only you got paid to be sick, eh?" I don't mention that some people in Bethania do just that. I get an instant mental picture of Hayley licking toilet seats and eating out of rubbish bins: doing her traineeship in welfare dependence. Putting in the hard yards. She already has, in a way, living with Pisshead Mum. One look at the underside of her arms tells you that.

"That'd be good, eh!" Hayley brightens at this prospect. "It'd be too easy."

"You kidding? That'd be such a crappy job," Nikky says, looking for joy in a one-dollar scratchie as she coughs in perfect harmony with her best friend. I know where Hayley's coming from, though. Sickness is the perfect job for an introvert. It's something that happens to you; it doesn't ask you to go out into the world and risk anything.

Hayley doesn't really want to be as sick as she is, of course. I know this, because ever since she moved in, she's been talking about Her Tonsillectomy.

She describes it the way kids in other suburbs talk about the perfect OP score: not exactly an impossible dream, but definitely in that neighborhood.

No doctor in Brisbane wants to take the tonsils out. Apparently the idea these days is to leave the bloody things in where they can do the most harm, reinfecting the kid and making her sick for months on end. So Hayley gets better for a day, gets herself out of bed, goes to class, and promptly picks up the next bug on the conveyor belt of disease that she calls her alternative school. She's been in class for seven weeks total since the beginning of the year, and it's Ekka time now, August. Mostly she lies around the house, coughing. Infecting things. If I knew how to take tonsils out, I'd do it myself.

"What'd your mum say about the doctor?" Nikky asks, abandoning the useless scratchie and flicking through the pirated DVDs instead. Because she's an ambo driver and has seen Actual Dead People, Hayley's mum is considered by both teenagers to be a medical authority of the highest order. Plus, yesterday was a breakthrough—Hayley went to visit, ten stops away on the train, and by all accounts they didn't fight. This is a big step forward.

"She reckons I should go and get a prescription, but not take the antibiotics. Then, when my tonsils get to level four, she'll talk someone into taking them out. They're at level three now." Hayley is pleased with this new plan of her mum's. She is being *proactive*, engaging in *forward thinking*. The plan encapsulates her basic philosophy: things have to get far, far worse in order for them to get any better.

"Do you know any free clinics open on a Sunday?" Hayley asks, launching into another coughing fit.

"Well, I'll go up and look," I say, even though I don't have much faith in this mad scheme. At fifteen bucks a pop for cough medicine and twenty bucks for a course of antibiotics, Hayley's tonsils are sending me broke fast. There's got to be a better way.

That feeling follows me up to the computer in the lounge room, where I just manage to sit down before Hayley's mum shows up. I'm bolting back downstairs as soon as I see the uniform heading up the driveway.

By the time I make it outside, she's screaming at Nikky that we've stolen her daughter—that we don't care about Hayley, not like she does. We're just in it for her homeless allowance, and Hayley's too dumb to see it. That'll be Angry Mum, then. Crying Mum will be along in about fifteen minutes.

I walk over and stand beside my daughter, letting my right forearm drift up to Nikky's bony shoulder. I'm hoping Angry Mum doesn't realize it, but the maneuver puts my fist about twelve inches from her sweating, yelling face.

"She's not here," I lie. "You may as well go home. Come back when you're sober, Liza."

While I talk I'm checking to see what weapons are in today's equation. A mop, a broom—not so hot, really. Blunt objects don't worry me all that much, because I was born with an abnormal ability to tolerate pain. I'm like Homer in the Lollapalooza episode, the one where they shoot the cannon ball into his guts. You could pull my hair out in chunks and it'd hurt, sure, but I wouldn't cry or scream or anything. As long as there's no fucking scissors in the equation. My very mild superpowers don't run to scissors.

Nikky has stepped wisely away from the argument now, up onto the back deck. Angry Mum has started screaming about lesbians, like now it's my fault her daughter's gay. I tell her not to get her fucken flaps in a knot about it. Christ allfuckenmighty, you'd think she'd be happy! No teenage pregnancies. No dumb-arse boyfriends bringing the jacks to your door. No HIV.

But I've crossed some kind of line, apparently, telling her not to get her flaps in a knot, because she gives a homophobic shriek and launches herself at me. I duck her fist and all sixty kilos of her—skinny and blonde and I guess petite in a skanky muffin-top-jeans kind of way—go flying by. There's nothing that scary about Liza, not unless you're a fourteen-year-old kid she's terrorized since infancy; not unless she's lost the plot and has a pair of scissors to your throat while you're trying to drive her to the Logan hospital where her daughter is waking up in the psych ward after swallowing thirty-five Panadol. There's no scissors, now, so I turn to face her and give her a good hard shove.

It puts her in the garden, away from the sliding glass door to Nikky's room. I tell her to knock off and get some sense into her thick head; you'd think an ambo would see enough drama and blood at work without looking to create more, but maybe she picked that job because she likes that stuff. Likes seeing people all cut up and dying and shit. Why does anyone do anything? People are complicated, that's about the sum total of what I've learned in life. Money's the thing, and people are complicated.

"Do you want me to ring someone?" Nikky yells from the deck, standing near the back door so she can run and lock herself inside if she has to. The jacks, she means, but she doesn't want to say the word out of fear it'll set Hayley's mum off again.

"Nah, it's all right," I tell her, faking extraordinary relaxation and calm. "We're finished here. You were just leaving, weren't you, love?"

As it turns out she's not ready to give up yet. She comes at me again, yelling about lezzos and the rent money and her phone bill that still hasn't been paid since last quarter and Hayley's homeless allowance, a whole litany of grievances that have led her, thirty-nine years old and full drunk, to throwing punches in my Bethania driveway at four o'clock on a winter afternoon. I sidestep her flailing arms once again, if not the litany, and she tumbles sideways into the wisteria vine that's gone all yellow and dead-looking from the frosty nights we've been having lately. The wisteria gets torn away from the narrow bit of steel weldmesh that I've planted it up against, and a whole two months of growth are gone in an instant.

I begin to get the shits now. She can settle down and tell me where there's a free clinic open, I tell her, or else she can fuck off quick smart. And knock off this tossing punches at me, or I might start to get proper cranky. Does she think I *want* to raise her daughter for her, for fuck's sake?

Angry Mum lying on the lawn there puts one hand beside the flattened wisteria. Her well-shaped nails are painted with that overdecorated artistic shit that some women go in for. A dotty silver design on a purple background, still perfect and complete—not flaking off or anything. She takes a big gulp of air, and then another. It's a long way up onto her feet from where she's lying. She starts to look pitiful, not murderous, and I begin to think we might be getting somewhere.

"But how am I going to pay my fucken phone bill?" she howls. "I *told* Hayley I needed her pay to cover it. And the vet was a hundred dollars!"

Money's the thing, all right. And fuck me days if Hayley doesn't go and yell out the upstairs window at me right then:

"Did you find a free clinic yet?"

Hearing her daughter, Angry Mum's back on her feet so fast it's a wonder she doesn't black out from the g-force. Oh, she's spitting chips now, you better believe it. She rips a bit of narrow weldmesh out of the ground, and while she's trying to clock me with it I discover that I'm a liar—

A skanky daughter-stealing ho,

A money-hungry bitch,

A bullshit artist,

A danger to underage youth,

And a fucking half-caste coon who—

That does it.

I'm not a violent person, I'm *not*. But a moment later I find myself lowering my bruised fist and telling Bleeding Mum, sprawled on my concrete driveway, that next time she'll get more than a tune-up from me. Next time I'll drive her teeth through the back of her head into the next fucken millennium. Money's the thing, all right, but it's not the only thing. Don't fuck too hard with Bethania blackfellas, I tell her as I walk back inside and slam the door. Add that one to the list.

CONTRIBUTORS

HENRY BEAN is a novelist, screenwriter, and occasional filmmaker. He wrote and directed *The Believer*, which won the Grand Jury Prize at the 2001 Sundance Film Festival, as well as many other awards.

AIMEE BENDER is the author of four books, including *The Girl in the Flammable Skirt* and *The Particular Sadness of Lemon Cake*. Her short fiction has been published in *Granta*, *Harper's*, the *Paris Review*, *Electric Literature*, and elsewhere, and has also been featured on *This American Life* and *Selected Shorts*. She lives in Los Angeles.

TONY BIRCH is a Koori writer. He is the author of three books, the latest of which is *Blood*.

RYAN BOUDINOT is the author of the story collection *The Littlest Hitler* and the novel *Misconception*.

JOHN BRANDON was raised on the Gulf Coast of Florida. His two previous novels are *Arkansas* and *Citrus County*.

SIBYLLA BRODZINSKY has spent more than twenty years writing about Latin American politics, human rights, and social issues in publications including the *Economist*, the *Christian Science Monitor*, and the *Guardian*.

KELSEY DAKE lives in the desert and draws pictures for a living.

CIROCCO DUNLAP is a writer and an actor based in Brooklyn. She enjoys scanning casting notices for the term *ethnically ambiguous*.

JOHN FLOWERS is a writer and TV producer based in New York City. He's currently working on his first collection of essays, *The World's Largest Outhouse*.

CHRIS FLYNN is the books editor at *The Big Issue* and author of the novel *A Tiger in Eden*.

J. MALCOLM GARCIA's work has been featured in *The Best American Travel Writing* and *The Best American Nonrequired Reading*.

JOWHOR ILE was raised in the coastal city of Port Harcourt, Nigeria. Not content with being an accountant, he currently walks the streets of London.

CASSANDRA C. JONES's work has been shown throughout the U.S., Canada, and Europe. She is represented by Eli Ridgway Gallery in San Francisco.

JULIEN LALLEMAND has lived and worked in France, Hong Kong, and the U.S. His illustrations and designs have appeared in *McSweeney's*, the *Guardian*, the *South China Morning Post*, and elsewhere.

GRACIA LAM was born in Hong Kong and raised in Toronto, Canada. Her illustrations have been exhibited widely and have won many awards.

DAVID LIDA is the author of several books about Mexico, including *First Stop in the New World* and *The Keys of the City*. When he is not writing, he works for defense lawyers in the U.S. who defend Mexican nationals facing the death penalty. His website is *davidlida.com*.

MELISSA LUCASHENKO is a Murri woman of Yugambeh, Bundjalung, and European descent, with affiliations to the Arrente and Waanyi people. She has written four novels.

DOUGLAS MCCULLOH is a photographer, writer, and curator. His fifth book, *The Great Picture: Making the World's Largest Photograph*, was released in January 2012.

THOMAS MCGUANE's latest novel is *Driving on the Rim*.

VIVECA MELLEGARD is a writer and filmmaker. She lives in London.

STEVEN MILLHAUSER's most recent book is *We Others: New and Selected Stories*, winner of the 2012 Story Prize.

ELLEN VAN NEERVEN-CURRIE is of Munanjali, Yugambeh, and Dutch descent. She graduated from Queensland University of Technology in 2010, with a degree in fine arts in creative-writing production.

JASON POLAN is a member of the 53rd Street Biological Society and the Taco Bell Drawing Club. He has exhibited work all over the United States, Europe, and Asia, and is currently drawing every person in New York. He also has a weekly column in the *New York Times* called "Things I Saw."

MATT ROTA is an illustrator based in New York, and an instructor at the School of Visual Art and the Maryland Institute College of Art.

MAX SHOENING is a researcher in the Americas Division of Human Rights Watch. He contributed research to *Violentology: A Manual of the Colombian Conflict*, a photography book by Stephen Ferry.

KEITH SHORE's work has been exhibited across the U.S., and internationally in Denmark, England, Italy, and Sweden.

SUSAN STRAIGHT's newest novel, *Between Heaven and Here*, will be published by McSweeney's in September. It is a companion to *Take One Candle Light a Room* and *A Million Nightingales*.

BEDE TUNGUTALUM was born in Nguiu, Bathurst Island, in 1952. While attending Xavier Boys School in Nguiu, he was taught how to cut woodblocks for printing; his earliest prints date from the late 1960s. Tungutalum works in carved and painted wooden sculpture, lino and textile prints, etchings, and paintings. He has exhibited widely.

DEB OLIN UNFERTH is the author of the memoir *Revolution*, a finalist for the National Book Critics Circle Award; the story collection *Minor Robberies*; and the novel *Vacation*, winner of the Cabell First Novelist Award.

JESS WALTER's most recent novel is *Beautiful Ruins*.

TARA JUNE WINCH is from Wollongong, New South Wales, and is of Wiradjuri, Afghan, and English descent. Her novel *Swallow the Air* won the Queensland and Victorian Premier's Literary Awards.

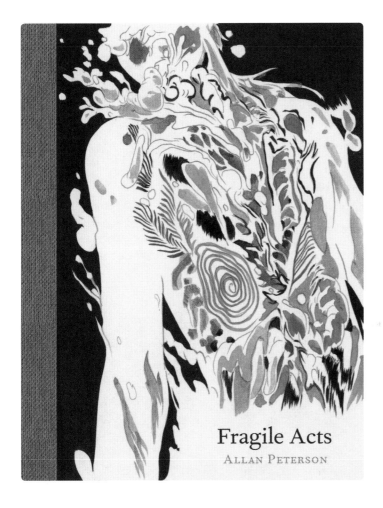

Wait—McSweeney's has a

Yes, we do. Our children's book department—called McSweeney's McMullens—has already published several excellent picture books, including the three brand-new titles shown here.

To order these books, and to check out our growing catalog, visit *store.mcsweeneys.net* or your favorite independent bookstore.

We also offer a subscription plan, which makes a great gift.

Stories 1, 2, 3, 4

by Eugène Ionesco & Etienne Delessert

"Among the most imaginative picture books of the last decade."
—Maurice Sendak

Back in print for the first time since the 1970s, these illustrated stories by one of the twentieth century's great playwrights make ideal bedtime reading for young children.

children's book department?

The Night Riders
by Matt Furie

Four nocturnal friends wake at midnight and strike off on an epic journey toward the sunrise. Matt Furie's glorious debut is warm, witty, and full of surprising detail on every hand-drawn page.

"AMAZING.
This book just jumped to
the top of my all-time-
favorite-kids'-books list."

—Jordan Crane

Benny's Brigade
by Arthur Bradford & Lisa Hanawalt

The hilarious and riveting tale of two sisters who accidentally find a tiny, very gentlemanly walrus named Benny inside an oversized wiggly walnut shell.

"A faithful account of my true story."

—Benny